ENIGMA FRONT: BURNT

NOW, EVERYTHING BURNS

edited by
Celeste A. Peters

co-editors
Justin Acton, Renée Bennett,
Ron S. Friedman, Kristine Saretsky

foreword by
Craig DiLouie

ANALEMMA BOOKS
analemmabooks.wordpress.com

Cover design and interior layout by Brent Nichols

Foreword by Craig DiLouie

First Print Edition:
August 2016

ISBN: 13: 978-1-5329667-2-9

Published Worldwide by

Analemma Books
Calgary, Alberta
Canada
analemmabooks.wordpress.com

CONTENTS

FOREWORD

By Craig DiLouie

Fire, so beautiful, so treacherous. Love it at your risk. It can leave you burned.

Fire has given humanity civilization. Light and heat. So wondrous were its benefits to the ancients that they considered it one of the basic elements of the universe. They believed harnessing fire set humans apart from animals. Fire and its light quickly became associated with enlightenment and progress. With life itself.

When I think of fire, the legend that immediately comes to mind is Prometheus. This Titan fought against the Greek gods before switching sides, helping Zeus claim the throne of Olympus. Hoping to ease humanity's struggle, Prometheus stole fire from the workshop of Hephaistos and Athena and gave it to them. More than fire, like the Snake in Genesis, he gave them knowledge.

Fire is difficult to control, however. Prometheus is a benefactor to humanity, but he's also a trickster who can't be trusted. And as fire is a gift, it is also a punishment, as it destroys as well as creates. It runs, it leaps, it consumes everything it touches. This can be purifying, as in the case of the phoenix, or punishing, as in the Christian concept of Hell.

Some apocalyptic myths hold that as God punished the world with water, next time it will be fire. Prometheus himself was to be eternally and painfully punished, just like the Snake in Genesis.

Whether fire purifies or destroys, the experience changes all who touch it. Fire is a transformative force. Some will come away enlightened, others damaged.

So it goes with the creative spark and the fire of imagination that join writer and reader. The burning desire to write, the intense burn of reading something powerful. A quote attributed to Nietzsche is that a single sentence can change your world. If that's true, a single word can be a spark. The mind, the kindling. Imagination, the fuel. For both reader and writer, the process can be supremely transformative.

Which brings me to this extraordinary collection of stories about people touched by fire and forever changed by it. Within these pages, you'll find devils and demons, climate change, Steampunk fire machines, radioactive alien artifacts, dragons, and a fire aboard a spaceship bound for Titan.

If these stories are the fire, their spark can be traced to the writers. These include award-winning talents like Robert J. Sawyer, Susan Forest, and Jayne Barnard as well as Writers of the Future honorable-mention recipients like Adria Laycraft and Ron Friedman. Many of the authors have been previously published, while for some, this is their first published work—a major event in their careers.

And if these stories are the fire, who's our Prometheus? The editors, of course, including Justin Acton, Renée Bennett, Ron Friedman, Celeste Peters, and Kristine Saretsky. Brent Nichols provided the cover and layout, and Selene O'Rourke did slush pile reading.

From Steampunk to fantasy to science fiction to mystery to horror, you'll feel the burn in *Burnt*. Turn the page and light the fire.

—Craig DiLouie
Author of *Suffer the Children*

THE DIM BENEATH THE LIGHTS

By R. Overwater

Hiram had been kneeling in the ashes, doing nothing for a good long while now. Not working, not thinking, just staring at the dark globe half-buried in the scorched ground. Exhaustion hung on him like wet clothing. He needed sleep, and he wasn't getting any under the glare of the damned northern lights.

He shook himself—as if the weariness would just fall away—and tried to figure which direction the sphere might have come from. Ahead, the charred corpse of a deer lay among the burnt trees, trapped by the inferno that erupted when the orb struck. There was no birdsong, no wind rustling through leaves, only dead stillness.

Beyond the trees, Addlestein muttered towards the sky, waving a pencil in one hand, a journal in the other.

Hiram blew on the sphere, smelling his own breath as fog condensed on its cool surface. When he polished it away, his warped reflection stared back at him. Brown and pitted, tobacco-stained where they weren't black with decay, his teeth were rotted by whiskey and molasses. How could any proper lady—a lady like Sarah Bethany—kiss a filthy pie-hole like that?

He resolved to see one of those tooth doctors when he and Addlestein got the orbs down south. It would cost plenty, but he'd get a good one, the kind you only found in the big city. Sarah would help.

"Is it another one or not?" a hoarse voice shouted over the thump of approaching hoof beats. It was Addlestein. Hiram didn't look up. He could see the man's reflection as he rode closer, distorted in the globe's smooth sheen.

"Well?" Addlestein shouted. "Is it?"

"Sorry, Boss," Hiram answered. "My mind keeps wandering."

Addlestein opened his mouth to issue another indignant prompt.

Hiram cut him off. "It's sunk in pretty deep, 'bout the size of a man's head. Cool to the touch, just like the others."

Addlestein dismounted, hobbling through a patch of blackened tree stumps. Puffs of fine ash billowed with each step. Out of habit, Hiram covered his mouth.

Addlestein leaned over Hiram's shoulder. "Well, I'll be damned. It is a big one." He coughed, spitting out a bloody clot.

Hiram looked up. "You sound worse. Can't hardly make out what you're saying."

The older man scowled. "Don't concern yourself. There's a pen and ink in my saddlebag. Put the orb with the others and mark an 'X' on the catalog page. I'll note its properties when we make camp." He shot Hiram a self-satisfied smile. "I'd leave it to you, if you could write more than your own name."

Stuck-up bastard. Lording over Hiram every chance he got. Sarah was teaching him to read and write. Soon, sons-of-bitches like Addlestein wouldn't always have the upper hand.

Bankers and businessmen, they didn't work any harder than Hiram did. They weren't any stronger, couldn't shoot any straighter, couldn't ride any harder. They pissed standing up no different than him. But they had power—power that came from words on paper. If you could read those words, make your own words, you could hold their kind of power. If you had that, all you needed was a good shave and a clean suit.

Hiram was going to get those things. Sarah had promised. But first, he needed to get Addlestein down to California and meet the men coming west from the Smithsonian museum. By Addlestein's account, the Smithsonian men had found an orb in some tar pit and were eager to compare it to his—and they were willing to pay.

Getting paid meant keeping Addlestein alive until then. Hiram wondered if the man would even make it out of Alaska. He looked like hell. Every time he spoke, it triggered a coughing fit. A yellow, flaking rash covered his skin and he scratched at it constantly.

Hiram was starting to show the wear of hard living, too; he'd seen that in the orb's reflection. After years on the trail, driving cattle, escorting settlers, any job he could find—and then gambling and drinking his pay away—it was time to put that all behind him. He needed to make sure this opportunity didn't slip by.

Some opportunity. If he'd known what he was in for when Sarah read him the newspaper advertisement, he might have said no.

"Wanted for immediate hire," she said, looking over the edge of the nickel paper to see if he was listening. "Experienced trail hand to accompany scientific expedition. Salary commensurate with length of journey."

Sarah urged him to reply. She needed the money to build them a better life and, hopefully, Hiram would make a name for himself, bringing him closer to the fancy world she missed so much. She had plans and he was lucky to be the man who would make them happen.

Addlestein paid well. If Hiram spent it on barbers, tailors and new teeth, he'd be civilized enough for Sarah's purposes.

He marked the catalog, packed the orb away and saddled up. The two men rode until they were back among living trees. It was late when they pitched camp.

Afterwards, Hiram finally worked up the nerve to ask Addlestein about the lights.

Every night, he'd lay awake. Above, a writhing canopy of pink and green spread to the horizon. Long streaks of white slid through the glimmering colors, hissing like burning snakes. They were bright enough to read by, not that Hiram could read. But he did know such a grand display was uncommon before winter. Knowing more might dampen his uneasiness. He should have kept his mouth shut.

"Ah-roar-ah ..."

"Aurora borealis," Addlestein said, finishing Hiram's sentence with trademark disdain. "Most natives up here think they're animal spirits or some such." The firelight colored his skin a sickly orange. "Some Eskimos think they're evil. The Fox Indians think they're slain enemies seeking revenge."

It was all horseshit. The boss wasn't just ill, he was crazy. There'd been plenty of examples, like that very night when they made camp.

Hiram had gone into the trees to gather firewood. When he returned, Addlestein jammed a map in his face, tapping a line of dots circled on it. "Equidistant across the longitude and parallel to the latitude!" he shouted, laughing, limping back and forth. He spat, and then laughed again.

"And this!" He held up his journal, a crude calendar scribbled on one page. "Another will fall close to here this very week." He wandered away, shaking his fistful of paper, shouting as if someone was there to hear.

Addlestein spooked Hiram almost as much as the lights did. When he laid out his bedroll, he tucked his pistol inside it.

Squirming on the hard ground until he found the right position between the rocks and lumps, he pulled out his worn picture of Sarah. He kept it folded so it fit his pocket, and a jagged crease now divided her into two halves. Hiram never noticed, his mind forming a complete image of her whenever he held it.

He squinted at the photograph until Addlestein's coughing

interrupted his thoughts. Watching him lie with his back to the fire, hacking and clawing at his skin, Hiram considered the cards life had dealt the retired schoolmaster. One of the only survivors in a town razed to the ground after the first orb fell, his family dead .... Hiram saw how a man could go half mad.

Addlestein said his quest was in the name of science. Probably, he was just trying to play a bad hand as best he could.

When he awoke later that night, Hiram's throat burned from smoke. It happened sometimes when the campfire needed stoking. Except it wasn't their fire. A short distance from the camp, flames roared through the willow branches.

He leapt up and scanned the clearing, worried the horses might bolt. But Addlestein was tending to them at the clearing's edge. He had one already saddled and stood half mounted, a foot in one stirrup, using his vantage point to peer through the flames.

When Hiram caught his eye, he pointed into the fire. "I saw it!" he yelled. "I saw it come down and land over there!"

They had to wait until late next evening for the blaze to subside and the smoke to clear. Addlestein found it first.

"Look," he whispered as Hiram walked up. It was almost three quarters sunken into the ground, about as round as a small washbasin. Its surface rippled with color, as if the northern lights were inside it.

Addlestein reached down hesitantly, feeling it with his palm. He emitted a strangled gasp. "Touch it."

Poking it with a fingertip, Hiram jumped back. He could feel the hot ground through his boot soles. Sweat dripped from the faces of both men. Yet, despite having fallen from above and igniting hundreds of yards of bush, the orb was icy to the touch. Not just cool like the others—cold as a frozen pond.

He could see Addlestein had no explanation. Hiram looked at the eerie luminescence above their heads. The end of this ride couldn't come soon enough.

They rode for another month, following the path scrawled on Addlestein's map.

By now, Hiram was packing all the supplies. Addlestein, protective of his prizes from the start, insisted on carrying the orbs himself. With the latest one, his horse couldn't bear any more weight.

They found one more. It was shiny silver, glinting in the noonday sun, maybe six feet across judging by the few inches of curved surface above ground. Addlestein clutched his head, murmuring, agonizing over what to do.

They had no choice but to bury it. Addlestein pulled out his map and compass, carefully noting their location. There was hope in his eyes when Hiram returned from stowing the spade.

"The Smithsonian will pay a tidy sum when we return for this one," he said. He spat a glob of ash-black saliva. "Whatever fortunes we make on this trip, we are poised to double that."

Hiram stayed quiet. They were never coming back this way.

The next day, the sky filled with dark, swirling clouds and a thunderstorm hammered them with rain shortly after sunset. They hunkered down near a stand of pines, doing their best to keep dry. Hiram was cold and wet, but grateful the clouds obscured the aurora's glow. It was the darkest night so far, illuminated only by lightning flashes. He thought he might get some sleep, when a movement caught the corner of his eye.

He ran to his pack and dug for his pistol. "Boss!"

"What?" Addlestein shouted, visibly alarmed.

"I thought there was ... look." Hiram pointed toward the tarpaulin covering the saddles and packs.

The tarpaulin bucked like something alive, and the sacks rolled from beneath them, tumbling on the wet ground. The one with the two largest globes careened off Addlestein, hurling him into the mud.

Hiram pulled out his Barlow knife and looked at

Addlestein, who nodded. Keeping his distance, he danced around the shifting sacks, slashing at them. The orbs spilled out and instantly smacked together in a tight clump. He stood back and let out a low whistle.

"I wonder ..." Addlestein said, getting to his feet. He took Hiram's knife and approached the cluster. The knife leapt from his fingers and clacked against the largest one, clinging tightly.

Then they were blind. Lightning shot down, engulfing the spheres in blue sparks. The men stumbled back, slipping and falling in the mud. Their ears rang from the thunder crack and the tang of ozone burned their nostrils.

Hiram and Addlestein lay there in the mud. The rain continued to beat down.

The orbs' grip relaxed and they settled apart, rolling to accommodate the uneven ground. Addlestein rose, blinking to regain his vision, and nudged one with his foot. "Whatever phenomenon we just witnessed, it now appears to be over."

Hiram rubbed his muddy hands on his pant legs. "For a minute, I figured we were gonna have a hard time sacking 'em up again."

They rode into Skagway two weeks before the *SS Aleutian* embarked for San Francisco. The first night, Hiram drew the hotel room curtains and vowed to never again underestimate the pleasure of sleeping in darkness.

Addlestein sold the horses and spent his days sending telegrams and making arrangements. Reluctantly, he helped Hiram telegraph Miss Sarah Bethany and arrange for her to come north and meet them.

Hiram was elated, and treated himself to a bath every day. He'd seen a barber immediately and spent a chunk of his next advance on a tan suit and patent leather shoes. At the tailor's advice, he'd picked a red silk kerchief to tuck into the breast pocket. It was the first suit he'd ever owned. Wearing it was like being hogtied.

"Good lord, Hiram." Sarah put her hand to her mouth when she saw him on the station platform. "Your skin is practically falling off your bones." She caught herself, softening her expression. Setting her case and parasol down, she stepped closer and touched his lapel.

"But look at you! Proper attire and grooming! Without any help whatsoever."

She pressed up, draping her arms loosely around his neck. Hiram leaned in to peck her on the lips. She turned slightly, letting it fall on her cheek. It was disappointing but he figured she needed to keep up appearances.

It also wouldn't do for a proper woman like Sarah to bunk with a man she wasn't married to. Hiram had seen her logic in that. Even though he ached to lie beside her, he could wait. He'd booked her hotel room close to his anyways.

With Addlestein's help, he secured a table at the hotel restaurant—the kind of place that normally wouldn't allow someone like him through the door. He did his best to mimic Sarah as she ate in measured bites. It was all he could do to keep from shoveling it in; after months of pemmican and molasses, it was the best food he'd ever tasted.

After the meal, over steaming cups of dark coffee, she beamed at him, reaching out and touching the back of his hand as he recounted his trip and described their strange cargo.

"We've done it, Hiram, exactly as we hoped we could." Her green eyes looked deep into his. "We're at the forefront of a scientific discovery, one that will astound the world." Hiram felt a grin spreading across his face.

"From here, our futures are assured," she continued. "With my education and—" the corners of her mouth barely dropped—"the respectable man a woman needs, we are all set."

Hiram crawled into his comfortable bed after they parted, imagining Sarah Bethany in her bedclothes only a few rooms away. He drifted off, pleased with himself.

In the morning, Addlestein joined them for breakfast

before they boarded the passenger liner. Sarah had no end of questions for him: several about the orbs and a few about seeking recognition.

"No, actually," he answered, looking thoughtful. "I hadn't thought about the newspapers. A story would certainly enhance my stature as a discoverer, wouldn't it?"

Sarah didn't respond. Hiram could tell she was staring at the sores on his cheeks. Addlestein could tell also, blushing slightly.

"And Hiram's stature as an able man in the field," she said finally. "Don't forget the seasoned trail hand whose skills helped precipitate this amazing discovery."

"Yes, yes," Addlestein answered, looking away as he dragged his nails down one arm. "It would have been impossible without an extra man."

Breakfast was quiet after that. Miss Bethany said nothing as they went back to their rooms and waited for the bellhop to come for their belongings.

On the deck of the *Aleutian*, Hiram ignored the unsteady, rolling sensation and marveled at the sight of receding land, the bustling harbor and busy ships.

Sarah took him by the elbow as they strolled the length of the promenade. "That man has some sort of consumption, and is most surely in denial," she said. "He will never speak before the prominent scientific community." She turned, stopping them where they stood. "He is dreadful. They will separate him from his discovery as soon as they can."

Hiram thought about it. Addlestein, watching his home and family burn, riding hell-bent every day through miles of devastated forest, chasing the things that had cost him his whole world. And then getting cut out of the deal that could bring his story full circle, offer some sort of redemption.

Sarah was peering into his eyes. "It will happen, despite the fact he is an articulate, learned man," she said. "When we dock in California, I will contract a photographer to capture us with the spheres."

Before Hiram could answer, she pressed on. "His ego will

allow this. Then we'll contact the press and your name will be synonymous with these discoveries. What he does after that, successful or not, will matter little to us."

Hiram was unsure, but he felt her excitement. He was too sheepish to ask what synonymous meant.

Addlestein all but collapsed at dinner the first night. Sarah, God bless her, saw him to his room and offered to spend the trip caring for him.

It made sense the way she explained it. "You worked so hard to get him here and our futures depend on him," she said. She put her arms around Hiram, squeezing him. "You've earned some leisure. The least I can do is this."

His nights unexpectedly free, Hiram found himself at the poker table. He'd forgotten how strong its call used to be, but he remembered now. He had enough money left to ride the ebb and flow of luck and, by the time they closed the gambling tables, he'd pocketed a good haul. Enough to buy something nice for Sarah.

Rising late the next morning, he shook off the previous evening's liquor and got right back at it. The cards liked Hiram. They were telling him that Miss Bethany was right, that this trip really was a new beginning. It occurred to him: he should squirrel away some money for a ring.

"You got the winning touch there, pard," a voice said over his shoulder as he made his way back from the water closet. Hiram turned to see a clean-cut man in his early thirties. He wore a white uniform with gold insignia on his chest.

Hiram remembered him; he'd seen him speaking to the captain before the *Aleutian* shoved off.

"I know a winner when I see one and I'm sitting on a good stake because of it," the crewman said. He looked around, then leaned in close. "'Course, it's no good for the bos'n to be seen gambling on duty."

"I suppose it ain't," Hiram said. "But, might be your captain won't mind you buying a man a drink." The bosun smiled and slapped Hiram's shoulder, motioning toward the bar.

His name was Dupris, and he'd obviously been doing this for a while. He saw Hiram as a winner and, hell, that's exactly what he was now.

Hiram spent the rest of the afternoon and all that night betting big, sometimes losing big, but mostly winning big.

He was so focused on the cards, he didn't notice the room growing slowly louder until it was impossible to ignore. When the dealer closed the table for a fifteen-minute recess, Hiram saw that half the crowd had filed out to the deck. He could hear excited voices.

"Lived here all my life, only saw this once," said a woman.

"Absolutely breathtaking," a man's voice answered.

Hiram's stomach dropped when he set foot on the deck. Everyone was staring skyward. Looking up, he could arrive at only one thought: the lights were following him.

The crowd gaped at the multi-hued spectacle. They were off the Washington coast by now, still far enough north this sight wasn't unheard of. But rarely was it this intense. Not down here.

They churned and flashed as vividly as they had in Alaska, but the lights didn't extend to the northern horizon. They were right above, reaching for only a few miles. Suddenly sober, Hiram returned to the table, ordered a double whiskey, and asked to be dealt back in.

When he met Dupris in his cabin afterwards, the bosun produced a bottle and poured two fingers of bourbon into a pair of dirty glasses. He handed one over, looking tired. "This is the only good thing to happen today," he said, shaking the handful of bills Hiram had won him. "Compass is off three degrees for some reason, and slowly getting worse."

He gulped back the drink and reached for the bottle. "Captain made me spend the whole shift double-checking our navigator. Had to account for the drift. Not even my job."

Hiram only half listened. Despite his best efforts, his mind was elsewhere. The sky outside had put a knot in his gut and all the whiskey he drank that night—a lot of whiskey—couldn't untie it.

Dupris was still talking, and Hiram made like he'd been listening. Dupris winked. "With a stack like yours, I can introduce you to a couple ladies who'll gladly take your company. Not dance hall girls. Real ladies."

It hit him: he hadn't seen Sarah for nearly two days. "I got a lady," Hiram said. He downed his drink and started for the door. He stopped and looked over his shoulder. "Thanks."

It was late. He wondered if Sarah would forgive him for waking her, but something already had. She leaned against the cabin doorframe, speaking to a tall porter.

"Hiram!" Sarah shoved past the porter, leaping on him. "I didn't know where you were. I've been terrified." Her cheeks were flushed and Hiram felt the moist heat of her skin through her nightdress.

The porter was still there, looking awkward, and she waved him away. She seized Hiram's wrist. "I fled that awful Mr. Addlestein a few hours ago," she said, closing the door behind them. "He's lost his mind."

Sarah loosened her collar, tugging it down a few inches, giving him a tantalizing glimpse of the uppermost portion of one breast. A purple welt bloomed above it.

"Do you see this? I tried to care for him, since he's clearly at death's door. But in his delirium, he's so jealous." She put one hand to her mouth. "He accused me of trying to smother him! Said we are conspiring against him!"

Sarah blinked, tears welling. "If he hadn't been in a weakened state when he attacked ..." She let the words hang.

Hiram's thoughts went black. He pushed Sarah away, fighting to check his anger. The mad bastard had finally gone too far. She sat on the rumpled bed, reading his grim expression.

Her voice was quiet when she finally spoke. "Do you still have your pistol?"

Hiram knocked once on the painted steel of Addlestein's cabin door, and then turned the door handle. It wrenched itself out of his grasp, as if someone pulled it from the other side. But no one was standing there. The tension lingering in his gut coiled tighter.

The door refused to open more than halfway and Hiram squeezed around it, pistol leveled at waist height. Before he got through, the gun jumped from his hand, banging against two steamer trunks in the corner, clinging to the side of one. Other metal objects—coins, a money clip, scissors—were stuck to the trunks as well.

A wet cough cut through the hum of the steamship. Addlestein's bed was in the corner opposite the trunks. Propped against the headboard, he peered over a grimy bed sheet, red-rimmed eyes punctuating a face more open sores than flesh. He convulsed, choking as he clawed at his skin. The sheet fell away and Hiram flinched at the sight.

Long fingernail grooves tracked down what little skin remained, most of it scraped away in desperate fits of itching. The sheets were stained red, bits of raw flesh stuck to them, and strands of hair lay fallen from a now bare, pocked scalp. Hiram had seen dead bodies before. Few looked as bad as this still-living man.

Addlestein raised a shaking hand, crooking one finger towards the pile of metal in the corner, voice barely more than a whisper. "These aren't accidental creations of nature. They are artifacts of unknown design."

For a moment, there was light behind the swollen vessels in his eyes. "Otherworldly perhaps. In the last two days ..." He coughed. "... intermittently magnetic, right to the exact hour."

Hiram knew what magnetism was. And he understood now why the ship's compass was off.

He stepped toward the bed. Addlestein nodded weakly, half smiling. "Yes, yes. You've come to finish what she failed to complete herself."

Hiram struggled to make sense of what he was saying. Sarah never could have—

"It's alright, Hiram," Addlestein coughed. "We both know

I'm finished. Take them. Seek your fortune." His back arched as he fought another round of spasms. It was a full minute before he continued. "I see it now—they emanate some undetectable, poisonous quality. You're lucky it was I who was packing them. This ..." He looked down at his body. "This is what you'll inherit."

Addlestein was uppity, ornery, a horse's ass. He looked down his nose at Hiram, ordered him about as he pleased, and left him all the backbreaking work. But he was not a liar or a cheat. Hiram had rode with the man. What he knew about him didn't square up with Sarah's story. Or what she wanted Hiram to do to him.

He could hardly believe Addlestein's accusations about her, either. He wrestled with the contradiction.

A woman like Sarah would surely value a man with some backbone. He would insist on finishing the job and see Addlestein to California like he'd been paid to. The wretch was as good as dead anyways and their plans would unfold without a shot fired. She'd see the wisdom.

Hiram got his next steps straight in his mind. "Here's how it's gonna be," he said. Before he could finish, the items hugging the steamer trunks clattered to the floor. He heard Addlestein inhale, saw his eyes go wide in amazement.

Right then, Hiram saw the purity of Addlestein's obsession. The old schoolmaster burned with curiosity right to the end, knowing the orbs were killing him. Knowing he would never see their mystery explained. There was a difference between the thing that drove him and the motivations of Sarah and Hiram.

The ship lurched, throwing him down on all fours. The room tilted, pictures fell from the wall and the steamer trunks and loose articles slid toward him in an avalanche of debris. A deep metallic groan shuddered through the compartment, through Hiram's bones, and the clang of bells pierced the cabin walls.

Voices rose outside, and through the half-open door Hiram saw people flooding into the passageway. "We've run aground," a panicked woman yelled.

"Ladies and gentlemen, proceed to the upper main deck," a deeper, authoritarian voice shouted.

The orbs could sink into the mud for all Hiram cared. He'd never learn what they were, where they came from, same as Addlestein. The difference was, he didn't give a damn.

He pushed himself up, noticing the pistol sliding towards him. He caught it and a shot rang out.

A red hole blossomed in Addlestein's chest and he rolled off the bed, face slack, a final pink bubble on his lips.

Hiram looked at his pistol. Impossible. How could he have—a second shot boomed and pain tore through Hiram's skull, blinding him, thrusting him face-first to the floor.

He strained to move his limbs. They were as dead as burnt timber. Around him he heard shuffling sounds. Blood stung his eyes and he blinked until he made out shadowy forms.

Two men carried Addlestein's trunks, one atop the other.

There, by the door, was Sarah, a pistol in one hand. The other hand rested on the cheek of the tall porter. She handed him the pistol and he tucked it inside his coat, turning for the door. The men with the trunks followed.

Sarah remained still for a moment, glancing around the room, scratching at her neck. She approached Hiram, leaned over, and looked deep into his eyes. There was no denying it; she thought he was dead.

"Sarah," he tried to call out. She looked for another moment, then went to the desk and rummaged through the drawers.

"Ah!" she said, raising Addlestein's journal. Stuffing it under her arm, she left, pulling the door tight behind her.

Hiram tried to call out again, hard as he could. Only a gasp emerged. The agony in his skull grew stronger above one ear. Sticky wetness pooled around his face.

The door pushed open again. Something gray and filmy crowded the edges of his vision but he could tell Sarah was there. She'd heard him after all.

His heart leapt as she leaned down, touching his chest. He felt his jacket open and she pulled out the wad of poker earnings.

Then she strode back to the door, pausing to look into the hallway. In the dimming light, on the back of her neck, red lines showed where her fingernails had broken the skin.

RICK OVERWATER is a Calgary-based author and songwriter. He loves craft beer, short sentences and spaghetti-western soundtracks. Rick can be found online at www.overwater.ca and on Twitter at @rjoverwater.

GOOD INTENTIONS

By Katie Harse

They say the Devil hunts at Midsummer, that the air is wild with the cries of ghost hounds and phantom horsemen, that his minions ride forth on toasting forks, of all things, to greet him. Well, out here the Devil drives a pick-up: a big, black truck, all heavy tint and blinding chrome. He cruises the back roads with one hand on the wheel and the other on a cigarette he doesn't need a Bic to light, and no one ever gets the number off his plates.

I should have stayed home, or stayed at Dinah's when she offered, but instead of letting her finish the sentence that began "tonight of all nights," I held up my left hand and whistled through my teeth like I would to calm a horse, and took the words away, leaving her sputtering and furious. Most other nights I wouldn't have dared; Dinah has tricks of her own, but on the evening of the longest day, she just looked at me with sad eyes, and let me walk away.

A spark leapt up to meet me as I unlocked my truck, and air too hot for an Alberta night crackled against my sunburnt skin—one of the lesser curses of being red-headed. The earth was panting in the heat, crying out for rain, and from the way the hair on my arms stood up, I might have said there was a storm coming. The proverbial *something* in the air, anyway, as I hit the road, driving to beat the dark.

Usually I like night driving, but I'd had a close call a few days before that left me seeing accidents at every turn, endless possibilities of twisted metal and glass, trajectories mapped out as clearly as the outcome of any given shot on a pool table. I've never been able to explain how I see, not to Dinah, not to anyone, except that it isn't as useful as you'd think, and when I dwell on it, it makes my head hurt. You see, there isn't one future to know, just an infinite series of possible courses, each leading to another. Any choice limits the outcome for the length of a breath, then more paths open up, spreading out in front of you like all those tiny lines on a road map, except that the destination changes with every turn you make. That night I only knew that all roads led to disaster, and I couldn't see just what it was.

By the time I hit gravel I could almost feel the impact, the dead weight of a deer across the windshield, the scrape of metal against metal, the fast-elevator feeling as the truck plunged off a cliff, tires spinning in the air. There are no cliffs in these parts, which gives you some idea of the shape I was in. A million ways to die on the road.

I opened the window against the heat, but the air rushing past was as dry and stale as the air inside the cab. The rearview blazed with lights coming out of nowhere like they do when you're driving and thinking of something else, and I had a moment to wonder *where'd this guy* come *from?* before I slowed right down and pulled over to let him pass, because I wanted the road to myself. The other car—no, a truck by the height of the lights—slowed too, and waited patiently behind me. When I started up again, adjusting the mirror for night, his lights bobbed upward for a moment, then settled just as bright in the center of my view, and the thumping of my heart drowned out the engine.

Just over the hill I could see the telltale halo that meant another car, and dipped the lights for him. The feeble low beams barely scratched the darkness-*how did it get so dark so fast?*—and the air was still too hot and dry to breathe. I see well enough in the dark, and I just waited for the other guy to come over the hill, and wondered why no one had the sense to stay at home on such a night. Little pools of light raced to meet each other, but he hadn't dipped his, and they reached me faster, drilled into my tired eyes until there was nothing else left in the world, and at that moment I understood why deer stand staring into the lights of the cars that kill them. It was all I could do not to drive straight into him, meet him head on. I put the thought from my mind and blinked the dark flashes from my eyes just in time to see a figure standing in the road, thumb extended. I hit the brake, and my truck slewed across the gravel sideways. The wheel yanked out of my hands and slammed into my ribs, then cracked me in the forehead on the next bounce before I could brace myself. Probably for the best—you can't shoe a horse with a broken arm, and I've got six brothers and a handful of ex-girlfriends who'd tell you I might benefit from a head injury.

When the truck slid to a stop, facing the wrong way in the middle of the road, there was no sign of the hitcher, the guy with the lights, or the truck that was following me, and I sat there shaking like the truck was shaking, trying to recover from someone else's life passing before my eyes. Because the hitchhiker who'd mysteriously vanished looked an awful lot like the driver of the white Camaro that had cut me off in the city three days before.

He'd come out of nowhere, too, changing lanes without looking, and, needless to say, without a signal in sight. He barely missed me and took off weaving through traffic to the sound of squealing brakes and horns blaring. Then he found himself stopped at the same light as me and I wondered exactly what the point had been. I got a good look at him then, a thin face with bluer eyes than mine and teeth as white as his car. When he pulled away from the light with a screech, and ran the next one, just outside the school that my niece Carly will attend next year, I thought *that's it* and spared another thought for him as he sped towards the highway.

I'd just been to see Carly and her mother while my brother Will was at work—he doesn't like me spending time with his daughter. As if I'd ever hurt a kid! I told myself I had the best of intentions: get this idiot off the road before he kills someone, and I had Carly in mind when I wished the worst for him. But you know where good intentions get you.

Blood dripped into my eyes, staining my fingers when I tried to wipe it away. The truck grumbled in protest but I managed to get it moving and turned around, when the hitcher reappeared, his eyes glowing catlike under the dark smudge of a cut on his face. Then his head twisted around on his neck like an owl's, and he went limp, and was gone.

The next few miles had me seeing things again, wondering for a moment what Dinah had put in the wine we'd been drinking that afternoon, but I wasn't drunk, any more than *he* had been when he set out that sunny afternoon to terrify everyone on the road. I tried to get his grinning face out of my head, even pulled over and shut my eyes, but the image stuck to the backs of my eyelids like the aftereffect of staring at the sun. I used to do that, too, when everyone told me not to.

When I looked up gravel had become asphalt, and I was on the highway with the scene flickering across the windshield like an old movie on a screen, exactly the way it had happened, exactly the way I'd known it would when I'd pictured him losing control of the speeding car on the wrong side of a double yellow line, heard the sickening crunch as the metal crumpled around him, felt the heat of the flames.

The truth is, I didn't think at all; I was mad, and it just happened. I just *made* it happen. Everyone's done it, wished disaster on someone else, but a wish is as good as a fact for a red-haired, left-handed seventh son, and when I thought of what I'd like to have happen, I heard the echo in the darkest corner of my mind: *so be it.* And when I saw the smoke rising in the distance, and the smell of burning gasoline with it, I thought I wouldn't lose any sleep over it. I was wrong. I couldn't close my eyes for days without imagining this very stretch of road, and what happened here.

A black truck passed by, casually, its engine buzzing like a thousand flies. I couldn't make out the driver, only a shadow a little darker than the others. Something glinted in the ditch, and when I took my eyes off the road, I saw the dead shells of maybe a dozen cars, all in a row, rust like old blood showing through rough prairie grass, the earth trying to break the metal down, reclaim it. Last in line was the Camaro, still exposed. The grass hadn't reached it yet, and the paint gleamed the color of sun-bleached bone.

He wasn't the only one in my dreams. That night I saw on the news that it hadn't been *his* car on fire. The woman who was driving got out okay, but they couldn't free her four-year-old daughter, who was strapped in safely in the back. They showed a picture of the little girl, and she reminded me of Carly.

I should think that *he* killed her, but I can't.

A host of black trucks surrounded me now, circling driverless, unmindful of whether there was a road under them or not. Each had that extra row of little bright lights under the front bumper, which made it look as if it had crushed a small car earlier, and was now looking for its next meal.

I stopped, turned the engine off, paused with my hand on the door, wishing that the gun rack held something more substantial than a dusty umbrella. Or that I'd taken Dinah's advice, or even the sprig of Saint John's wort she'd held out silently just before I left. But she knows I don't go for that stuff. I have enough problems.

The night smelled of diesel and burning rubber, and the trucks as they circled whined like the air through a poorly sealed window, but stirred up no wind. Then there was only the Camaro, lying in the ditch with its nose caved in, and a station wagon in flames. I was about to get out of the cab when the radio crackled. Now, the radio in my old Ford hasn't worked since I bought it from Tim Johnson for more than it was worth, and anyway, I had the keys in my hand. Even so, I could have sworn I heard the static, then the deejay's voice speaking my name. "This one's for you, Rob Wayland." Then more static, and I didn't wait to find out what the song was. I couldn't hear it, and without the lights I couldn't see it, but I could feel the massive pickup and its driver, waiting in the shadows near the two wrecked cars.

"What do you *want*?" As if I didn't know. Like the moves on a chess board: you plan a move, think of all the possible ways your opponent can respond, then all the ways you can respond to all his responses, and act accordingly. Of course, most people don't play chess that way, but I'm not most people, never have been. I stepped out into the darkness and stood, dazed, in the middle of the highway.

"I put my mark on you when you were born, Rob Wayland." The radio crackled again at my back, and twin orbs of fire blazed in front of me, the black truck crouching ready behind them. A crack about taking my name in vain occurred to me, then withered and died like Dinah's words had done. Because it's true. There's a reason my brothers don't want me playing with their kids. They know that I came into this world at midnight on October thirty first, and any one of them will tell you about the birthmark, or the fact that I spoke Latin before anyone taught me how. So I just stood there, frozen in the Devil's headlights.

A moan came from the burning car, and the truck's windshield reflected the flames. "You can save her, you know," said the radio, as if in casual conversation. "You can make it as if this never happened."

I heard my own voice rough in my ears, talking around a piece of barbed wire caught in my throat. "Can't change the past." The past is like a road you've already driven over, and it disappears behind you. There's probably a legend about that, and if there isn't, there should be.

"You changed the future."

"I made a choice." There is no fixed future. I wish there were, I wish I didn't have to worry about the outcome of everything I do, and then when I don't think about it *this* happens, I wish—

"I can give you that." The voice wasn't coming from my broken radio any more. The red, forest-fire glow of the black truck's cab brightened as the door opened with a creak, and I had the vague impression of a ball cap and scuffed black boots. Somebody's uncle, or the car salesman you see on TV. He wore dark glasses, or maybe his eyes swallowed the light spilling from the high beams. "Come back to me, and I'll give you one future. And I'll fix the past for you. Just open the door and pull her out."

The image of the little girl flashed across my brain, and this time she looked exactly like Carly, which was his mistake. If I'd seen her real face in that car, I might have done it, but he took the theatrics too far. Still, I was up and moving, and had to do something, so I headed for the Camaro instead.

The door handle burned like hot iron, but I work with the stuff for a living, and I know things about pain that the Devil himself couldn't tell you. So now I focused on the metal searing into the flesh of my left hand as something real, that and only that, and it gave me the strength to get the door open, and to reach for the man inside.

He groaned when I touched him, the kind of groan that would have been a scream if he'd had the strength for it, and I wondered what he saw. When I finally got him free of the car, and he lay broken and bleeding on the highway, I saw my own face looking up at me through a mask of shattered teeth and bone, head lolling at an impossible angle. But for the Grace of God. And I held that thought as I turned to face the black pickup and its driver's disappointment.

He didn't even give me that satisfaction. When I looked, he was driving away, one manicured hand dangling the cigarette out the window for a moment. Then the butt fell with a hiss onto the asphalt, and lay there, smoldering. I went over and ground it out with the toe of my boot.

Shadows oozed through the windows of the driverless trucks and flowed over the fallen man, like tar, but cold on a stifling June night. His face contorted so it hurt to watch, and he made a sound like he was suffocating, and his body shuddered and jerked, then lay still and empty-eyed. A dark shape rose out of him, limped towards the nearest truck, and got in without opening the door. Then there was only a dark stain on the highway, and one by one, the driverless trucks peeled off into the night, leaving fiery tracks on the road, and me alone with the burning station wagon. You can't change the past, and God help you if you believe someone who says you can. I knelt next to the car, looked at the little girl inside, and I could swear she smiled. As her mouth opened, white light split the sky with a crash, and rain fell on the parched earth, and put out the flames.

When I looked up again there was only my beat-up Ford, and the highway stretching smooth and straight in front of it. I turned back onto the gravel instead, and took the long way home, not minding that the road was full of ruts and potholes and crazy turns and half washed out by the downpour. Not the easy way, but *my* choice, and safer, maybe—at least until Hallowe'en.

KATIE HARSE has been a member of the Imaginative Fiction Writers' Association for most of her adult life. She is an Aurora Award nominee, and her fiction has appeared in *Tesseracts6*, *Tesseracts13*, and on CBC radio. Nights spent driving on the country roads of southern Alberta, combined with her past academic life specializing in Gothic and speculative fiction, make her wonder why rural fantasy isn't more of a thing.

FIRE BORN, WATER MADE

By Adria Laycraft

Chahna let the babe suckle, yet still no milk would come. He cried, and she sparked a trickle of fire to run along her fingertips. Her little firelord only cried harder, fists punching the air.

She let the fire die and his panic settled into mere cries of hunger. Exhaustion made her body heavy. She put him to her shoulder.

"Please, Taksheel, don't cry," she whispered, but nothing would sooth him. Chahna clucked and cooed and cried right along with him.

When she rose to walk him, her father stood in the doorway. She caught her breath, and held Taksheel tighter. By some small grace of the gods, the babe quieted.

"Give him to me." Fire licked along his bare arms and trailed from his fingertips.

"Father—"

"His ceremony approaches." His glower warned her. "I will not risk public shame. Bad enough you are now spoiled for any decent marriage contract. Give him to me."

His fire grew and she stepped back. He seemed almost hungry for the child. There was only one way to forestall him.

Chahna looked up at her father through a veil of saltwater mist. “Let me take the babe to a Vaidya.”

He studied her for a long moment, and she feared he would not even allow this one concession. Then he gave a sharp nod. “I am leaving to meet with our merchants. If you don't have proof of his firelord status when I return, then you will be forced to surrender him to me. Understood?”

She simply stood with her gaze downcast, chin tucked to her chest. When she finally dared look, her father was gone.

Taksheel began to cry again. Chahna sighed, and set him on blankets of silk so she could heat more goats' milk. In drips and dribbles, he drank from the cloth until his eyes drooped closed. She changed his wraps, glad for this moment of peace, but she saw his ribs, his sunken cheeks, his weakness.

What stupidity made her believe Jalesh when he claimed to be born of a high family? As a firelord Kumara, she knew she could only be paired with a true Kanwar, a prince of equal caste. In her deepest heart, she must have known he wasn't worthy, or she never would have kept their affair secret from her parents.

Why hadn't she demanded the truth of him?

She knew why. He had soothed her fires and watered the garden of her heart. She knew, she *knew*, but she never believed it would come to this, Jalesh dead of firefever and their child in danger.

But if Taksheel passed the ceremony as a proven firelord baby, it would no longer matter who his father was before the fever. All she had to do was ensure he did pass.

Chahna called for her servant girl. “Bring me one of your saris.”

Pani brought the simple wool sari, blue to mark her as a water slave. Chahna held the rough fabric between trembling fingers.

“Mistress?”

“Yes, Pani?”

“What do you intend?”

Chahna held Pani's fearful gaze until the girl looked away. She kept her head down after that, just as Chahna had before her father.

"Be sure no one enters my chambers tonight."

"Yes, Mistress."

Chahna changed into the homespun sari, flinching as it chafed her flesh. With teeth set hard against her fears, she took her son and left the palace through her private gardens.

Mandore, the Sun City of daily fire and heat. The markets teemed around her as the day waned into evening. Vendors hawked anything one might need—jewelry, cushions, spices, and candles, as well as lesser silks and food for every taste.

Chahna tucked Pani's wool sari over her face, doing her best to blend in with the other women in the market. She needed to assuage her suspicions without risk of being gossiped about, and that meant a Vaidya that did not know any high caste families. She entered a doorway under the sign of holy fire, Taksheel tucked within the folds of the rough sari. A low caste Vaidya crouched on the rug crushing herbs, his gray beard stained with tobacco. Scattered around him were baskets of cardamom and black cumin seeds, and bundles of mint and basil in various stages of drying. Tea steamed in a pot, and glass bottles with strange stoppers lined the shelves behind him. He rolled his eyes up to peer at her. Flies hounded him, and the fragrance of the turmeric he crushed could not overpower his stench.

Chahna swallowed. This man was nothing like the high-caste Vaidya she was used to seeing when illness or injury struck. She tried to speak, swallowed hard, and tried again.

"My milk will not come," she said. She pulled back her sari to reveal the babe. "He fades away before my eyes."

Her health, diet, and sleep patterns were questioned, as well as the quality of water she drank. She assured him all was better than he could imagine and passed him two gold coins, fire no doubt flickering in her eyes.

"Please just examine the babe."

The man's eyes narrowed as he took in her blue slave

clothing. He opened his mouth, his gaze meeting hers again, then closed it tight, asking no more questions. He indicated where she could lay the child as he tucked the gold away.

He examined Taksheel, muttering prayers while he laid out different element stones. One by one he laid a sliver of each against the babe's skin. The gold made Taksheel flinch and wail and left a red welt. Chahna blinked away tears, holding back the fire of her protectiveness in fists clenched. A piece of oxide had no effect, but the polished sliver of limestone from the enemy lands of the waterborn made Taksheel stop crying, suck in his breath, and hiccup. When the Vaidya lifted the element away, the welt was gone.

"I am sorry, this boy is no fireborn," said the Vaidya. He watched her, though he tried not to be obvious about it. "What do you know of the father?"

This question, spoken so light, woke all her fear.

"A good man," she replied, lifting Taksheel back into the safety of her embrace.

"Where is he now?"

"Dead."

The Vaidya raised an eyebrow. "If the babe is waterlord ..."

Chahna rose on shaking legs and pressed more gold into his hand. "Thank you, kind Vaidya."

He stopped her retreat with a hand on her forearm, waking fire in her. He released her, eyes wide, but still spoke his mind. "It would be a kindness to end it. He cannot thrive here, nor can you feed one such as him."

Chahna gazed down at the tiny sleeping form. "I know." She raised a hopeful face to the Vaidya. "Although, maybe ..." she began, but the twist of disgust in the old man's face made the thought die inside, unuttered.

"You would soil another by taking their birthright?"

Shame soured her stomach, and she hung her head.

"No."

His expression softened, and he patted her arm. "Call for me when you are ready, Kumara. I will make it quick and painless."

She had other ideas.

She braved the blood-hot streets now shrouded in the depths of night. The crowds had thinned, and wild monkey packs hooted at her as she descended into the bowels of Mandore. With a piece of gold she purchased both a guide and safety in a teenage cinder. No firelord, he would endure a low caste all his life. The gold would at least let him buy comfort and sustenance, if he spent it wisely.

The cinder boy led her into streets so dirty she covered Taksheel completely with her sari. The cinder ran ahead, dodging through crowds of people, goats, carts, and vendors. It took her a moment to understand why he did not treat her as befitted her rank. Then she realized the blue sari and plain sandals marked her as a slave, not worthy of any respect at all.

Chahna hurried after him as best she could. Her head spun as the cinder ducked this way and that, turning her completely around. Then, at a doorway like hundreds of others they had passed, he pushed aside a dirty woven rug and waved her into the dimly lit room beyond. Within, she found a place so foul the rug over the doorway was blissful in comparison. She wished she had thought to bring a satchel of cinnamon or a press of jasmine to place under her nose. Better, she wished she could fire this hole until it burned clean.

"Pretty lady, please be welcome, sit here. I am Sandeep. Tell me what this humble servant can do for you."

His smile spoke of greed, not kindness, but Chahna sat. "I have a need for your services, kind ramanah," she said. "I need a birthright."

"Pah, I can see the fire in you, my lady. You have no need of me, surely …"

She let her sari fall open enough to see the baby hidden there.

"By all the gods," he said, his voice harsh. He sat hard on the small goatskin stool across from her chair. "Is this babe yours?" When she nodded, he spat to one side in disgust. "The man who raped you, I curse him to the seventh watery hell. Such an abomination should never be allowed to live."

His assumptions angered her, but she held her wrath tight within and fingered two more gold pieces in her hidden purse in case it was needed. She wondered if a knife might have been wiser insurance.

"Please, good ramanah, tell me you can change this poor child's fate. I cannot bear to kill him."

He shook his head in disgust, but his greed won over. "I have no one immediately available, my lady, but I can send the boy when one comes along."

She released the hidden gold, took a deep breath, and said, "No, good ramanah, I do not wish to steal a birthright from another. You will take mine."

He stared so long she took a breath to repeat herself, only to have the ramanah bark out a laugh that stole all her hope away.

"You cannot give an adult's fire to an infant … it is a boy, no? Even worse!" he cried when she nodded. "No, my lady, I cannot help you today. Find me a fireborn boy child, no more than a year old. Only then will it work."

The cinder boy was gone when she emerged into the narrow street, but the light of dawn pinked the sky, guiding her home. By the time she stumbled into her courtyard, Taksheel screamed in hunger and seemed to weigh double what he did an hour before.

Pani came at once, taking the boy and following Chahna into the chambers. Taksheel needed to be fed, but she couldn't even bear to try to nurse again.

"Feed him best you can, Pani," she said, turning away before the girl even answered. Chahna went into her bathing chambers and let a whirlwind of fire and sand score her clean. What good was it to be of the powerful firelord caste if she could not save her son?

Chahna let the fire burn away any tears that dared fall. She stepped out calm, took up a fresh silk sari, and wrapped, tucked, and draped it, finding comfort in the ritual and the fine touch of luxury.

Then she sought out her mother. She was not with her

ladies or in the gardens, so Chahna climbed the tower to find her on a balcony staring out over the city.

Her mother turned at the sound of her approach. Chahna wanted to run to her as if she were still a girl and bury her face in the warm folds of sari. Instead, she was stopped short by a fierce gaze.

"Daughter."

There would be no understanding, yet still Chahna tried.

"He said he was a true prince."

Her mother turned away. "I fear he told you the truth. This is the problem. You have borne a waterlord child, and if you will not do what needs done, the ceremony will reveal his source to your father."

Chahna's fire leaked beyond her control. "You would have me kill a babe, my get, to save yourself some embarrassment?"

Her mother's nostrils flared. "Embarrassment? No, daughter, it will be much worse than that. The elements don't mix, and water drowns fire. Your father and his kin have sought a way to conquer fire for generations. What do you think they will do to the babe? And how do you think they will treat you?" Now her mother's gaze narrowed, cold, hard. "If you don't make that thing disappear before your father returns, you will suffer far worse than embarrassment, my daughter. The child will be taken from you. You will be disowned, sold, and branded as a slave, your birthright stripped away, your face scored forever. There is no worse fate for a firelord princess. Death would be a kindness, for both of you."

Chahna turned away. Her father's hungry look made more sense now.

Taksheel's feeble gasps and protests echoed through her chambers as she made her way back to him. Pani fussed and fawned over the babe, praying in a steady stream of foreign water words as she held the milk-soaked cloth for Taksheel to suck.

Chahna leaned against the doorway, the stone cool against

her cheek. She must be strong. He should not suffer for her stupidity. Once she put him out of his misery, she would end her own life and send her soul to join him and his father in the water depths of hell.

She drew upon her fire, bringing it forth in a rush of sound that sent Pani scrambling aside with a cry. Taksheel began to wail, and with every step closer he howled louder, barely able to gasp a breath in between, little body stiff with terror, and still she moved closer, and closer, body enveloped in flame.

The tiny wisps of hair on his head shriveled away. His silk wrap began to curl and darken at the edges, his skin reddened, and blisters rose on exposed flesh. She stepped closer still, forcing her body forward, wanting to close her eyes and scream but knowing she deserved to watch this…and that it would haunt her all her days.

The smell of burnt hair filled her nostrils.

Pani screamed somewhere to her right. Chahna faltered.

It was too late. He already burned.

Then water arced through the air, gathering and growing. Chahna looked to Pani for its source and saw that Pani's tears flowed away from her face. But there was more. From her. Tears, the saltwater of the soul, flowing from both women, became a sheet winding through the air to settle over Taksheel and wrap him, dousing the fire, soothing his burns. His cries abated.

What magic was this? Chahna stood quiet, her fire gone, and stared at her son. Pani fell to the floor to press her forehead to the tiles.

But she did not bow at Chahna. No, she bowed to Taksheel. She chanted a word in her own language again and again.

Waterlord. Her mother was right.

Chahna's fear rose to new heights. There was no saving him from her father now. He was a threat to all Firelord people, and she could never change him. She stepped forward, ready to battle the water of this tiny being, turn it to steam and end it all.

"Please, Mistress, please."

"Please what?" She did not mean to sound so sharp, but grief engulfed her in a terrible wave, and her weakness made her angry.

"Please, Kumara, you must not kill him."

"And what would you have me do?" Chahna demanded. "He is no watersnake like you—he is powerful. My father will do worse than burn him alive. Why make him suffer so? Death would be a blessing," she said, echoing her mother's words.

Taksheel cooed, a tiny sound that caught in her heart.

Pani beseeched her. "If you will free me from my bond to you, and let me take him to my lands, Kumara, he will be all you are here, and I will serve him to my dying day. I can sneak him—"

"So he can grow to be one who can douse my people's fire?"

Pani recoiled from Chahna, shaking her head but unable to voice her protests.

Chahna leaned over the woman, the heat rolling off her making the girl flinch. "I will fix this, not you," she said, unable to constrain her anger.

Pani's mouth tightened. Chahna's gut twisted in shame. Pani loved and cared for Taksheel as well—or better—than she ever could.

Chahna left them, the fires of guilt and grief trailing off her to blister the flowers of her gardens. She would have to kill Taksheel if she could not purge his waterlord birthright and replace it with a firelord status.

Chahna paced the city streets again, only this time wearing flames and expensive silk. The way cleared before her, many bowing or prostrating on the ground.

She needed a child, an infant boy. A firelord. How would she possibly gain one? She made her way along the richest streets, remembering a cousin and his pregnant wife.

At the cousin's palace she heard the cries only a woman in labor could make. Chahna's own memories were only too fresh, and she flinched with remembered pain. Guards stood at the ornate gate, but let her pass without a glance. She was a cousin, after all. She didn't doubt the expression she wore discouraged them just as much as her caste and family ties.

Once out of their sight she slipped into the side gardens, passing trees laden with fruit and flower before finding a quiet doorway in. All attention in the hall was focused on the celebrating father.

The cries from within the room beyond quieted.

Chahna waited, her heart as hard as sunbaked earth. She would fix her son, make him a firelord as he was meant to be, raise him and love him and feed him…

A slave brought the precious wrapped bundle to the firelord and he took it into his arms. His gaze lowered, his face softened, all firelord gone to reveal only adoration and joy.

That is what Jalesh could have looked like, holding Taksheel.

Chahna stood in the shadows a long time, unable to move. Finally she retreated, returning to the streets.

There was only one way left to her.

She returned to the market and purchased a small sharp blade that could be strapped onto her arm beneath her sari. Then she sought out the cinder boy. She saw him talking with his friends, his back to her. She walked up to them, the others scattering as she approached, and tapped the boy on his shoulder.

He turned, irritated look melting away to awe, and then fear as he recognized the woman he had helped the day before. Falling to his knees, he shoved his face into the dirt, his muffled voice begging her forgiveness.

"I did not know, Kumara, I did not know," he repeated like a mantra. Chahna bent to touch his head and quiet him.

"Take me back to the ramanah."

He guided her back to the hovel, the streets now crowded with vendors and carts in the heat of the day. Children ran shouting after monkeys, chasing them from the fruit carts in return for a mango. A donkey brayed close by, loud to her ears but ignored by everyone else. Some stared to see a firelord walking through their streets. Others simply bowed and backed away.

If the ramanah was surprised to see her as she really was, he let nothing show. Again she sat on the only chair, folding her hands in her lap.

"I am at your service, fire princess." He licked his lips as his eyes travelled over her sari, no doubt noting the missing babe. "Have you found a suitable fireborn child so soon?"

"You are despicable, and the fires of heaven will shun you," she said with no emotion at all. She knew she spoke out of her own guilt, yet it felt good to scorn him in her place.

His eyes widened only a little. "My apologies for my presumptions, princess. Please, this one begs to know how to serve you."

Fire trailed unbidden along her fingers, as if it made its own protest at what she considered doing. "You must have clients interested in rising to the firelord caste."

He only hesitated for the barest moment. "Of course. There are always those who would buy what birth did not give them, although it is rare to find one who will sell it. But your son has nothing to sell, Kumara. Why do you trouble me?"

An insult she could not let pass. "Your veils are so thin, Sandeep, I see right through to the greed in your heart. No matter. Bring your client that they may buy my birthright. You will pay me the full price that they pay, and not a coin less."

Shock froze his tongue. He blinked a few times. "My princess?"

"No, I am not yours and never will be." Fire danced over her, licking dangerously close to the wood shelves and wall hangings. She did not have time for this man's greedy thoughts to work it through. "Do it, now, as I command!"

Sandeep tripped and scrambled for the doorway, shouting for the boy. For now she ruled him with fire—how would it be once her fire was gone? Chahna stepped out of the tiny room and looked to the sun in the sky. Her time was running out, and soon she would have no fire at all. She watched Sandeep yelling at the cinder boy and pointing up at the palaces of firelords. The boy glanced once at her, only to receive a blow to the side of the head. He scrambled aside, dodging the second swing, and took off up the hill.

Chahna hid her fear deep within, burying it in ashes, and readied herself for what must come.

Sandeep ushered her back into his room and laid out a mat for her. He lit incense, praying under his breath, and laid out gold nuggets in star burst patterns over her heart and on her third eye. Then he mixed bits of this and that into a marble mortar, releasing a horrid smell when he ground it with the pestle.

Chahna met his gaze as he sat back. "It is ready," he said.

"Where is your client, ramanah? My time runs short."

"Soon, soon," Sandeep said, licking his lips. He rose and paced outside the doorway, muttering quietly. Chahna shivered. This was her only chance, and the gold from it as important as the change it would wreak in her. She must be ready. She must be brave. She must be quick.

Finally Sandeep led a pretty young girl and a firelord prince she vaguely recognized into the small room. The cousin fell to his knees beside her, palms pressed together. "Thank you, Kumara," he said, his own eyes smoldering. "My family would never allow us to be together otherwise."

Chahna studied the two faces that hovered over her. She recognized the love that filled the air between them, just as it had with her and Jalesh, and the pain of that loss was soothed in knowing she could at least give these two a chance.

Sandeep crouched at her other side. "Make it so, ramanah," she said.

He bowed his head in acknowledgement. He dipped a trembling finger into a bowl of foul paste and marked her. Pain seared along her skin, heat flaring high, and she bit her tongue so hard blood filled her mouth. Sandeep chanted breathlessly as he marked her again and again, each time more painful than before.

Chahna's awareness faded, and some small voice within screamed at her to stay conscious. She must not let the ramanah take her coin, and she must not die, not here, not like this, not after such a sacrifice. Only she could rescue her son.

"You must let go now, Kumara," Sandeep said in a whisper at her ear. The girl knelt at her other side, her hands pressed to Chahna's belly, her eyes closed and arms swathed in fire. "Let the fire go."

He dipped his finger, steady now, a small smile creeping over his face, and drew the final mark.

Chahna's back arched and the girl screamed. Every bit of Kumara's fire magic poured out of her in a rush, leaving her cold as death. Sandeep let out a happy sigh.

"It is done."

With a flick of her wrist Chahna bared the steel of her hidden blade and thrust it up to nestle under Sandeep's chin. "Slowly now, ramanah," she choked out. "Help me up so that I may not slice your neck by mistake."

Sandeep, his face pale as limestone, took her other hand and pulled her to her feet. The young firelord prince and his newly gifted girl backed away, eyes wide.

"Drop your payment there, cousin," Chahna said, counting on his gratitude and family loyalty to save the moment. He hesitated, and Chahna wondered if all was lost, until the girl elbowed him in the ribs. He grunted, pulled out a bulging pouch of bright red fabric, and let it fall. It made a satisfying clink.

Chahna pushed the tip of her blade hard enough to draw blood, then shoved Sandeep back so he tripped over his own stool with a cry of dismay.

Scooping up the bag of coin, Chahna ran full tilt, praying to every god she knew that the cinder was not lying in wait, that Sandeep would not follow, that her father would not have returned home yet. She dashed through lines of saris hung for sale, past crowds that stared, around donkeys and monkeys and children. She reached the gardens outside her room, scattering birds in every direction, and burst into her chambers. Pani looked around, eyes wide, and Chahna saw Taksheel beside her. A rush of love nearly took her to her knees.

"Quickly, Pani," she gasped, her fingers tight around the heavy pouch of gold. "We must go before we are found."

Pani gaped at the markings still painted on Chahna. "What have you done?"

"What had to be done. Quickly, or it will be all for nothing."

Soon they rode through the gates of the city on newly bought camels and headed west into the desert. Chahna gazed at her son, and his wide eyes regarded her back. She opened the stopper on her waterskin, and dipped her finger to place it on her babe's forehead. He blinked and sighed, content. Peace washed over her.

Fire no longer sprouted from her fingertips.

Pani led them west and south and west again, on towards the legends of great waters beyond the sand. And when Taksheel, their waterlord, cried out to the world his demanding, Chahna smiled and opened her sari to his questing mouth so he could nestle up against her full breast to feed.

ADRIA LAYCRAFT is an author and freelance editor that once upon a time earned honors in journalism school. She co-edited the *Urban Green Man* anthology in 2013, which was nominated for an Aurora Award. Look for her stories in *Orson Scott Card's IGMS*, the Third Flatiron anthologies *Abbreviated Epics* and *Only Disconnect*, *FAE* and *Corvidae* anthologies, *Tesseracts 16*, *Neo-opsis*, *On-Spec*, James Gunn's *Ad Astra*, *Hypersonic Tales*, among others. Adria is a grateful member of IFWA and a proud survivor of the Odyssey Writers Workshop. She is also a member of the Calgary Association of Freelance Editors (CAFÉ).

WHEN THE TIDE BURNS

By Jayne Barnard

Debris scraped along the weathered hull. Wood echoed on wood, resonating up the underwater amplifier to Selva's ear-cans. Some new current was stirring the submerged layers of floating garbage within the cove's rocky arms. In the dim of the barge's waxed-canvas shelter, she lifted the ear-cans clear and listened instead to the above-water murmurs of sea and air. Ripples stirred the lighter surface trash. Zephyrs ruffled the sail's slack edge. Was it weather, or just the tide?

The tide she could survive. Had survived many times on this barge, but never without a shudder of remembrance for that long, dark night on the rock. A storm, though… They would be driven against the cliff. If they weren't, they'd still die. The soapberry wax, all that protected their clothing and equipment from the acid spray, was down to its last sheen in the tin's bottom corners. They'd never survive a gale. Was the wind freshening, or just the tide?

"Pugh," she called, and rapped her stylus on a support pole to get his attention. "How's the sky?"

"Fine, far as I can see," he said, from his post outside. But was he seeing far enough? His eyes, graying over from years of exposure to the polluted coastal climate, could no longer read a chart. She had navigated their voyage up the coast while he steered. "Light, high cloud to the west," he added. "Barely a breeze. Get your ears back on. I'll yell if it changes."

She cupped the cans over her ears again. She had to trust him. He'd kept her alive all these years, a picker's orphan with no blood claim, spat on by townsfolk who could ill afford another useless mouth. Eyes closed, she faded into the sound from below the barge, focusing on the search wire's movement. The upper ball clicked steadily as its clockwork unwound. Faint thumps and whispers followed the lower ball as it skittered over the unseen bottom. How many hours of underwater sounds today? Sand, sand, gully, small rocky pile, and more sand. The balls stopped beside the barge, their wire vertical at last. No wreck on this pass either.

If she'd missed some vital clue in the journal, or made a calculation error, this might not be the right cove at all. What would Pugh do to her? He'd joked often enough about trading her for a strapping lad. All his years of picking, dredging, and shady deals to finance this search couldn't be re-done overnight. Hearing the whine as he reeled up the heavy balls, she detangled from the cans and picked up her hood. Securing the eye-pieces and sealing the neck, she pushed out to the antechamber. Gloves next, before the outer flap. No exposed skin.

On the wide deck, its cages crammed with sorted flotsam, Pugh wound the wire with bared forearms, standing well upwind of the fine mist that spun off as it rose from the foul sea. She said nothing, but scanned the sky through the yellow tinge of her lenses, wishing she dared open the mask for a breath of air that didn't taste of berry, or raise the goggles for a proper view of those clouds to the west. Too risky. If her eyes scarred over, Pugh would hire another hand to do the seeing. Another mouth, another share of the takings. And someone else to trust with the chart, as Pugh had to trust her. He eased the dripping balls onto the deck. She moved over to assist, her long gloves brushing his short ones as they dunked the clicker and its heavier drag-ball into the neutralizer bucket.

"Almost out of berry," she said loudly, sliding her glove into the tin. "Barely enough for two more sweeps." Or one good coating of her hood and suit, but she knew better than to mention that.

"Molo will bring more." Pugh's huge hands held the drag ball while she worked waxy film into the wire. His next cast was as clean as the rest had been; a neat arc out to a spot one barge-length to the left of the previous cast. "Go below. I want this one done before dark."

Back at her narrow shelf in the shelter, she settled the cans over her ears and listened, tuning past the shifting garbage and Pugh's feet shuffling on the deck. The clicker sent its monotonous ticking through the water toward her. She marked the distance on the chart. Three quarters of the circle searched. If it wasn't here, if it was buried in sediment or slipped down to deeper water, they'd lost. The flimsy, half-dissolved plastics they'd dredged between throws wouldn't pay for the berry bought to get them through the whole month.

Pugh would blame her for that. *Look at me,* he'd say, pointing to his bare arms with their light stippling of white spray-burn. *I don't huddle in berry-cloth and I'm fine.* Then he'd pound his chest. *I breathe the air, and I'm fine.* Then his face would close up and her nerves would tighten, sensing his mental calculation. Was a teen girl worth her keep, all the extra berry she used up on her own protection, or could he cut her loose and start over with a new hand? If they found the wreck, he'd keep her rather than risk the news spreading before salvage was complete. Any neutralizing chemical was worth more than gold nowadays. A whole cargo had incalculable value. He'd buy her more berry to finish the job, even though he sneered at her need for the security of the fully waxed suit.

But it wasn't Pugh who had clung onto that rocky outcrop through the dark hours, while the tide pounded in and the surf swirled at their feet, throwing up the acid ocean in millions of tiny droplets that settled on Pa's hair, his eyelids, and sucked themselves into his nose and lungs with every breath he dared take. It was four-year-old Selva, not big Pugh, who had huddled inside Pa's coat, the last of the berry slathered on a shirt pulled over her head to neutralize the searing spray. It was that little girl's week of tears while the acid burned out through Pa's nose and dissolved his ribs from the inside.

Ten years ago, she told herself, and not this cove, even though it felt frighteningly similar. That one was miles away down the shore, said Pugh. The coves and bays looked alike all along the coast, he said, surrounded by high, undercut cliffs. No way up if the deadly tide cut you off from the ladders. Pa should have watched the water, not put his little girl in danger.

No ladders in this cove nowadays. A few corroded spikes had shed their rusting stain down the rocks, but nobody had visited here in a decade or more. Tidewrack piled deep against the cliffs, mounded around outcrops. So much plastic to sell to the recycling plant. They could fill the barge a dozen times over, if they could get it out over the reef at the cove's mouth. Only a full-moon tide had let them in past those teeth, and only the next would let them leave. Few pickers would risk staying afloat so long. Without the fully waxed shelter, they couldn't have done it either.

If they found the right wreck, though, and if it had not been salvaged long ago, she would never have to eat garbage-fed goat again. With her share of the finder's fee, she could leave the shore forever. Leave the sneers and the memories behind with the sharp vinegary sea-tang. Dine on plump vegetables, grass-fed beef, maybe try a slice of freshwater fish from a rehabilitated inland pond. Well worth the risk of being here, on the water, for the full moon cycle.

Pugh roared, "You asleep in there, girl?"

Selva jumped. Her ears homed in on the clicker, and the slow scrape as the bottom ball climbed something hard.

"Rock," she yelled, and clanked on the pipe. Pugh's reeling slowed. Click, click, and a glissade as the heavy ball slid through a patch of soft sediment. Wait, an echo. More than one click out of time. She banged the pipe twice. "Stop."

With the drag gone, only the clicker remained. She listened with growing excitement, her brain busily plotting the undersea structure from the echoes and re-echoes of the little clockwork's repetitive tick. It floated between two widely separated uprights, with a solid flat space beneath it. Only one twentieth-century cargo ship was recorded as wrecked on this stretch of coast. Was this it, or had some later vessel blown over the cove's teeth and gone down without leaving a record? If the drag ball fell off the deck cleanly, a few seconds after the clicker cleared the uprights, that would be a fair indicator of the wreck's width. She smacked the pipe.

"Ahead slow."

The lateral echoes vanished after twelve seconds. One drag, two drag, three…the ball dropped, landing with a dull thud in muffling silt. She sketched the position in two curved lines, the scant outline of a hull, with a hand that trembled slightly, and banged the pipe.

"It's a ship," she said when she joined Pugh on the deck. "We need to put the Eye down. We need measurements."

"We need," said Pugh, "to get on top of her and drop our heaviest anchor through her deck. First bit of cargo that floats up will tell us all we need to know."

The remaining day vanished while they poled the barge forward and heaved out the push-boom to force a working perimeter. Garbage from deep below bobbed up as they pushed aside the surface layer of shredded bags and pitted bottles. Normally they'd rake it all into the drain pit to be sorted for sale, but tonight, with the golden rays of the big score dancing in both their sights, they forked it over the boom to rejoin the muddled mass.

At last Pugh dropped the anchor. Oh, the whoosh it sent through the ear-cans as it fell through the water, the cracking, smashing, rending as it punched through the final, fragile bonds keeping the corroded deck-plating together. The boom swayed; the garbage beyond it barely rising where the ripples passed. As they heaved at the capstan to lift the anchor, a half-dozen yellow barrels rose sluggishly into the cleared perimeter. Heavy plastic, almost pristine. That much plastic would cover the month's berry and food. Surely empties, though, or they wouldn't float so high. But empty of what?

Pugh slung one alongside and together they hoisted it into the barge. He splashed it with neutralizer and, not waiting for it to drain off, prised off the top. It was not quite empty after all, but half filled with clear plastic bags, a loaf's worth of powder in each. Each label had black type, a stripe of black-and-white lines, a square of squiggly black. All unreadable through her scarred goggles. Pugh shoved one at her mask.

"What is it? Is it the calsi stuff?"

She peered at the letters but couldn't be sure of anything beyond a 'C'. "It might say 'Cargo'."

Pugh took his turn peering. After a moment he let the loaf slide onto her gloved palm. "Wish we'd paid for lamp-fat now, so we could find out tonight."

He reached his hook out for the next barrel. Selva watched his rhythmic swing, poke, pull. How he worked with the garbage and the slick water to bring the choice pieces closer without splashes. A lifetime's experience in every motion. As long as she'd known him he had dreamed of this moment. Sent her to school to learn reading and navigation, so she could decipher his great-granddaddy's logbook and find this cove. Saved up to buy the barge, moved them both out from shore picking to richer off-shore garbage patches. Invested in the waxed shelter, higher-quality berry, the clockwork clicker to augment the drag-ball. All toward staying out longer, finding this one cargo. Wait for daylight before they were sure, all because they hadn't bought lamp-fat? No. She clumsily thumbed the catch on the side of her left lens. One eye. Ten seconds. How bad could it be?

$CaCO_3$. Calcium Carbonate. The multi-use neutralizing agent. They'd done it.

By moonrise they had seven barrels aboard. Selva's eyes both stung about equally, from exhaustion. She had not tried to read any more labels, and yeah, things would go faster if she took off the hood. But no. Not when she finally had something to lose.

Pugh was determined to continue, clearing the push-boom as fast as the barrels bobbed up. But eventually her tired arms dropped her end, sending up a splash. He stumbled backward to avoid it.

"Go below. Molo can help if you're not awake by dawn."

"I can't believe you told that slithy mollusk where we'd be."

"Somebody has to broker for us." Pugh pulled a mouthful of neutral water from the condenser, rinsed, and swallowed. "Go sleep. I'll sit up a while." She went, leaving him to the moonlight that gleamed as impartially on his bare arms as on the pale, plastic barrels.

In the night the gyre shifted again, agitated by tidal inrush. As her brain staggered up from sleep, something clattered against the hull by her head. Molo had arrived on the high-moon tide, floating over the reef in his flat scow. His oily voice, pitched loud, complained that Pugh's buoy off the point was invisible in the dark. Every hour's sail showed more crumbling headlands or rocky arms littered with garbage. How'd Pugh ever find this one cove, anyway, when he couldn't see half a chain in full sun?

"Selva worked it out on the chart, from the journal. Navigated us straight here."

Molo laughed. "Ten years food and finally she pays her way."

Selva gritted her teeth but reminded herself he was just the broker. A middleman to the port authority, and another pair of arms to haul in the precious barrels. If the old captain's journal was accurate, there was enough $CaCO_3$ to make them all rich. The port authority would set aside some for the town, to restore more wells and rehabilitate the least-burnt agricultural land. The rest would go up and down the shore, spreading out a wave of new possibilities where acidification had blighted lives for four generations. Wealth beyond measure would flow to the town, enough to move homes far uphill, away from the spray. To start businesses that didn't rely on the dangerous work of picking. As the gyre rocked her back to sleep, she dreamed of buying a place in the Eden Project for herself, of fleshy fruits and vegetables, of sturdy livestock, healthy children at play in once-polluted lands.

Dawn's light showed barrels two-high all along the cages. Two dozen now, with half again as many bobbing inside the booms. Somewhere down below, hundreds more would jostle inside the smashed cargo hold, waiting for the current to ease them out.

Molo was there, small and swarthy, his rotted teeth leering. "Still hiding that sweet-cream skin, hey, girlie? Give yourself some sunshine. Get a tan."

Expose herself not only to the stinging spray but to his abrasive gaze? Bad enough the way it roamed her ashore, plotting her curves through her clothes like she plotted underwater reefs from the clicker. Ashore, she could disappear to the school or the barren fields. Out here, working side by side, nowhere to go? No. She pulled a half-measure of neutral water to take back inside, ran a finger over her teeth and cupped the rest to splash yesterday's sweat from her face. Soon she'd never have to see him again.

At midday, Pugh called a halt. Standing atop a barrel, his scarred forearm resting on a second layer, he surveyed the treasure stacked around his deck. "Still coming up, and we'll never get this lot home unless we can secure them somehow. Ain't enough wire, is there, Sel?"

"Not that we can treat enough for sailing two days down the coast." Because Molo, the skeevy shite, brought only two small cans of berry, remarking that they shouldn't need more before tomorrow's moon-tide. Selva sweated inside her treated suit, the berry-odor rancid under the baking sun, but she wouldn't strip off. The cove water dripped everywhere as the barrels came aboard. Evaporating under the sultry sky, it freed its gaseous nature to the air, invisibly attacking lungs, sinuses, eyes.

Pugh and Molo exchanged looks. "Ashore it is, then," said Pugh.

"Ashore?" She stared through her steamed-up lenses. "What's the point? We have to show them to the brokers before we'll get the fee." And to leave them on the beach for the full moon cycle? That was just crazy, even if nobody else could get over the teeth at the entrance either. What about storms? If the barrels washed from the sand, they'd be invisible amid the myriad shapes and shades of the constantly-shifting garbage pack. The whole cove would need to be raked clean of lighter plastics before they'd find them all again. This was some bright idea of Molo's, sure to result in more profit for him. But how?

"Molo can certify the contents," said Pugh. "And we don't want to give them crooked port bastards a free run at our treasure, do we? Give us a hand here. See if we can fit six at a time on the scow without sinking her." When the flat boat's gunwales were all but awash, Pugh and Molo set off for shore, one to each oar, standing as they sculled slowly through the accumulation to the strip of beach. Trip after trip they made, debris closing over their wake faster each time as the sub-surface mass shifted to fill it.

Between fishing out barrels and raking garbage aside, Selva scanned the sky anxiously. It remained clear. Only the foul sea was restless, sending pulses of noxious spume over the cove's teeth from some storm beyond the horizon. Could they get out over the teeth? They wouldn't last another month here with the little bit of berry that remained. Not to mention food. And all for naught if the port authority demanded their chart and then pretended to discover the wreck itself. That was what Molo said could happen, what Pugh most feared. As the men set off across the darkening water with the final load, she thought of Molo's complaint, how all the coves looked the same from the sea. Pugh was sure to move his marker on the way out, to confuse any scavengers. She could alter the chart, too, in case the port authority men were as crooked as Molo.

By the last light angling through the shelter's roof panel, she carefully shifted all her tidy chart markings from this cove to one further up the coast. Returning to the deck, she opened both her lenses and eyeballed the chart up against the pink sunset, to make sure she'd removed any trace of the true search area. Nobody was taking these barrels away from her, from the town.

To make sure she could find the wreck again, she dropped the clicker ball down beside the ship and hurried below to don the ear-cans. Distance to the north arm, noted. Up on deck to rotate the clicker toward the teeth. Noted. Rotate to the south arm. Then two equidistant points on the beach. A five-pointed star with the wreck in the middle. She repeated the numbers to herself, beginning with north, as she scanned the cliff faces for eye-marks to help her find the exact spot again. Traces of the old picker ladder on the south end lined up over her clicker points, and a tumble of rocks like giant stairs at the north. She'd find it. The wind freshened, driving spray before it, sending her below to huddle in her berth while the barge clanked and shuddered amid shifting garbage. Repeat the numbers.

Molo returned alone. "Get your gear and some food. We're spending the night ashore."

"We can't."

"Want to be out here alone if the anchor drags?"

Even Molo's company was better than being alone with the night and the vengeful gyre. She gathered up the last jerked goat and dried roots, filled a water bottle from the condenser, and made a clumsy pack from her waxed bed-cover. Barely big enough to roll herself once over, but it would keep her off the acid-damp sand, and keep acid spray off her suit. After a nerve-stretching scull, queasy from watching the rise and fall of floating debris on all sides, she leaped onto the beach and helped Pugh yank the scow as far up as it would go. He ran an anchor line to the cliff base.

Under an overhang scoured from the rock, a long natural passage sloped upward into the hillside. It opened to a high, sandy cave, half filled with the salvaged barrels. No storm-driven waves would reach them here, nor would spray penetrate this far. She took off her gloves, then the hood. The air, on her first, cautious breath, was dry and had no bitter aftertaste. Nectar after a month on the water, and whole days in the sweaty, berry-smelling suit. A small driftwood fire burned and the last of Pugh's water already bubbled. She made soup. Goat jerky soup. Never again. Once the finder's fee paid out, she was gone.

"Off to sea on the morning tide," Pugh told her. "Get some rest." While Pugh and Molo sat by the fire, passing a bottle back and forth, she crawled behind two rows of barrels and settled herself where the cave wall met the sand. Overhead, firelight was only a flickering gleam. The waves on the shore whispered up the passage, and for a time she lay wakeful, in irrational terror that the sea would find a way to reach her even here. At last she fell into exhausted sleep and dreamed of a clean cottage on a high, green hill, where the breeze carried no scent but sweet meadow blossoms, no sound but a laughing rill of clean water and the buzz of insects pollinating. Like a giant Eden dome, without the dome.

Molo's choking laugh echoed down the cave's curved wall, rattling her awake. "Eight barrels on the barge in the morning, that's all we need." Too easy to picture his sideways glance, the leering curl to his mouth. "Eight's flotsam, not salvage."

"Ours to trade as we choose, eh?"

"Not from a wreck, no way. Caught up in that mess three bays back, maybe."

"Could happen there. Wouldn't be worth as much as the finder's fee."

Selva held her breath. Could Pugh really consider keeping this precious shipload of neutralizer for his own gain? When the acid sea choked and starved the entire region? He'd done some shady dealing in the past, but only to find the cargo. To make the big score. To earn his place in the town's memory. Was money a stronger lure than reputation?

"Not by themselves," Molo said. "We take off six, eight barrels each moon-tide, alternate selling up coast and down. Couple years, we can leave the shore forever, live in high style up on the plateau. Yer granddaddy was a sharp dealer; he'd want you to work his last load proper."

"Great-granddaddy," said Pugh automatically. Selva could almost hear the numbers adding up in his head. "One load a year for any port, keep supplies low so price stays high. The girl won't need but one to stop her mouth."

Pugh would cheat her? After he'd fed and trained her for ten years? Worse, he'd condemn the next generation to the same stunted lives and early deaths. The waves' echo mocked her dream.

"Why give her any?" Molo's words brought her upright, the stiffened cover crackling so loud she feared he'd hear it even if Pugh didn't.

"She's kin." Kin to Pugh? He'd always said he took her as his last act of friendship. "Her daddy, my cousin, he had that journal what brought us here. We was scouting this cove from the land side when he took a lungful of tide-spray."

The same cove? Out there was the rock she had huddled on all night while Pa breathed the toxic air to keep her safe? The gyre whispered. *You know it's true. You've known us in your bones all month. Now we have you back. We'll never let you go.*

She realized her hands were clapped over her ears; she switched them to cover her mouth and nose against spray. Then she realized her foolishness and removed them. Forced herself to breathe the dry air. The polluted water wasn't the biggest danger. That danger lurked here, in the cave, in the men who would cheat her of her father's legacy, her double-great grandfather's precious neutralizing cargo of $CaCO_3$. No finder's fee, no reclamation of wells or gardens. No life beyond the shore. Only the price of a single barrel, and that entirely dependent on Molo and Pugh and their non-existent honesty.

Rage boiled in her chest, scalding her breath, hissing between her teeth. She'd kill them. Push them both into the gyre to join the other garbage. Hear them scream like Pa screamed as the acid burned them too, and stay to watch them rot.

The lifetime's caution that kept her alive on shore and water held her back from leaping out to confront them. She could not tackle them both together. Pugh might spare her but Molo would not stick at killing her for one more barrel. Tomorrow, somehow…

The bottle moved between them, the talk eddied. By the time they drifted off, they had convinced each other she would take them at their word while they got obscenely rich. Her anger congealed as she turned over ideas for vengeance, for prevention.

It was already done. She had not been alone with Pugh for a moment to tell him of the chart changes. Let them take her home with eight barrels and the promise of a fake finder's fee. Let them set out without her next moon-tide, to search the wrong cove for a wreck that wasn't there. And keep searching until they died of the sea air.

Beyond the cave, the relentless waves eased their clawing at the beach. The gyre, she felt, agreed with her. It had not killed her ten years ago, it would not consume her now. If she had to wait another decade to line things up, so be it. She could come back with her own barge, reclaim the wreck, take her finder's fee, and watch the whole region celebrate her family name instead of spitting on it. For now, she laid back and watched the firelight's glow ebbing on the cave's roof like the tide draining back to the sea, waiting for dawn.

JAYNE BARNARD's award-winning short fiction draws inspiration from history, mystery, and fantastical tales like those of HG Wells. Her YA novella, *Maddie Hatter and the*

Deadly Diamond (Tyche Books, 2015), a Steampunk adventure for ages 12 to 92, is nominated for the Prix Aurora. Her full-length mysteries have been shortlisted for the Unhanged Arthur in Canada and the Debut Dagger in the UK. Building on her theatrical and psychology training, she regularly presents craft and vocal workshops for authors.

THE UNFLAPPABLE MARTA

By Valerie King

The whole neighborhood agreed; Marta was an unflappable woman. When the troublesome boy down the street threw rocks at the gnomes in her garden, she quietly took them into the garage, repaired their chips and repainted them bright, cheery red, yellow, green, and blue.

One of her beloved gnomes lost an arm when a speeding car crashed into their oak tree out front. She sent the injured driver flowers from her garden and reattached the arm using a very strong *papier maché.*

Her zen attitude amazed her husband when her favorite gnome was kidnapped by a world traveler and spent a year touring before being returned. It came home a little worse for wear but with an envelope full of pictures of its travels. Marta loved to show them to visitors.

One day she tripped on the garden hose and sprained her ankle. It was the night of her fortieth wedding anniversary and she was supposed to be spending it dancing with her beloved. Instead, she set a healthy stack of books by her bed. She'd been meaning to get to them for a while and it seemed the perfect time to take a bite out of the pile.

However, if there was ever a time for the unflappable

Marta to be flapped it was now. She startled at the sound of thunder—twice. The first crack was thunder. And the second, which followed right behind, was their neighbor's poplar tree splitting and smashing through the bedroom ceiling. Insult to injury was the ice-cold drenching rain that now poured down upon her. So much for her wonderful fortieth anniversary supper in bed. She shivered from the chill, wishing that she'd climbed under the covers earlier in the evening. But she'd wanted to read the novel she'd just purchased that all the bridge women were gossiping about. Its sodden pages lay on her chest.

Her husband came running in from the kitchen.

"Are you alright, Marta?" Robert frantically scrambled among the branches, trying to find and extract her before the tree and the roof shifted and flattened her.

"I'm okay. For now." She tried to part some of the branches entangling her. "It seems I'm a bit stuck, dear."

"I'm trying to get you out." Robert tore a small branch or two off the tree. However, it was the larger branches that pinned her down.

"Well, I didn't think that you were going to leave me here like this."

Robert's voice cracked. "I have to. I'm going to get Travis to help. Oh, God, Marta. Don't die on me."

"Oh, for heaven's sake, Robert. I'm pinned down is all. I'll be fine."

"I'll be back as soon as I can."

This time it was Marta's turn to sigh. "All right, dear. I'll try to dislodge myself while you're out."

"I'll be right back." Marta heard the slam of the front door as Robert left.

"It's getting a bit chilly with all this rain," she said to herself, as she tried to slide her knees up to give herself some leverage. She wondered if she could slide out from under the branches, fall to the floor and roll out from there.

Another crunch sounded as the tree slipped closer, with more roof and rain following. "Robert, dearest. Hurry." She was pinned even tighter.

A prickle of panic slipped through her otherwise calm demeanor. “Robert? Robert!” She smelled it—smoke. Fire? In this deluge? “Robert Charles Franklin!” No response came. “Robert!” Still nothing. Had Robert left the fried chicken cooking on the stove?

Wet branches cut and tore at her as she fought them with all her strength. “Robert! What's happening?” Something caught on the sleeve of her nightie and was holding her fast. To hell with it. She strained against the entrapment, heard the fabric tear and felt it give way.

She could now see a glow at her bedroom doorway. “RAW-BERRRT!” No answer. “Aaah.” She forced herself to move the next inch. “Aaaaaaah.” Another inch.

She heard popping. The fire from the kitchen reached the wet bedroom. The rain-soaked carpet and wet everything held the fire at bay, for now. However, it created smoke. She coughed. No use calling for Robert any more.

“Arrrrrrrr.” She fought harder to break through the branches. Oh, how she wished he were still in the room with her, to help calm her. “Arrrrrrrrr.” She strained against the limbs. He would be back to rescue her soon.

Another inch gained. Where could she go if she finally did get out? Flames licked at the doorframe and the tree blocked the bedroom window.

Oh, who am I kidding, she thought. I haven't even gotten out of bed yet. She almost laughed, except she was in a dire situation and her husband wasn’t with her.

Their neighbor Travis looked at the tree that once stood proudly in his back yard, but now lay like a fallen giant reaching into Robert and Marta's home.

“I'm mighty glad that you and the Missus are all right.” He held his rain poncho tightly around himself. “Should've cut that sucker down last summer, but she gave the best shade and the grandkids enjoyed the swing hung on it. Poplars.

Freakin' unreliable when they get that big."

Robert wasn't wearing a rain poncho but a terry bathrobe. It felt heavy, wet and cold. "I need you to help get Marta out from under it."

Travis shook his head, "Do you think I should get my chainsaw? Is it that bad? Holy heifers, I can't believe that Marta survived that." Travis shuffled nervously between his house and Robert's.

"Well, she's not really okay, she's stuck under the tree and can't move. Can you help to get her out from under the tree?"

"Don't know how we're going to manage that. That's one big suckin' tree."

"I'm not leaving her there." Robert started to pace.

"Jiminy Cricket," Travis stiffened. "I'm thinkin' that we should call the fire department."

"Hell, between the two of us, we should be able to get her out."

Travis pointed at the front of the house, where smoke billowed out of the now broken kitchen window. "Holy smokes. I'm callin' the fire department." Travis grabbed his cell phone from his pocket and dialed while still pacing frantically.

Robert ran to the front door of his home, but the knob was too hot to open. "Marta!" he shouted over the crackling and popping. He sprinted to the fallen tree, as fast as his arthritic knees would allow, and started to claw his way to the bedroom window. He'd need an axe or chainsaw to get to it. Scrambling about, Robert tripped on one of Marta's garden gnomes and fell, splat, onto the wet lawn. "Marta! Are you okay?" He could hear her coughing, but she didn't answer.

Marta could hear Robert. It was nice to hear him. He was alive. He'd do his part to get her out, so she'd do her part. She would soldier on. Marta didn't want to breathe in too much smoke. And there was more than enough to go around. With her right hand she could feel the edge of the bed, and a very large, unmoving branch squashed up against it. There was no moving that, or coaxing it out of her way. Inch-worming her way down towards the foot of the bed then to the side was the next grand plan. It seemed to work until her other sleeve caught. She allowed her arm to slip out of the nightie. Modesty? To hell with it.

The fire engine could be heard blocks away. It came to a stop but the men inside it didn't. Like birds startled from a bush, firemen scrambled every which way.

"My wife is still in there!" Robert yelled to the closest fireman while pointing towards the back of the house. "She's inside the house, pinned under that tree." Robert didn't like the look on the fireman's face. It was almost pity. Robert tried to ignore that thought. Marta always told him he was bad at understanding her feelings. He knew that. He couldn't tell Marta's bored face from her darn-right pissed at him face. They looked a lot alike to him. But that fireman. Damn it to hell if that wasn't a pity face. Robert tried to go around the house looking for other ways in, but the fireman grabbed his arm, stopping him, and told him to stand back. Robert looked over to Travis, who was now standing in his own front yard. Again. Pity face.

Robert's mind wandered. No more Marta. No more bridge night with the Arlingtons. No more suppers in b— Holy Jesus! Supper! He brought his hands up to his face and stared at the flames licking out of the kitchen window. This was his fault. He was so plumb caught up with the tree that he forgot about the fried chicken on the stove. He fell to his knees and began to cry.

Marta tried to breathe more slowly. The only way that could happen was to stay calm. Calm. It was what was required. An uncomfortable thought struck her: as she slid down the bed, twisting onto her belly, she was now sans nightgown. She imagined herself, prone, bare butt peeking out between branches as the first sight her rescuers got. She nearly laughed, but coughed instead. Keep to the sane thoughts, she chided herself as she twisted yet again. Keep your head about you. She didn't think that she'd be able to last much longer. She was tired and heard sirens close by. She hoped that they were for her. That Robert had gotten help.

Help, she thought. Help, as she coughed yet again.

Marta forced herself to focus. Still under the tree. Wet. Smoky. She could hear the buzzing of what she imagined were chainsaws. But closer than that was the chittering of creatures. There were creatures in her house! She saw a flash of red. In her bedroom! What were they doing? This couldn't be the end of the world with the thunder, fire and rain and creatures. All in her house. Something hard and cold brushed her ankle. There was a quick flash of blue. She twitched. "Who's there?"

There wasn't an answer. Why should there be. There wasn't anyone in the room with her. A flash of green. Well, there was something in the room with her, what it was or what it wanted she wished she knew.

She could hear the snapping of twigs. Was that her rescuer? No. Snap. Snap. More than one. Definitely more than one. A flash of yellow. Maybe two or three. Marta looked around, but there were too many wet leaves dripping onto her face and the smoke in the room didn't help either. She imagined squirrels and beavers nibbling away at the smaller branches, making a path for her to escape. "Push through!" She imagined them saying.

She got a tiny glimpse of one of her rescuers. It wore a—red conical hat? No, she thought. Just the stress, lack of air, and the water dripping into her eyes.

She had to do her part. Pushing her body with all her might, Marta felt the limbs ripping at her skin. Trying to hold her down.

Then she felt it. A space. A space at the edge of the bed that gave way. Branches parted more easily. She slipped off the bed to the soggy carpet and sticky leaves.

The bathroom window creaked open ever so slightly. Closer to the fire, further from the tree and the glass. She rolled that way.

Making it to the window she reached out an arm and tried to yell for help, but all that came out was a croak. Maybe more effective than yelling, help, help, she took a towel and waved it out the window. Flap, flap.

Years passed since the unflappable Marta faced the disasters that befell her home that day. Things changed. Marta wasn't quite as unflappable anymore. She became obsessive over her gnomes. Moved them to the back yard away from the kid down the street and from speeding cars. Named them all and made Robert build them a little home by the back steps.

Marta wasn't zen at all when it came to the repairs to her home. She spent most of her time in the back yard with her gnomes talking to them about the interlopers in her home. The work needed to be done, but did they have to saw and hammer so loudly?

Then there came an afternoon that changed things even more. Enough was enough. That was the day Travis planted another poplar tree. And that's when Marta had Robert plant a For Sale sign.

VALERIE KING is a long-time member of the Imaginative Fiction Writers Association. She likes to write mostly urban fantasy, and likes to read fantasy, science fiction and mystery. As a writer of short fiction, she has workshopped with authors such as Robert J. Sawyer, Mike Resnik, Connie Willis, David B. Coe, and others.

THE RED BULB

By Erin Sneath

The overhead light in the kitchen is the third to die in one week, leaving a sharp electrical smell in the air and low visibility. The room has no windows. It's a nightmare for anyone who cares about safety.

The middle basement unit of this four-story high-rise belongs to Darius, or did until he disappeared. His sister Justine keeps it for his return, and in case it provides any clues to his whereabouts. She couldn't afford to pay rent for two people, however, so she let her own lease lapse and moved in a couple of weeks ago.

His appliances are all second hand, except for those that came with the place. His dryer doesn't work. He apparently uses it to store jugs of water. Only his shredder is new. Justine occasionally picks ramen-width strips of paper from the thin carpet. These strips provide no clues that she can tell, other than his fear that the authorities would get him. Every evening she seeks out another one of his friends, but either she does not have the correct contact information, or they have disappeared as well.

Darius was outspoken about his theories on the clean water crisis, the chain reaction of collapsing treaties, and his support for the displaced masses climbing northward and inland away from the seas, whose movements tend to complicate said treaties.

He is, not was, Justine reminds herself. She holds out hope.

The quiet is unnerving. Her brother nearly always had friends over. There was Eddie, who specialized in old-fashioned protest fliers; Patience was their game master; a guy known only as Arr made fun of them all for their earnestness but attended every event. Liv, Darius' definitely-not-a-girlfriend, specialized in drunken rants. According to her, They (the Government, the Corporations, a different "they" every time she spoke on the subject) plan to cull the population so that the wealthy would have space and resources, or so that the survivors would cower and fall in line. Justine is certain that such extremes wouldn't be necessary. There are more effective ways to muscle people from their homes or frighten them.

Liv is among the missing. Eddie's family believes he's gone to find himself.

The police haven't done a damn thing to find any of them. Most of the individual cops Justine asks aren't rude about it so much as agitated, forgetful. She sees in them all the signs of sleep deprivation.

Justine finds Darius' bathroom frustrating to use, cluttered as he left it with obsolete photography equipment. She hauls heavy buckets of chemicals from the tub whenever she needs a shower. To make it worse, the only lightbulb is red, (not counting the one in his enlarger, which she would remove and use in the kitchen except it is an old tungsten, and so will not fit in the socket.) The thought of changing or replacing her brother's things makes her uneasy.

Justine has already searched through the only box she could find containing his prints and negatives. These are mostly portraits of his activist buddies wearing masks. She recognizes a burn scar on one of the quiet younger guys who she never formally met, and the tattoo adorning Patience's wrist.

Besides the portraits, Justine discovers a few negatives of landscapes. To examine them, she climbs onto the couch and presses them against the small window in the living room. She does this every few days in case she missed an important detail when last she looked.

After work, Justine watches the news, or she tries to. Over the course of a week, a handful of pixels permanently black out, which would be less annoying if they weren't in the dead center of the screen. She tries to use Darius' obsolete gaming monitor. The power port sparks when she turns it on the first time. Nothing happens at all when she tries again. This is probably for the best. Lately, the news has alternated between warm fuzzies and dread, depending on the source. A standoff with, depending on the news source, either rebels or human smugglers at Olympic Plaza, which thankfully resulted in no fatalities. Highway blockades. Neutral zones. Look, a baby sloth!

Clunking noises wake Justine in the night. She pulls the tire iron out from under Darius' bed and tiptoes to the kitchen. All of the cupboards are open. The room is silent now. She stays awake on the couch, tire iron in hand, until daylight. The intruder must have left before she came in, and for some reason locked the door behind them. The only items missing are non-perishable food, all of it in fact, save for one sad can of Algaeghetti. Darius hates Algaeghetti almost as much as she does. Why it's there at all is a mystery on its own. Darius must be the culprit: in hiding but alive and free, if hungry. Justine's heart shines.

She makes a trip to the grocery store before her evening shift at the hospital. She replaces the cans and some of her brother's favorite snacks, in case he returns.

Cans of food disappear again the next night and the night after that, leaving the Algaeghetti behind to taunt her. Their mutual hatred of that so-called food is infamous. There's nothing redeeming about it. Even the label looks as if it's been slapped on with school glue. Darius would find that comment funny if she says it out loud. Why doesn't he reveal himself? Plausible deniability? If he's going to raid the cupboards, the least he can do is leave a note to say that he's alright. The thought creeps up in her that it may not be Darius after all, but someone else with a key. Replacing food every day is a nuisance, and her wallet isn't pleased about it either. Again, a note would be nice.

On the fourth night she stays awake, ready to catch the thief in the act. Someone who steals canned goods and locks the door afterwards probably won't act violently. In her mind, she plays out a scenario in which she scolds her brother for frightening her, and then forgives him, and then they share a coffee while he tells her as much as he can about his underground activism. She would joke that Darius could have stayed home, that the apartment itself is underground. The two of them would laugh. This is the extent of her fantasy reunion. Any more hope might jinx it.

Justine sets a trap: a string of bottle caps tied to the door knob. The moment she hears the slightest jingle, she pounces into the kitchen, but the intruder is once again nowhere to be seen.

"Are you kidding me with this? Get your skinny moron ass back here and ask me like an adult!" No answer. "I'll change the lock if you don't."

Neither Darius' skinny moron ass, nor anyone else's, appears. Justine throws open all of the cupboards, and the closet door. She pulls the couch from the wall, and even her bed, in case the someone is still there. She finds no one at all, but she does find the Algaeghetti and the black and white landscape negatives that she is ninety-nine percent certain she put back in the box.

She never believed in ghosts before, nor is she entirely sure she does now. There is no conclusive answer online as to whether a ghost could carry canned goods.

The box where she originally found the negatives is closed, and still tucked in the closet. She opens it up to see if the contents are intact. Maybe the negatives she found in the cupboard were always in there, moved forward to where she can see them when the thief took the most recent cans. No, these are the same ones she examined a few days ago.

Ghost or no ghost, Justine is now certain that these images are important. She has to print them, if she can figure out how. She does not change the lock.

She finds some photosensitive paper sealed up in black plastic, which he'd left poking out from the padded envelope it came in. The return address says he ordered it from Chicago. How much did he pay for this? Justine pulls a hardcover paper book on analogue photography for beginners out from under one leg of his otherwise wobbly table. She reads bits and pieces, jumping over details that sound like they might only matter to the serious artist. She takes it as a given, for instance, that Darius' paper, and the contents of the buckets labeled Developer, Stop and Fixative are compatible with one another. She tests the enlarger to see whether the timer still works, which thankfully it does.

Photography, she learns, is the result of chemistry, light and time. Like plants, she realizes. Like wine.

Following the basic instructions, and triple-checking to make sure she doesn't forget anything, Justine slips one of the negative strips through the film carrier, and chooses an image. She plays around with the machine to find a size she likes for her print—in this case a traditional four-by-six—and to get it in focus. She turns on the red light and closes the door.

As much as the red bulb makes it difficult to rely on the bathroom mirror when getting ready for work, Justine admits to herself that there is a soothing quality to the darkness here, and the redness. A sacred space. She smiles for the first time in over a week. This was, no, is Darius' heart. The outside world beyond the darkroom is full of fear and hatred and threats, along with the occasional cute animal story, but not here.

Click. Justine jumps a little when she starts the timer and the enlarger light turns on. The timer softly whines. The light clicks off. The words "This is my first print," come to her mind and then, to make it official, she says it out loud.

Bathing the exposed paper, she learns, could qualify as a meditation. The soft, splashing rhythms of it. The image appearing slowly, fading in from nothing, as she sloshes it around in the tray. Developer, Stop, Fixative, Rinse. Drip dry clipped to a string. She triple-checks that there are no more steps to follow, and then leaves the room with her print, a few water droplets still clinging to the surface.

The subject of the photo is a canola field in bloom. The focus is sharp and goes deep into the distance. Chinook clouds arch in the sky. Too bad Darius shot this in black and white; canola flowers are an intense yellow, to the point that they appear to vibrate if you stare at them.

Hours pass. Justine loses track of time as she makes prints for Darius' other negatives. She rushes around at the last minute to avoid being late for her shift, only to arrive in the middle of a natural disaster drill. Again? This is the third time in two months.

Justine finds it difficult to concentrate on her work. For the first time since Darius disappeared, thoughts of making something, rather than thoughts of losing someone, occupy her stray thoughts. She can finish making the four-by-six versions. She can redo the last couple of prints, because either Darius didn't focus his camera lens properly (unlikely) or she bumped the enlarger at some point and let the focus ring slip. She can make larger prints for Darius' best shots, and frame them as a welcome home gift, or, if Justine is honest with herself, a form of memorial.

Some of the other nurses believe that a crowd of people were killed at the standoff the other day, despite the official story. It is a matter of debate as to whether the victims were demonstrators, or smugglers, or an organized diversion so migrants could slip away from their designated zones to who the hell knows where. To Justine, this is all speculation. Wouldn't the emergency ward see an increase in gunshot wounds?

She doesn't go to bed when she gets home, but continues her project. In the near future when the chemicals run out, which should happen long before the paper does, she will have to get more. Does Darius order concentrated versions from Chicago? Does he make his own? If Justine prints as many as she can per session, she won't waste as much, unless each print depletes the chemicals. She'll have to look that up.

She makes an eight-by-ten print of the canola field shot. The process is the same. Red light. Paper. Timer. Wait. Developer. Wait. Stop. Wait. Fix. Wait. Rinse. Dry. Wait.

The canola field looks different this time, and not because the print is bigger. Now there is a fuzzy, meandering shadow in the middle of the grain. The shadow is definitely not present in that first print, but otherwise it is the exact same picture, right down to the individual flowers. There must be something wrong with that sheet of photo paper. Better try another.

Justine's next attempt at an eight-by-ten yields an even worse result. The blob is darker, with sharper edges. How can that happen? She flips through Darius' beginner book for any clues.

Aha! You can make sections of the image paler by covering it for part of the time during exposure. It's called dodging. The opposite, giving part of the image more time in the light, is called burning. The blob in the canola field was burned somehow. What did she do differently? Maybe light is leaking through the top of the wrapper.

Justine tries again, this time using paper from the bottom of the stack and double-checking that she has sealed the wrapper properly. She steps away when the timer clicks and the light on the enlarger beams down. Developer, stop, fix, rinse. Chemistry, light and time.

The dark blob looms darker and sharper than ever. She sees it while the paper is still in the developer bath. The blob is a word, and it starts with the letter S. Without bothering to examine the print more closely, she immediately makes another.

This time, when the timer clicks and the projector light dims, there is a wheezy pop noise that Justine recognizes all too well as the sound of a bulb as it dies.

Much to her shock, a white light flickers back into existence, not from the enlarger but on the ceiling. It's small and it flutters like the reflection off an old wristwatch. Justine turns the exposed paper over to shield it from that impossible stray light source. She follows the light as it works its way down the wall and onto the cupboard under the sink. It stays there, hovering over the handle, twitching as if agitated.

Justine opens the cupboard. The fluttering light whooshes in and illuminates… cans. All of the canned goods that went missing are there, as well as a manual can opener. Justine laughs, not because it's funny but because she expects to wake up at any moment and get ready for her shift. Nothing in her life could be realistically this weird. She runs her thumb across a can of peaches. It feels cold and solid. The label is frayed along the edges. Not a dream, unless her mind is trying to convince her that she's awake by giving her the impression that she's experiencing vivid sensory details. She stops second-guessing. If this is a dream, she can ride it out.

The white flicker disappears.

"Hey!"

After a minute, Justine drowns her new print in the developer tray. The sky fades in, and the canola, and the unmistakable word SORRY burnt into the center.

Her chest tightens into an icy knot. She leaps to the door and turns the handle. Nothing. The door isn't locked, it's blocked by something. She throws the weight of her whole body into it, hoping she might knock loose whatever is keeping her in there. She slams on it again and again until her shoulder hurts too much to continue. She tries her other shoulder.

The sound of an air horn wails. Playoffs? No. The pitch rises, then goes silent. The noise repeats, repeats, repeats, rising at the end each time like a question. This isn't an air horn. It isn't the building's fire alarm. Tornado warning. Yes, this was the sound they broadcasted before the tornado hit last summer. It isn't windy out, or it wasn't the last time she looked out a window.

The walls vibrate. The mirror shatters. The lenses on the enlarger crack. The red bulb bursts with a "ffft!"

The blast doesn't come as a boom but as a rising roar, which after a few seconds throws Justine in the air, or maybe she fainted and didn't feel the floor for a second before her face hit the tub on the other side of the bathroom. No windows, no lights, no ghost. She might as well be blind.

A bomb. Darius knew this was coming eventually. Did an insidious "They" take him, even execute him, for trying to warn people, or did he escape to somewhere off the grid to cook up a real action plan? The former might explain the presence of a ghost.

The world goes quiet, except for a ringing in Justine's ears, but then darkroom heats up like a sauna. Water sprays onto Justine's shirt. She worries for a moment that it may be the darkroom chemicals, or even her own blood. Feeling around, she finds the sink cracked and the faucet broken off. There are other hissing water noises, but she suspects that most of the leaks are inside the walls.

She runs her fingers over the burning metal exterior of the dryer and retrieves some of the water her brother stored there. The plastic on the most exposed of the water jugs is half-melted, giving it a new hole wide enough that Justine can poke her thumb inside. This is when she notices the numbness in her thumb, and on much of her skin. There isn't much she can do about it until she has some light. She gulps some of the warm water down.

The ringing in her ear subsides. There are far off screams from beyond the apartment or outside the building. The basement walls insulate well from sound. She can't tell who is screaming or from how far away, but they also wouldn't hear her properly. She screams back anyway. The bathroom door still won't open. She still can't see.

Time is impossible to track. When her stomach rumbles

enough that she can't ignore her hunger any longer, Justine pries open the now-broken cupboard door. The labels slough off the cans as she touches them, wet from the broken pipes, or glue damaged in the heat. Even if there were some light, these would remain mystery meals. For all she knows, the one she pulls out could be the dreaded Algaeghetti.

Justine laughs like only a person surviving a trauma can laugh, with gasps and with giggles that take forever to trail off, whether the joke merits the attention or not. School glue. The label on the Algaeghetti can felt wrong before. Of course she wouldn't eat it until she had to, because Algaeghetti is revolting. Of course she wouldn't throw it away, because wasting food is stupid. She would keep the can and Darius knows that. Knew that. He left it behind with a label he'd peeled off and then glued back on. A message. To say what? Another "Sorry," in case she didn't take the bait with the photography stuff?

Justine isn't laughing anymore.

She waits. She doesn't decide to sleep. When she wakes, the only way she knows she slept at all is because she had a muddled dream she can't even narrow down to an idea, let alone something worth remembering.

Her tactile sense returns slowly, as a stinging itch on her arms and face. Justine learns that her skin has lumpy burn marks. They will infect if she doesn't treat them soon. The medicine cabinet feels bare save for broken shards of mirror. If Darius had any antibiotic cream, it must be somewhere on the floor by the toilet, amid the broken glass. If she can't find a way to escape from the darkroom today, she'll take the risk of searching for it, but not before then.

The door is cheap wooden veneer. Lightweight. Knocking loudly is easy. Maybe she can puncture it and tear it apart enough to climb through. She finds the enlarger beside the toilet and picks it up. Heavy. Maybe it's heavy enough but that's hard to tell.

"I'm sorry too, Darius."

With all her strength, Justine uses the enlarger as a

battering ram. She hears the wood crack and splinter. A good sign. She hits it again and again. First the base breaks off, and then the enlarger head, which gets stuck in the hole in the door. She can't pull it out. She can't push it through, even when she kicks it. Not only is she stuck in the room, she now has a great metal obstacle that will likely fall on her and break an already bleeding foot even if she manages to get through with something else as a ram.

Wait, that isn't true. This is a bathroom, with a bath, which means somewhere in this mess there is a shower curtain rod, heavy enough to make dents in the door and long enough that when the enlarger head comes loose it won't crash directly on her.

The curtain rod works, at least enough to knock the enlarger head out. The size of the hole she made before, though, is too small for her to climb through, and the rod is too light to be efficient at poking holes into the wood.

When she drops the curtain rod to catch her breath, the monotone drumroll of a helicopter fades in and grows. If it lands, its passengers will make a sweep of the area. If Justine remains hidden too far inside the building, they won't find her and they won't take her to safety with whomever they do find. Justine works faster, pounding at the door with whatever might she has, over and over and over. The chopper sound slows to a halt. Justine screams as she bashes away.

Finally, the hole in the door feels wide enough for her to climb through. Before she does, though, she throws cans of food over to the other side. The sound they make upon landing will give her a sense of what she's walking into, and if she becomes trapped there too, she doesn't want to starve.

The coast is clear as far as she can tell. She starts squeezing her body through the hole in the door, scraping her already shredded skin as she goes. She squints at the light that beams in beyond a mound of rubble. A literal sight for sore eyes. Most of the ceiling caved in during the blast. If she'd been in the living room or anywhere else she would be dead now. It rains outside. Giant drops of black water splash into the apartment.

A nuclear bomb. She suspected as much the moment it happened. If they don't leave the area soon, the survivors will die from radiation and all that comes from it. Light and time and chemistry. Boy could Justine ever use some wine right about now.

Climbing through the hole in the door takes longer than expected, then the wood splits down further under her weight and wedges her in. No. Not now. At least in the darkroom she could move around. Now, it's as if she's caught in a pair of scissors.

Heavy-booted footsteps thump overhead.

"HELP!"

A small bouncy light flickers through from outside. The ghost. Darius. No, a flashlight.

As her rescuers help her onto a stretcher, Justine scoops up a now label-free dented can covered in permanent marker. Only fragments of words remain:

JU TINE GO O OLYMP P ZA WE AKE YOU W S TO SA F TY

The thought "He didn't abandon me," flickers into her mind, followed by a dull shame. He must be dead. He is dead. Exhaustion filters out the searing heartbreak she expected to have.

Outside, the sun glows red through the ash-stained rain.

ERIN SNEATH grew up on a lake in rural Ontario. She studied film at Ryerson University, and dabbled in animation before her love of screenwriting took over. She has been a freelance video editor, a barista, a luggage salesperson and a nanny. She once sang on tour in northern Europe with her choir. Now she lives in Calgary, where she still writes screenplays but also horror novels and short stories. You may find her in summer tent camping with her wonderfully supportive husband, friends, acquaintances and musical instruments in the middle of a prairie ghost town.

THE CURE

By Celeste A. Peters

Prime Yb glanced away from the latest issue of *Galactic Gourmet* displayed across the bridge's forward monitor. In the room's portal stood the ship's second in command, head crest curled to the right, a clear sign of supressed angst.

"What is it, Zal? Has your latest brood hatched?" Zal had been on edge, awaiting word. The capable officer's previous broods had all failed to crack through their pod shells before running out of energy and dying. Sad, indeed.

"No. But thank you for asking, Prime." Zal dipped, then straightened. "The auction results have come in."

"Excellent! Who won?"

Zal's crest coiled even tighter. "The Glyphins. At 42,000 rills."

The Glyphins! No wonder the officer displayed discomfort. Yb's own fifth stomach tied itself around the fourth. Still, 42,000 rills was a fortune. All the time spent tending this consignment might be worthwhile after all. Might.

"Let me consider how best to proceed ... given its destination," mused Yb. "In the meantime, do we have the latest sampling results?"

"Yes, Prime. They're averaging 5.8 percent."

"Hmmm. Needs a bit more." Yb's primary appendage manipulated symbols on the display monitor. "Another one hundred seventy-five loads should suffice. Make it happen, Number Two."

The second in command extended to full-height, saluted, and left.

Yb's attention returned to the monitor, all five stomachs knotting around one another. Hopefully a search would turn up adequate information on the Glyphins. There were rumors…

Davina Wilson stooped down and lifted a twig bristling with brown needles from the forest floor.

"What's that, Mom?" Eight-year-old Wally slowly bent forward, holding on to his mother's arm for balance.

"It's a small branch from an evergreen tree."

Wally scrunched up his nose. "I don't think so, Mom. My teacher says evergreen trees don't change color."

"See those trees over there?" She pointed to a small patch of healthy pines at the base of a nearby hill and Wally nodded. "All the brown trees around us were just like those before."

"So…" Wally's brow knit. "My teacher was wrong?"

Davina felt a wry grin form. *He's so young. So trusting that authority figures are always right.* "No. She wasn't wrong. But these brown trees got sick and died."

Wally's eyes went big. "Trees can catch the flu, too?"

She felt a shiver come and go through her son's close-pressed body, a tremble she surmised had nothing to do with the cold breeze that had just come up. A new strain of bird flu had swept the globe over winter leaving millions dead in its wake, including two children from Wally's third-grade class.

"No, dear. These trees were attacked by beetles."

Wally surveyed the landscape. "Wow. There must be a lot of beetles around here."

Davina sighed, remembering summer walks in this same forest when she was a child, the smell of pine sap and the sound of breezes rustling the green canopy—life before invasions of pine beetles and drought rang the death knell for billions of acres of forestland around the world.

No one but a few attention addicts doubted climate change at this point. The arguments now centered on how hot, how fast. And she had news that was going to shake the socks off her fellow oceanographers at the 2026 United Nations Climate Change conference in November. This rustic walk in the woods was simply the calm before the storm of controversy her findings were bound to spawn.

A single storm among many these days, one of which broke overhead, splatting large drops onto the crunchy ground cover she and Wally hobbled over, arm in arm, back to Wilson Cottage. They hurried inside through the squeaky screen door and stopped on the entrance carpet to remove their soaked coats and shoes.

The three-bedroom log house had been in her family for four generations. Davina marvelled that its deteriorating roof and dry rot-infested walls had withstood the onslaught of severe weather that had been hammering the area for the past decade. If she was correct, the storms would only be growing in number and magnitude. A warm tear mingled with the cold water already coating her face. This could very well be her last visit before the cabin succumbed.

Before she succumbed to the scorn of her colleagues.

Especially her ex, the almighty Dr. Curtis McNaughton, an academic prima donna. Her once-favorite doctoral adviser at Scripps Institution of Oceanography in California. Her primary reason for accepting a post-doctorate position at Woods Hole Oceanographic Institute on the other side of the continent.

And Wally's father. Before he decided he didn't want the burden of raising a child with Duchenne's Muscular Dystrophy. A child destined to become weaker and weaker, until he could no longer breathe on his own.

Yb looked away from the data device, sighed and pulled together. No good having one of the crew enter the prime's quarters and find the occupant puddled on the floor in a posture of utter fear.

Research on the Glyphins was turning up information Yb wished were entirely false. The wide-spread gossip didn't come close to the facts he'd uncovered. There were picky, vengeful, unpleasant species out there, but none as ruthless as the Glyphins. Only their tremendous wealth and willingness to pay exorbitant fees made it worth letting them sign on to the trade pact. Yb had no intention of raising their ire. Just the opposite.

The prime remembered long ago coming across a juicy tidbit about something the Glyphins found particularly appealing. Something perhaps applicable to the consignment Yb's fleet was to deliver them. But what was it?

Davina stood at the podium. A time plot of salinity readings within the North Atlantic Gyre, including her own measurements over the past year, glared out into the small conference room. By its light, she scanned the faces of the dozen or so researchers attending her presentation, Curtis among them, as they took in the material on screen. Two pairs of raised eyebrows, a cocked head, more than a few frowns. One bit lip, Curtis'.

She grabbed a corner of the wooden note stand, willing herself as rock solid as her watery data. "It's right here in front of us. Undeniable. The salinity of the saltiest region of Earth's oceans is continuing to increase at unprecedented rates." She gestured to the right-hand side of the graph. "Frankly, at first, I didn't trust the data for this steep upturn during the past three months. So I asked our tech team to double check the sampling buoys and upstream data analysis for bugs. Everything checked out fine."

A rotund older man in the front row raised his arm but

didn't bother waiting for her acknowledgement before bellowing out, "That's absolutely ridiculous. Something is clearly wrong, young lady." Murmurs throughout the room punctuated his inhale for another salvo. "Clearly you need human sampling done on the spot for verification. Have you bothered to do so?"

Davina had prepared herself for this very response, but expected it to come from Curtis, not Dr. Wake. "No," she said, calmly. "Troubling as it is, this latest data doesn't matter." The murmurs amplified, yet Curtis just sat there, silent and grinning.

She raised her voice, as much to overcome the unease of Curtis' unexpected behavior as to overcome the noise. "I only showed it to you to illustrate how far we are from understanding what's going on out there. Our current model assumes the increase in salinity is due to evaporation, evaporation brought about by global warming and the concurrent increase in wind speeds over the North Atlantic. I've done a set of calculations, though." She advanced the screen image through a set of visuals showing her every step, going just slowly enough to let her colleagues see her methodology. "The results clearly show that even the most severe warming and winds measured to date cannot account for the rise in salinity levels we've seen over the—"

A security guard entered the room. "Sorry," he said, then paused momentarily, breathing like he'd just run a marathon, "but we're evacuating the building ... Protesters got inside ... Things are ugly."

The room's occupants hurriedly gathered their belongings. Davina sighed. At least she'd had time to deliver the meat of her presentation. But had anyone taken her material seriously? She might never know.

"Follow me and stay close," said the guard.

The small group hustled along a second-floor landing. Davina guessed the fire escape door at the other side was their destination, not the elevators. Below, in the lobby, a line of armed police and building guards prevented a horde of fist-shaking men and women from getting any further into the conference complex. The mob chanted, “Do something!” as a bright blue banner sporting the words “Less Talk! More Action!” danced above their heads.

Her muscles tensed, both in fear for herself and in sympathy with their frustration. Not millions but billions of eco-refugees had fled homelands no longer viable due to drought or rising sea levels. A no-win situation for everyone.

A hand fell on her shoulder and she nearly dropped her briefcase.

“Davina…”

She turned to see Curtis had come up beside her and her muscles tightened even more.

“Can we talk once we’re clear of here?” he said as they hustled into the stairwell. “Maybe I can buy you a drink?”

A drink? Was this the same man who cheated on her the night they got news of Wally’s diagnosis? The man who, since their divorce, had attempted to belittle her before their colleagues at every chance? Something was up—something that might be worth swallowing her pride to discover, especially if it might impact Wally.

She shrugged her shoulders, playing it cool. “Whatever.”

They emerged onto Spokane Falls Boulevard amid the painful blare of sirens and the bull-horn-amplified barks of a police officer. He stood a hundred yards to their right, ordering the crowd out front of the Conference Center’s main doors to disperse immediately. Angry return shouts from the mob indicated their intent to stay put.

The last thing Davina wanted was to stick around.

The two separated from the mob and half-ran in silence, making their way south, then west, and finally ducked into a pub across the street from the Historic Davenport Hotel. Far enough to be out of harm’s way and as far as she was willing to go with Curtis.

Davina ordered a chilled cider and gave her ex an equally chilled stare across the table. “So. What’s on your mind, Curtis?”

"I just wanted to reconnect," he leaned back, placing his arms atop the booth seat. "You gave a good presentation."

Oh boy. A compliment. He definitely had something up his sleeve.

"Thanks."

They chatted for a few minutes, commenting on the protesters, and matter-of-factly tossing around half-, but only half-, plausible theories regarding the cause behind the unprecedented saline levels. Then their drinks arrived, and Curtis leaned forward.

"How's Wally?"

The son of a bitch. What right does he have… Oh. I get it.

"So. You heard about the cure." A method to replace the dysfunctional dystrophin gene had been announced two weeks earlier and clinical trials were about to begin.

"Of course," said Curtis. "And I couldn't be happier." He reached out, but stopped short of touching her hand.

"So now you care? Now that there's a 'fix'? A chance of getting back the perfect little you 2.0 you thought we had at first, before we found out …"

Davina grabbed her briefcase, making to stand and leave, but he jumped up and blocked her way.

"I've always cared. For Wally and …" he grabbed her by the shoulders, "for you."

She could see other patrons of the pub staring at them, so she jerked away and slid back into the seat, shaking. No way did she buy that line about him caring for her. But Wally? Maybe. Just maybe.

"The Glyphins are getting restless. How many loads left, Zal?"

"Fifty-two. Shouldn't take more than a quarter revolution around the star, Prime."

"Excellent, but speed up the process any way you can. We don't want the Glyphins doing to our home system what they did to the Bolutins' when their order for glummer grease was delivered late. Right?"

Zal's facial appendages waggled furiously then froze in place.

"Well, get on with it!" shouted Yb. Zal did a near-complete reverse roll backing out the door.

Three months after the convention, Davina searched the horizon from a small fishing craft that bounced gently beneath her. She and the crew were heading east-south-east from Georgia, three days out, and about to arrive at their destination, the saltiest area in the mid North Atlantic Ocean. The sun was about to set behind them, yet dense smoke high in the atmosphere masked any hint of brightening in that, or any other, direction. One third of Earth's forests were on fire; she'd never seen the effect of pyroclastic clouds stretch this far out to sea. Davina sighed. *Fitting, I guess. My dwindling research budget has had to stretch further than ever too. I'm taking readings from off a trawler, for crying out loud.*

A velvety black ink washed across the sky, blotting out her watery vista. She turned to join the crew below deck but stopped short as her cell phone rang. Wally was calling.

"Hey, big boy. How are you doing?"

"Okay. I guess."

The tension in his voice reached across the miles and squeezed her heart. "What's wrong, Wally?"

"I don't like it here."

"But I thought you loved it at your father's house." She'd been right that afternoon in Spokane. Curtis couldn't care less for her, but their son was another matter. Curtis had gone out of his way to make amends. To be the father Wally needed. He'd even offered to look after him during her research trip.

"I did. But now he has a new house."

"A new house?" Davina took a calming breath. "Do you know where you are, Wally?"

"No. But it took a long time to get here," his voice quavered. "And nobody talks English. Except Dad. And his new wife." A short pause followed by a gush. "She's not going to be my new mom, is she?"

Davina steadied herself against the railing. "New wife? Who are you talking about, dear?"

"She's a mean lady, Mom."

The cool night air did nothing to abate the heat rising from beneath her jacket collar. "Wally, listen to me. Do you know her name?" It was a longshot, but maybe she'd recognize the name, a clue to the whereabouts of her son.

"Ya something. I think, maybe, Yajen?"

Yaw Zhen? At China's Institute of Oceanology? Had that bastard got himself a new girlfriend and taken their son half way around the world to visit her? Big breath. In. Out.

"Okay, dear. That's good. Now, can you tell me what it looks like outside?"

"Uh huh," Wally sniffled. "It's strange and ugly."

Okay… Not much help. A lot of places were ugly these days. "What does that mean? Tell me exactly what you see when you look out the window."

"There's snow on the ground, but it's hot outside. And today I saw devils. Lots of them."

"Devils? Like the guy with the horns and pointy tail?"

"No, Mom. He's not real."

Davina desperately wanted to believe this conversation wasn't real, that she was somehow dreaming it all.

"Dust devils," he said, "like the ones in the desert when we drove to the cabin last summer. But these were huge!"

Hmm. The 'snow' might well be salts sitting atop derelict, over-irrigated farmland. No one wasted water that way anymore. The dust devils confirmed Wally was likely someplace pretty warm with a large expanse of flat, dry ground in the vicinity. And very little water. What the heck was Curtis thinking? She'd give him an earful when they all got back and he dropped Wally off. For now, her attention had to be on calming her distraught son.

"Look, Wally. I'm so sad you don't like it there. I'll make sure your father never takes you there again, okay? I can't wait to see you next week."

"So … You figured out where I am? You're coming to get me?"

"No. I mean, when you come home."

"But …" He broke into full sob. "Dad said … this is my new home … I can't go back."

Her entire body shook as she mouthed 'Bastard! Bastard, bastard!' She'd only just received email that morning saying Wally had been accepted into the clinical trials beginning next month in Boston—a chance at life she wasn't about to let Curtis compromise. Davina clicked into rescue mode. "Yes you can. I'm going to find you. But you can't tell Dad, okay?" Plans were forming in her head, even as she spoke.

"Okay. But I have to go. He's coming, and he said I wasn't supposed to call you."

It took all her might to wind up the sole connection with her son. "Love you, Wally."

"Bye, Mom." The call went dead.

Davina decided to stay on deck a few minutes longer, to calm down, and to figure out how in the world to convince the crew to head home immediately without the catch their livelihoods depended on.

Just then, a near-blinding vertical shaft of light as wide as a large city lot pierced the night and floodlit the ocean's surface not more than fifty feet away. At least four more shafts of light danced on the water further out. Davina threw up her arm to shield her dark-adapted eyes and peeked out from below her wrist. With a whoosh and a breeze, a shower of something fine-grained poured down the beam like sugar into a cup of coffee and roiled the sea, rocking their vessel in its wake.

Davina couldn't help but inhale and taste the dense dust billowing in a cloud surrounding it. Salt! Dumped into the sea by what? A UFO? What the hell was going on?

The shafts of light switched off as quickly as they had appeared, and the torrent of salt abated. A few seconds later, a much dimmer light came on behind her and Davina reeled around. Inside the bridge, she could see the captain and one of his crew, their jaws slack, seemingly frozen in place. She closed her stinging eyes and tried to relax. *Good. I'm not the only one who saw that. Just hope one of them took video.*

She headed for the stairs to the bridge, but stopped half way up, her head reeling. Something was wrong. The air smelled faintly of … What? Burning plastic? No. Carbon dioxide. The increased salt content was causing the whole bloody ocean around them to quietly belch the greenhouse gas into the atmosphere.

Davina clung to the rail and started up the stairs just as the captain leaned out the bridge door.

"Get in here, Doc."

Davina heard the urgency in his voice and hustled the rest of the way up.

Zal's facial appendages were at it again, wriggling so rapidly Yb had difficulty making out what was being said. Something about a craft on the surface … The second in command needed to unwind.

"Lateral stretch. Right now, Officer."

The poor thing appeared to be on the verge of exploding.

"Now! That's an order."

Zal moved away from the com center then, faster than Yb had ever seen someone do so, extended to full width and retracted. "One of our ships has just been seen dumping its load! By members of the planet's technically advanced species."

Not now. Not with our deadline so close, thought Yb. The species was smart enough to put two and two together, to peg what they called 'UFOs' as the enemy. The last thing Yb needed was the necessity and diversion of doing battle with these creatures.

"Have they spread word about us yet?"

Zal checked the com panel. "No, Prime. Perhaps their com devices are unworkable. Their craft was within our energy field during the dump."

"Then images could not have been obtained. Right?"

"Theoretically, correct, Prime," Zal replied a full tone higher than usual, betraying supressed fear. "But, they've turned their craft around and are heading for land. Can we take the chance?"

"I know," Yb leaned unusually close to the second in command. "You want to get home, intact and without threat of Glyphin retribution clouding the occasion. So do we all. Do what's necessary."

At a top speed of only seventeen knots a safe harbor was still days away. Davina was getting her wish to return post haste, but she'd never dreamed it would be for any other reason than to begin her search for Wally. Now her life and the lives of the crew depended on it.

The captain had been quick to point out, they weren't safe as long as another one of those 'damned things' might materialize overhead at any time and dump its load on the boat, either on purpose or by accident. He'd actually been apologetic about her having to chuck her research plans. Davina had had to resist the urge to hug the man.

Now they were racing along in the dark of night, nervously watching the starless skies. As much as Davina wanted to get on her cell and report the incident, the knots in her guts and shoulders kept her focus on figuring out how they'd survive being dumped on.

The craft was too small to accommodate a lifeboat, but when they'd embarked the crew had shown her where they stored a large inflatable raft. *Better than nothing. But will the captain and crew like my plan?*

Ten minutes later, Davina and her companions gasped in horror as a new shaft of light fell directly onto the trawler. Within seconds, tons of white, sandy soil piled atop the decks and housings, swamping the craft.

The navigator swiftly cut the tow rope attaching their life raft to the rapidly submerging trawler—the trawler carrying the captain and half the small crew into the ocean's depths. They'd agreed with Davina. It was unlikely both vessels might wind up under beams.

Simply grateful to have been in the remaining craft, Davina and the few other survivors sat bobbing in the dark, eyes stinging, heads swimming and stomachs heaving while the ocean briefly outgassed. They had two days of rations, a water purifier, and a transponder. They had hope.

"The final load's been dropped, Prime."

"Excellent. Excellent." Yb felt absolutely giddy.

"Better than excellent," countered Zal. "The predicted side effect of our salinization project has panned out, too."

"The accelerated climate shift?"

"Yes, Prime. The rise in sea level and extensive droughts have done most of the herding for us," reported Zal. "The planet's mammalian land creatures are congregating around the few fresh water sources left. We'll be able to catch and transport them to the drop area with relative ease."

"Fine work." Yb's head cocked. "And what about that craft of creatures who saw us?"

"The craft sank under the weight of the load dump. I assume the creatures went down with it, Prime. Let me check to make certain." Zal tapped at the com station interface, then paled. "Oh, no."

"Report, Officer."

Zal squirmed then stood erect. "My apologies, Prime. It looks like four of them survived. They are now on a much smaller, unpowered craft."

"Hmm …" Yb glanced sideways at Zal. "That might actually be a good thing. I have an idea."

Davina sat awake for the second night in a row, unable to sleep despite the lulling roll of the life raft. Too many unanswered questions vied for her mental focus. Would their distress beacon bring rescuers soon, if at all? Exactly where in

China had Curtis taken Wally and how could she get him back? Her phone–the only one on board—was useless without the transmitter that went down with the trawler.

And what about the UFO? She'd kept one fearful eye on the sky all night. *What the hell was that?* Had it deliberately sunk the trawler or was the whole thing a freakish coincidence? Why was it dumping salty soil into the ocean?…

A shiver bolted up Davina's spine. *Shit!* Someone—something—was playing god with Earth's climate system. The UFOs must have caused the unaccountable rise in salinity she'd monitored over the past several years. As she'd meant to point out in her truncated conference presentation, the increasing gradient between the salinity here and the adjacent conveyor current was fueling the rate of climate change. The UFOs had to be stopped or Earth's species hadn't a hope in Hades of adapting fast enough, let alone avoiding more devastating wars than were already being fought over shrinking fresh water supplies and mass migrations. Wally's pending future would be worse than bleak. *I've got to warn everyone!*

But how?

No phone. Dwindling hope of being found before rations ran out. And three traumatized crew mates babbling nonsense between bouts of eerie silence.

Reluctantly, she shifted her attention from the starless, smoke-filled sky to the life raft interior, turned on the emergency flashlight, and found what she was looking for—an empty, resealable ration packet. From under her life vest, she pulled out her phone. It had no connection, but it still had power and activated. She carefully tapped out a text message to her colleagues describing her encounters with the UFOs and a warning about the effect of their actions on climate change, texted a personal note to Wally, and grudgingly texted Curtis details of Wally's upcoming treatment. Then she turned off the phone and sealed it inside the water-proof packet. The first aid kit included a multi-tool which she used to cut a small hole in the non-pouch portion of the packet above the seal, then she cut an excess length from one of her shoelaces and tied the packet to the distress beacon's antenna. If she didn't survive, the phone's 'delayed send' feature would transmit her final words as soon as it was reactivated within cell range.

Davina sighed and lay back, surrendering to an overwhelming need to sleep, an urge so profound she awoke only just in time to feel her paralyzed body pulled upward into the light.

"How did the sample processing run turn out? Is the brine salty enough?"

"Absolutely perfect, Prime. We've also done inventory and have plenty of wrapping for the final step." Zal inched closer to Yb. "By the way, my brood hatched—every last egg. Seems they sensed I would be coming home soon."

"Congratulations! Wonderful news."

Yb and Zal exchanged slaps of their primary appendage tips.

"We should, indeed, be concluding this miserably long procurement trip soon. There's just one more thing I'd like you to take care of before we carry out the harvest, Zal.

"I've been able to retrieve an arcane fact and have modified my recipe accordingly. Set fire to the rest of the forests. It seems the Glyphins like their cured meats smoked."

CELESTE A. PETERS has lived a lifetime of great adventures that include: taking the images used to calculate the precise orbits of Jupiter's moons so Voyagers I and II wouldn't slam into them; translating two of Canada's major cuneiform text collections, and being kissed by Isaac Asimov in the back seat of a New York taxi. She's traveled extensively, authored six published non-fiction books and penned a growing list of published short stories. Celeste resides in Calgary, Alberta, where she's found a wonderful family of fellow writers in the Imaginative Fiction Writers Association. For more, see: www.celestepeters.com.

THE FIRE INSIDE

By Renée Bennett

"Petey Jamie sitting on a wall, dreaming of the time he's tall ..." Peter Quick's sister Barbara sang and kicked her heels against the wall they both perched on back to back. He faced in, watching the Queen's Elemental Guards lined up in morning parade. Barbara faced out, watching messengers trotting their horses to and from the Tower. Neither was supposed to be on the wall.

Peter aimed a punch; Barbara avoided it. "Dreaming of Air and Fire and Sky ..." Barbara sang. Then, "Da's awake. He'll be in the garden in a few minutes." She drew her feet up to crouch on the wall. "If you wait to see the Fire drill, he'll beat you." She stood and trotted east along the wall toward the ladder. "If he beats you, you'll not do well in your Fire test."

He tore his gaze away from the parading Guards. "I'm doing Air, not Fire."

She just shrugged and skidded down the ladder.

He wanted to be an Air Guard, better even than their father had been, but she knew that. Barbara knew everything. Just three years older than his eleven years, she knew him and his father and the Tower administrators and even the garden.

She had known when and how he'd break his wrist. Everything.

Did she know where their mother had gone? She only smiled when he asked.

With one last regretful glance at the parade–they were still in the middle of Earth drills–he headed for the ladder. It wasn't that he minded the beating Da would give him; it was that he'd mind the time it would take to heal, and how nothing would work right until he did.

Wait: there was one thing Barbara didn't know. She didn't know how to become a Guard, not even the auxiliary kind because she was just a girl. She had failed all of her tests, these three years gone. Cheered, he skidded down the ladder after her and hauled it with him to the garden at the base of the Tower.

By the time Da showed up, Peter was cleaning windows and Barbara was pulling weeds. The elder Quick stood watching them for a long moment, swaying, while his children pretended not to notice him. Peter thought this hangover seemed worse than usual; no wonder Barbara had warned him off annoying Da today.

"Brats." Roderick Quick stomped onto the lawn. "Nine of the morning and this is all you've done? I'll have you working!" He aimed a cuff at Barbara, who pretended to cringe, but she had already shifted half a pace right, so the blow missed. Roderick stumbled into the shafts of her wheelbarrow, half full of weeds, and he went down in a swearing, leafy mess.

Peter couldn't help himself; he snickered. Served Da right, going after Barbara like that. No one could surprise Barbara, not unless she wanted to be surprised. He'd learned that the hard way years ago. Da was a fool if he hadn't.

Da wasn't so much a fool that he didn't see his son laughing at him. "You bloody bugger! Come down here for a licking!"

As if. "I'm doing windows, Da! Like you said last night. The Warden won't want dirty windows." Peter cursed his timing; he knew better than to tick off Da when he was hung over. But it wasn't as if Da wouldn't find an excuse anyway, so Peter couldn't really feel too guilty. Roderick Quick went through life permanently resentful, what with his own Da turning his back on him and the relatives looking down their noses and Ma leaving. But it was the way he was.

"Don't you tell me what the Warden won't want, you bloody brat!" Roderick slapped the wheelbarrow aside with Air, sending it across the lawn. It shattered in the roadway.

"Great," Peter muttered, feeling the pulse behind his breastbone. His father was old and his Air inconsistent, which was why he was a gardener now and not a Guard. But trust Da to get wasted and get a hand on his magic at the same time.

Roderick roared and grabbed the ladder, yanking it away from the wall. Peter leaped for the windowsill, kicking his bucket aside to grip with fingertips and toes at the stone. He twisted in place to yell, "Da! The Warden—" but Roderick bashed the top of the ladder into him. He crashed backward through the window, splinters of wood and shards of glass raining down with him. He hit the floor and the world went dark on him for a long moment, save for spinning stars.

Roderick roared.

Oh. This was one of *those* days.

Peter scrambled to his feet—never mind the broken glass. Unswerving, drink-fueled rage howled around him, filling his ears and pulsing in his breast, where his own Air lived. His father was coming for him. Damn it. Peter's Guard tests were in two days—two! And he'd pass for Air and he'd be out of his father's house and in barracks and he wouldn't ever have to deal with this shite again!

Except if Roderick caught him, there'd be no tests and the shite would last for at least six months until the next round of tests. Damn it!

Someone grabbed his arm, yelling. Peter spun in place and popped the man in the face with Air, had a brief glimpse of shock and disarranged hair–no one he knew–and he was free again. He pushed the man, who went down with a yelp and pinwheeling arms.

His vision cleared further. He was in a long room, chairs against the wall, a table down the center, half a dozen men in suits and Guard uniforms. Peter felt his father leap to the window embrasure behind him. Roderick roared. Peter could sense what his hands were doing and the boy dove under the table.

A gale slammed into it behind him, cracking boards, scattering papers and chairs and yelling men. Peter shot out the far side of the table, dodged a hefty man in brown tweed, and bolted for the double doors at the end of the room. The Guardsman there—red coat, blue facings, white cross—Water Guard running for him with both bare hands reaching.

No way Peter was getting caught by a Dripper, his guts in knots, spewing at both ends. He bared his teeth, felt the storm behind him pulse again, and hopped the wave of it like a salmon surging up a stream as it hit, up to skim under the ceiling just out of reach of the Drip's fingers. He somersaulted down the far side of the wave to land in front of the door. He spun, shoved the turbulent air into an eddy that caught the Drip up and flung him halfway back down the room. Then he yanked on the door and dashed out.

The next room had a pair of startled Drips in it. He was past them before they realized it, heading for the stairs. They yelled, but then the doors to the first room blasted outward and Roderick hammered them aside. Peter put a hand out and caught the stairwell doorjamb, still tracking Roderick through the vibrating Air behind him and the shiver of magic in his bones. He could feel the shape of his Da blasting the Drips with bullets of Air, half a hundred tiny bursts in under a second. Both dropped.

Peter was going to have to learn that technique. Later. He skidded down the stairs, took the last turn too fast and hit the wall, and shoved off just as Roderick hit the stone above his head. Rock chips spalled into Peter's hair as he rabbited into the first floor.

He had to get out. Roderick would catch him outside, but bloody hell! His Da was tearing the Tower apart, and tests or no tests, the Guards would have both their hides pinned over the gates if this kept up. The Warden wouldn't keep him on as gardener after this. If Da wasn't gardener, Peter wouldn't be gardener's assistant, and that would mean no Guard tests.

Devil take Roderick Quick and his temper with him!

The best door out was diagonally across the whole Tower from the stairwell, with counters and cabinets and columns in the way. Nothing for it; Peter sprinted for the door.

A wall of wind followed him, caught him, lifted him into the air and flung him forward. He wasn't a salmon but a pebble, a mote, caught in the tidal wave of Air that lifted desks and chairs and men and him and washed them all to the walls.

He hit stone hard and felt his ribs crack. He fell to the floor and tried to push up, failed, as the wind slammed another wave across him. He couldn't fight it, it was Da, with thirty-seven years in the Guards before drink and age retired him from active service. He couldn't even breathe, shards of pain lancing through him as he tried to suck air, to build a bubble of Air to ride the next wave to the door.

"There you are, you little bugger." Da hauled him up from the floor by his collar. "Laugh at me, will you? I'll have none of that." His hand cracked across Peter's face.

Peter's head snapped sideways and he tasted blood. He gasped and that hurt, whimpered and that hurt, raged inside because this wasn't his fault, it was Da, but Da was stuck in his bottle and that was his problem, it always had been, it was why Ma ran away—

Another slap and Peter's head snapped the other way. He had a white moment, pure nothing, not even pain. His vision melted back to reality from the center out, like ice. Da was screaming at him, but Barbara stood where Peter could see her, arms crossed, looking expectant. She tapped her foot.

Da hit him again and Peter was staring at a different wall, the giant fireplace with the fire laid but not lit. It was a warm day, cool inside but not too cool, of course it wasn't lit ...

What had Barbara said? If Da beat him, he wouldn't do his test?

He felt that spot behind his breastbone ignite. There was being beat, and then there was being beaten.

Peter howled and his body contorted. Everything screamed, broken bones grating against each other, but they were already broken and Da was going to break more and no, no, a thousand times no, he was eleven and he was damn well going to be tested for the Guards and no damn drunk was going to stop him even if that drunk was Da!

He broke free, landed awkwardly on the floor and fell back to find a wall there, holding him up. Pain blossomed through him. Roderick snarled, "Defy me, will you, you sniveling pissant!" He flicked fingers in the old forms and Air answered him, sucking toward him as a hurricane blast.

Peter couldn't match that. He couldn't even use Air himself, with Da's magic wrapping the air all up in itself. But he reached anyway and something answered, because, no, he would not be beaten, not by Roderick Quick, not today nor ever again. He called it to him.

Every flame in the room answered.

He had a moment of stuttering shock. He'd called candles before, made them dance, but this was torches and lanterns and every other open flame in the room, in the Tower, and from the sudden surprised howls outside, from the Fire drill on the parade field.

Fire wreathed both Quicks. It licked the tops of Peter's ears, crawled along his arms and across his hands, flowing toward Roderick with the air. Roderick screamed and his hold on the air shattered.

It took a moment for Peter to realize that he wasn't burning, but Roderick was. It took another for him to decide to rescue Da from the flame. Fingers flexed in a pattern learned from watching Fire drills and the fire pushed outward into a ring, flames dancing in the wreckage of broken furniture and tattered paper around them.

Roderick was badly singed, most of his hair gone and his face bright red and going puffy. His lips cracked as he worked his jaw. But his eyes were clear and fierce when he opened them. Hate crackled in the air between father and son.

"So." Roderick coughed. "You want me dead, do you?"

"So," Peter replied. "It's what you want of me. Why not?"

Roderick spat. "You're your bitch mother's get. None of mine."

"Good. I always hated having a sodden Puff for a Da."

Roderick snarled. Peter flicked a match's worth of flame into his open mouth and his Da choked and staggered back until he tripped on a broken chair and sat down on the floor.

"Gentlemen!" Major Odom, Warden of the Tower, marched from the stairs toward them. Behind him came a dozen Guards in uniform and as many men in suits, who might be Guards, too. Odom came to a precise stop just outside Peter's circle, hands clasped behind his back. "Gentlemen. This is over."

Peter stared into Roderick's eyes and nodded. "Yes, sir. It is."

After they let him out of the infirmary, Barbara found him in the barracks. He was trying to make his new bunk, but the broken and bound ribs interfered, never mind what going through the window had done to him. She blew in, outraging the barrack's lead, and headed straight for him. "Peter!"

He cringed, which made the ribs squeal, but she only took him by the shoulders and kissed his cheek. "You did well, brother. Very nice control. That decided it, you know, so you didn't need a formal test."

"I got lucky." He blinked at her. "But you knew I would."

"I knew you could," she said, and smirked. Then she made his bunk in about three shakes while he digested the fact that she wore a brand-new blue cadet dress.

"You got tested? You passed?"

"I stopped lying on my tests." She patted his pillow into

place. "You didn't think I'd leave you alone with Da, little brother?"

He opened his mouth and closed it, opened it again. "I remember hoping you wouldn't."

She turned back to him and put her hand on his cheek, feather light, because of the bruising. "Remember I love you and I will never leave you to face these things alone."

He wrinkled his nose. "I'll grow up someday, you know!"

Another grin. "You will! I'll be able to leave you with someone who will take care of you when I can't!"

"Oh, no you won't!"

She laughed and slithered away from him and back out of the barracks. The lead came over to yell at him, because girls weren't allowed in the boys' barracks and that included sisters. Peter yes sirred and no sirred in all the appropriate places, and tried very hard to stand up straight for his tongue lashing, and considered that spot behind his breastbone where his magic lived.

He'd thought it was just Air, but this morning, he'd found Fire there, too. It had always contained Barbara.

It always would.

RENÉE BENNETT arrived in Calgary in 1972 and has been endlessly entertained watching the city grow ever since. In 1992 she joined IFWA, the Imaginative Fiction Writers Association, and is now their vice president. She runs In Places Between, the Robyn Herrington Memorial Short Story Contest, and coordinates the Author Liaison table at When Words Collide. Her own fiction has appeared on CBC Radio, *Year's Best Fantasy*, and *Rigor Amortis*, among other places, and she has been a finalist in Canada's Aurora Awards five times.

HOT BLOODED

By Robert Bose

Hammond House burned. Eldritch flames danced and roared over the peeling yellow siding, a spectacle of pyrotechnic glory.

No one noticed.

A couple walked their dog down the adjacent sidewalk. A teenage girl jammed a bundle of flyers into a dented tin mailbox across the street. A boy piled pinecones on a tree stump next door. He grinned and waved.

Once upon a time I might have waved back, nodded, or even cracked a smile, but that was before one of those degenerates cleaned out my car. I clicked the remote alarm on the aging Austin Mini convertible parked along the curve and fumed. A curse. A bloody curse. It had to be.

I closed the gate bisecting the white picket fence, stopped, and stared up at the second floor. A face peered out from a tall, narrow window, piercing the fire. Young. Pale. Eyes like icy blue diamonds. They widened when they saw me frowning and the head disappeared, the blinds swaying for a second. There was a subtle whine and a light scratching sound. I opened the gate again to let Rex into the yard. "Sorry, boy." The black mastiff, little more than a puppy, rubbed his head against my leg and growled at the spectral flames like only a hellhound born in the Seventh Circle of Hell could.

A metal sign tucked between the perennials of a flowerbed read 'Hammond House. Century Home and Heritage Site. Closed for Renovations. Check in with the foreman before entering.'

Rules. Rules were for regular people, not young ladies of equal parts heaven and hell. I made my own rules, thank you very much.

I knocked once, to be polite, and opened the locked door. Turn-of-the-century furniture filled the front room. Workers had laid white sheets over an ornate couch pulled away from the back wall. Stacks of bricks sat on plastic sheets next to a disassembled fireplace.

"Hello?" My voice echoed. I wandered through the private museum of a house, checking each room. Despite the face in the window, the place was empty. My temper, already on a short fuse, started to ignite. "Mary. Boys. Quit screwing around. I don't have all day." Still nothing.

"Orior Oriri Ortus!" A sword appeared in my hand, golden flame crackling. I didn't need to say the words, but I went for effect.

The top of a semi-translucent head poked out of the fireplace mantle, rising until the entire face was visible. The face from the window. "We don't want to come out."

"Why the hell not?"

"You looked ... You look angry. Bad things happen when you're angry."

"I am angry."

The head disappeared.

Rex padded over and scratched at the bricks, carving a row of deep grooves. I shooed him away, willed the sword to disappear, and sat on an artistic yet uncomfortable chair. "Mary. Look, I'm sorry, please come talk to me."

The spirit of Mary Hammond, a spectral teenage girl in a burned and tattered dress, took shape astride the hearth. She, along with her two older brothers, had died in a terrible house fire some ninety years ago and had haunted the house ever since. Mary scratched Rex behind the ears. "What are you mad about, anyway?"

"Life. Stuff. The fire. Have you lost what tiny shreds of vapor pass for your brains? Do you think I'm the only one who can see it? It's like a beacon. It's a wonder some predator hasn't already found you."

The shades of two young men, one short and chubby, the other tall and gaunt, appeared on either side of Mary. The ample one coughed. "Not our fault this time, Lil."

"Fine, John, tell me what happened."

George cut his brother off. "We were watching Netflix last night, thanks for setting that up for us by the way, and there was the whoosh of rushing wind. An explosion of light. The flames crawled out of the fireplace bricks the workers dismantled yesterday."

Of course, the bricks. I should have realized that right away. The focal point of the original fire, one I thought eliminated when I'd cleansed this haunted estate weeks ago.

I walked over and hefted a brick. A phantom aura of purplish flame erupted around me. "I'll have to redo the ritual."

"Now?" said Mary, her face falling.

"Tomorrow. Nothing is going to bother you while I'm around."

"Grand! Let's play a game. We are bored. So very bored."

Poker. They'd set up a card table in a long forgotten, and well hidden, wine cellar. We slid down a set of steep steps. Pulled up chairs. George picked up the dog-eared deck and shuffled like only the dead could do. Before I asked, a frosty can of hard cider appeared by my left hand. Fat John waved the phantom stogie he clutched in his meaty fingers and raised his glass. "Cheers."

We drank. I glanced around at the mounds of junk lining

the walls like a bad episode of *Hoarders.* Boxes, bags, and makeshift containers overflowed with shiny bits of glass, tin cans, papers, and books.

John blew out a spectral smoke ring. "So, what is it going to be? Texas hold'em? Five-card draw? Your choice, Lil."

"Five-card draw."

"Dealer's choice of wild cards." said Mary.

"With a hundred-dollar buy-in, one dollar ante." George dropped the deck on the table and pulled out a roll of crisp new bills.

"Twenty, with a quarter ante. You think I'm made of money?"

"Well, yes," said John, "your grandfather *is* the Devil. Lucifer, Beelzebub, the Grand Duke of Hell. I'd imagine he's rolling in it."

"He, yes; me, not so much."

Junk hands, one after another. Out five dollars before I knew it, I consoled myself by chugging the cider like water.

I pointed to a stack of blue recycling bins. "Do I even want to know where all this stuff came from?"

"Just lying around out there."

"Uh huh." More hands and my stake dwindled, eaten away by antes and bad bluffs.

"One-eyed jacks and the suicide king are wild," said Mary, spinning the cards across the table with perfect precision.

The jack of hearts, king of diamonds, the king of spades, and some trash. Three of a kind. I raised a buck and they all called, matching my feeble bet.

"I'll take two." The ten of hearts and the ten of clubs. Hot damn! Full house. I raised a couple more dollars. John grunted and raised again. Bastard was bluffing, I could tell. The other two called and I re-raised, going all in with my last few dollars. Everyone matched. I tossed my cards onto the table. "Eat hot brimstone, losers!"

George smiled and laid down his cards. Four queens. John was next with four aces. Mary flipped over a straight flush and raked the chips in. Smug smiles. Dancing eyes. Laughter.

"You cheating bastards. You god-damned cheating bastards."

Mary stood up and gave a dainty bow. "Took you long enough. I thought you had special sight, spectral awareness and all that. So easy." She pushed her shades, expensive silver Pradas, into her hair. I used to have a pair just like them. Until they were nicked from my car ...

My temper, already simmering, exploded. I summoned my sword and chopped through the table, sending cards, drinks, cash, and flaming fragments of wood across the room. "Damn you all. Damn you all to the Burning Hells!" Three small pops, like bubbles bursting, and the ghosts vanished. John's cigar dropped to the floor, spinning, until it dissolved in a puff of red tinged smoke.

Rex got up, yawned, and belched a bit of matching smoke. He gave me a look that said, "I can't believe you just did that."

I stopped and watched my grandfather through the window of the cafe before going inside. The Devil leaned back in a carved wooden chair, legs out and crossed, wearing a black pinstripe suit worth more than the entire place. Flirting with a waitress by the look of it. He noticed me watching and smiled.

"Lil!" He got up as I entered and gave me a sweeping hug and a kiss on the forehead. "It's good to see you, darling. I ordered you a double espresso."

I gave him a peck on the cheek and sat down. "Thanks, Nonno."

The Devil watched me, the corners of his green eyes crinkling. "How have you been?"

I stared into my cup. "You know that curse you taught me? The one you said never to use in anger?" I took a hot hurried sip. "Well, I used it. In anger."

He ran his hand through his coiffed black hair. "Bound to happen. I'm surprised it worked; the old ones are not very reliable in this day and age. Tell me what happened. All of it."

So I did.

A chuckle. "Evil. Sounds like some ratty old haunts cheated at cards and got what they deserved."

"I'm not evil."

"Half-evil."

"Nonno, please, I messed up. I can't leave them down there."

He thought for a moment. "They would have ended up in the Eighth Circle, the Hall of Serpents. Full of rogues, thieves, frauds, and such. Guarded by a dragon." He had a faraway look. "The dragon."

"Can't you just expel them? They're ghosts. In-betweeners. They don't belong there."

"It's not that easy. Protocol and such."

"Then send me down. I'll find them myself."

"Absolutely not."

"Why not? I can take care of myself."

"Lil. I don't doubt your strength, and I certainly don't doubt your courage, but the Eighth Circle is no place for a half-trained young lady. I can't let you risk your soul over three worthless ghosts."

I balled my hands into fists. "You don't understand. I need to fix this. Everything I touch takes a hard turn. A bad turn. Not this time."

He shook his head.

"But—"

"Lil. Darling. Trust me on this one. Just let it be." He stood and patted my shoulder. "I'll talk to you later. Bloody imps are riled up and I need to attend their union meeting."

Grandfather hadn't mentioned my most applicable attribute. Stubbornness. I'd gotten it from him, after all.

I tiptoed down the dark hallway of his old country lodge and prayed his meeting would drag on. My plan, if you could call it that, depended on a few serendipitous factors. The

Devil's prolonged absence, my strength and courage, and a faint memory from my childhood.

His office door slid open with a creak. I summoned a tiny flame, just enough to illuminate the immediate vicinity and, heart hammering, stepped across the threshold. A swirl of embers coalesced into a fiery humanoid apparition. Butler stared at me. I stared back.

A voice like a roaring fireplace. "Lilim."

"Butler."

"Entry is forbidden. You, of all people, know this."

"It's okay. Grandfather sent me to fetch some papers. Let me pass."

"You know I cannot."

A burning tornado engulfed me, lifting me into the air and pinning me to the wall. Not as hot as I'd imagined, but still an inescapable prison. Rex growled in the hall, eyes aglow and raw flame leaking from his mouth. He started to claw through the invisible barrier blocking the doorway.

I pulled a small carton of ice cream and a spoon from my coat pocket. "I was going to share this, but I guess I'll just have to eat it before it melts."

"Is that ... chocolate?" Hesitation.

I had a small taste, smiled, and closed my eyes. "Mmmm, so good."

The treat, guardian, and tornado vanished in a cloud of sparks. I dropped to the ground and took long deep breaths, amazed my idea had actually worked. Thank heavens for birthday parties.

The rich walnut roll-top desk sat open, covered in papers. I dug around in the left bottom drawer and dug out a flat wooden case. Nine polished stones that resembled ornate dominos. The eighth, fashioned from fire coral and rubies, bore the device of a dragon. I grabbed it and a small pouch of blood coins. Time to go.

A red brass ring, fashioned of angel feathers etched with tiny harps and trumpets, sat atop the papers. Without thinking, and for no particular reason except that it seemed like the right thing to do, I slipped it on and dashed back into the hallway.

A note waited on the kitchen table when I got home. A message from my mother. "Working late. Wok Box in the fridge. Love you."

I mouthed a silent thank you, gorged on noodles, and put on my nicest black getting-into-trouble clothes. Rex bumped against my leg, tongue hanging from the side of his mouth and drool making a mess of the hardwood. "I wouldn't dream about going without you, boy. Ready?" He barked and ran around me, full of puppy exuberance. I cut my palm with a steak knife and gripped the scarlet stone tight, letting the blood flow. Rex crowded in. The air grew hot and we found ourselves in the depths of Hell.

Crumbling red brick stairs wound down to an unmarked silver gate. No handle. No lock. Just two towering sheets of gleaming adamant. I placed my hands on the silvery metal and warmth streamed into me. My pulse raced. The ancient gate, built during the first war, resisted my will. I dug deeper, summoning strength from the heavens to augment the demonic spell. It was enough. Just.

The great doors opened, sliding inwards and away, to reveal a comfortable white room dominated by a squared obsidian desk. It reminded me of the waiting room at my dentist, including the requisite hint of antiseptic. There were no other exits. An elfin woman with long golden hair and emerald eyes highlighted by brass spectacles sat behind it, reading from a leather-bound tome. She didn't look up as we entered.

"Dropping off or picking up?" Words repeated a thousand times.

"Picking up."

"Case number and authorization?"

Bureaucrats. Hell overflowed with them. I looked at Rex. He sniffed a hanging tapestry and began circling a potted tree.

Sigh. Time to improvise. Nothing beats a bit of bravado when dealing with clerks.

"Not important. I'm here to collect three souls. They should be waiting."

The woman raised a perfect eyebrow. "Not without a case number and authorization."

Rex didn't like the tone of her voice. He growled, his eyes burning red and smoke leaking from his nostrils.

"Fine, fine. Tell your hound to mind his manners. Names?"

"John, George and Mary Hammond. Ghosts. They arrived earlier today."

She flipped through her book, running her finger across several pages. A tap. "Banished for cheating at cards. Why in the Hells would you want them?"

"That—" I fixed her with a frown and smoothed my jacket. "That's not your concern. Just release them into my custody and we'll be on our way."

"Hmm." The woman stood up, dropped her glasses and the book, and walked around the desk. She wore a shirt of black scales over tight leggings. Knee high boots. There was a glowing purple gem on her forehead. "Who sent you? Onoskelis? Valefar?"

I put my hands on my hips and glowered. "No one sent us."

"Then who are you?"

"Fetch the ghosts. NOW!"

"No, I think not." A sword of crimson fire appeared in her hand and she swept it around, intent on a quick kill. I turned the blade with my own, the golden flame leaving a bright arc. She paused to look at me, my weapon, and Rex. Recognition flashed across her face. "So HE sent you, did he? That good for nothing rat bastard." She smiled, a terrible frightening smile, and attacked with a flurry of lightning cuts, forcing me back.

"Well, damn you then." The curse was an explosive blast across the room.

She laughed and didn't miss a beat. "That spell won't work here. You can't damn the damned." It was all I could do to stay on the defensive, reversing step-by-step towards the gate. Rex darted around behind her, looking for an opening where he could put his teeth and claws to good use. The woman was strong. Skilled. I knew at once I was outclassed. She did too. A vicious overhand strike smashed through my guard, leaving a deep cut in my coat and shoulder, then another across my thigh. "Go home, little girl. Come back when you learn how to fight."

Damn it.

She neglected Rex for a moment. Just a second, but it was enough. He got his razor sharp teeth around the back of her calf and bit down hard. She screamed, taking her eyes off of me, and turned to deal with the ravaging hellhound. She kicked him hard, flinging him across the room and over the desk. My blade, relegated to my off hand, flicked out. Insane reflexes. The slice, meant to take her head off, merely licked her forehead.

She slid back and wiped the blood from her eyes, her beautiful face twisted with demonic fury. Red-black drops hit the tiled floor, scarring the white stone. "You'll regret that."

An aura of darkness manifested, turning her skin jet black and twisting her features until they became serpentine. She drew in a deep breath and gave me a draconic smile.

Double damn it. I held my sword in a guard position, knowing it wouldn't help, and grasped for a spell, any spell that might help. Nothing came to mind.

She let out the pent up air, a superheated cone of dragon fire. The inferno washed over me, disintegrating the colorful tapestries and scorching the walls. I closed my eyes and screamed in defiance.

A dull roar, a warm summer breeze; somehow I expected more. Pain maybe? A tingle crept up my arm from the red brass ring forgotten on my finger, a cool cocoon of angelic light.

The dragon lady poured it on, intent on turning me into

pile of ash. I pushed through the billowing fire until the point of my sword pressed against her throat. "Enough."

The flames died away.

I held the blade as steady as I could. "I don't know anything about your issues with my grandfather and, frankly, I don't care. I'm just here for the bloody ghosts."

She gave me a hard look and clicked her tongue, still pissed off, but wavering. "Fine." The dark aura and sword faded away and a doorway appeared at the back of the room. "Fine. You'll find them out there with the rest of the gutter trash."

We staggered through the door, healing as only our kind are capable of, and looked out onto an endless, smouldering cityscape.

"Tell your grandfather this isn't over. Not remotely." The edge was back in her voice.

The door faded behind us.

A car idled on the street. Some sort of glorified golf cart. A thin man with Elvis hair and a pencil moustache rushed up and gave an exaggerated bow. "Ma'am. Need a lift? A guide? Honest Thom is here to help."

"I need to get to the Hall of Serpents. Know it?"

His mouth opened, black cigarette hanging from his lip, and squinted at me. When he realized I was serious he said, "Of course I know it."

I flipped him a blood coin.

It disappeared into a pocket. "It's not far. Your hound can ride in the back."

The burning neon streets teamed with all manner of demons, from tiny imps to monstrous elementals, a supercharged Vegas mixed with Mardi Gras and Day of the Dead. Slow instrumental jazz drifted through the stifling air.

Thom turned on a small fan. "Sorry, no air conditioning. Prohibited."

"I'll live," I said, taking off my jacket.

"So you're a dancer?"

"What makes you say that?"

"Beautiful up-circle girls don't walk out of *that* door and ask to go to the Hall unless they're working. And you move like a dancer."

"Hmm." I used to dance. Ballet, tap, hip-hop, you name it. Guess it still showed. I had a thought. Not a great one, mind you, but I was winging it.

Rex barked at someone or something that appeared canine. It barked back.

"A rough place, but they always get the best talent. You'll be a hit in that outfit," said Thom.

We pulled up to a pub, its faded hanging sign displaying a bucket of snakes. "I'll come by later and check out the show. Save me a seat." He winked.

"Thanks." I rolled out and scratched Rex between the ears. "Well, boy, here we are."

A heavy beat came from inside, bass low enough to shake the sidewalk. The huge slab of a doorman blocked the way as we limped up, crossing his thick arms in front of his chest.

"Backstage is the fancy glowing portal to the left of the bar. Missy will get you settled in." He gave Rex an eye. "And no dogs allowed."

Even heaven had fewer rules than this bloody place. "I need him. He's my ... He's part of the ... my routine."

The man blinked for a second, his imagination kicking into overdrive. "I. Uh. Okay." He waved us by, muttering to himself. What little I heard made me blush.

Every patron within sight looked up as we pushed through the door. They leaned on the bar and sat along endless white oak tables, guzzling grog from tall steins. A band played in one corner while a semi-nude woman, some sort of albino succubus, hung from a silver pole by her tail, grinding her hips in time with the music. Her small stage was covered with coins.

I was tempted to give it a go, get a picture, leave it somewhere by accident. Grandfather would have a cow, to say nothing of my mother. The thought made me smile.

Rex growled, dragging me back to reality. Three large, bull headed nightmares flowed out of the shadows to surround us. Grey leather skin festooned with rough tattoos. Spiked hooves, beards of scarlet flame. Horns pierced with metal rings.

The largest one leered at me. "New blood. Finally! Come give old Aym a private show." He patted his thighs and his companions laughed.

More of the bull men, all with matching clan symbols, crowded around. They groped, pawed at my hair, and made their intentions clear. Screw that. My sword sheared through the closest one, spraying molten ichor. Rex snarled, shredded another with tooth and claw, forcing the rest to take an uncertain step back.

The leader bellowed an angry, "Take her, kill the hound." The remaining half dozen circled, angry blades replacing happy fingers while my sword wove a defensive net. I cut another down and spun, waiting for the inevitable knife in the back.

A terrible crunching noise and one dropped like a rock. The doorman threw himself into the fray, meat hooks lashing out in every direction. Aym, meanwhile, had stopped yelling. He clawed at his throat, a white rope cutting through his beard and growing tighter. His eyes bulged. Pleaded. Dimmed.

The owner of the rope, or tail as it turned out, floated over and touched my arm. She was drop dead gorgeous.

"You can put the sword away now, darling." She purred, the same way my grandfather did.

"Thank you." I checked on Rex. He sat gnawing on a broken piece of horn, happy as could be.

The succubus put her hands on her hips. Thrust her chest out. Gave me a critical eye. "You aren't the new dancer are you?"

"No. I—" She put a finger to my lips and smiled. My temperature went up a couple of degrees.

"Too bad. You have it."

She spun and walked back to the stage, pausing for a second to whisper over her shoulder. "When you change your mind, come talk to Meridiana."

My heart pounded, and not from the fight. Grandfather had been right; this wasn't a place for a half-trained young lady. I was way out of my league, running on adrenaline and luck. Neither would last. But. Always the "but." I'd defied my grandfather, stolen his treasures, and forced my way across a deep corner of Hell. I couldn't quit. I wouldn't quit.

Wiping the sweat from my forehead, I pushed myself between a couple of bleary-eyed ghouls and dropped a coin on the bar top. The grizzled old tender nodded once and slid over a ceramic mug ringed with tiny skulls. The drink tasted dark and stormy, strong yet smooth. Liquid courage.

"I'm looking for three ghosts. Probably showed up a few hours ago."

He rubbed his chin and thought for a moment, then tilted his head to the far back of the room.

It didn't take long to find them, holding court at a battered table surrounded by various underworld fiends. I stopped and watched them fan the flames of avarice. They were good at it.

Mary ran over to throw her arms around me. "Lil! What on earth are you doing here?"

"I got you into this mess; I thought I'd better get you out of it."

"Oh." The three of them looked at me, looked at the huge pile of coins on the table in front of them, and then looked at the rest of their card-playing entourage. The entourage, an odious collection of infernal thieves and crooks, all turned to look at me.

I knew what she was going to say before she said it.

"You shouldn't have! We like it here. A bit warm, but our new friends are making us comfortable." Their big stupid grins were back. "Join us for a game? Texas hold'em. Two blood coin ante. No limit."

One of the players, a weasel in more ways than one,

offered up his chair.

"Let me get this straight. You don't *want* to leave?"

"Hell no," said George.

"Never," said John.

"Why would we?" asked Mary.

I didn't know whether to laugh or cry. For the first time in a long time, I wasn't even mad. Just tired. And a trifle vengeful. "Fine. Then give me my stuff back. All of it."

With sheepish smiles they pulled out items and tossed them into a pile. A handful of change. A necklace. Two pairs of earrings. Sunglasses. Everything valuable I'd misplaced near their house, including the bracelet I'd worn to the afternoon's poker game.

"Really?" I felt my wrist. Sure enough it was gone. "For Heaven's sake!"

Pop ... pop ... pop ...

Cards fluttered to the table.

The Devil sat at the kitchen table reading the newspaper. The smell of toast filled the air and a tall glass of chocolate milk waited at my usual seat. Tipped off by my growling stomach, or sensing our arrival by more mystical means, he pointed to the section he was reading. "The sum of all evil can be summed up in four words. Letters to the Editor."

I dug in and Rex, famished, leaped to his bowl, a massive dish overflowing with grim and glistening chunks of who knows what.

"Mission accomplished?" he asked.

"Sort of."

A twinkle in his eye. He picked up the red brass ring I'd dropped on the table and spun it on his finger. "And what did you learn from your little adventure, besides my poor butler's singular weakness?"

I wiped the crumbs and milk off my lips with my sleeve. "Always know your case number and authorization."

He laughed.

"Oh, and I need a loan."

"For what? You already owe me."

"Studio fees. I'm going to take up dancing again."

ROBERT BOSE grew up on a farm in southern Alberta making up stories that entertained his mother, himself, and maybe his dog. His recent short stories have appeared in *nEvermore! Tales of Murder, Mystery, and the Macabre* and *AB Negative*. He is working on a couple of novels while annoying his wife, raising three troublesome children, running, and working for a small Calgary software company.

SHUT UP AND DRIVE

By Tim Reynolds

Juan sprinted through the downpour from the hangar to the Cessna parked on the tarmac, soaked to the skin before getting halfway to the single-engine mine-hopper. He started his flight-worthiness circle check with the starboard wing, but his ex-wife's shout from the hangar stopped him.

"Eh! Just get the damned umbrella and come get us!"

He looked to the woman with the perpetual scowl flanked by their six-year-old daughters. At that same moment lightning struck so close Juan's hair stood on end. In the brief second of stark, otherworldly illumination it seemed Consuelo and the girls were harsh, angry skeletons, judging him as inadequate. He shook his head to cast off the image and resumed his careful check of the aircraft's exterior.

"Stupido! Now! Or you can forget the girls coming to visit you at Christmas!"

No children at Christmas? First her infidelity broke his heart and now she would kill his spirit by taking his girls away? Was this what evil was? Juan surrendered and climbed up into the cockpit to fetch the umbrella. He was sure the aircraft was sound. He'd been up in it only last week and the flight to Bogotá was only two hours. He could get them to Consuelo's sister's third wedding and be back in time for lunch with his mother.

Thirty-two minutes into the bumpy flight, he gave up on trying to get above the storm and dropped down below the high ceiling of clouds to more rain but better visibility. The engine sputtered once, then continued whining just loud enough to drown out Consuelo's continuous complaining. Juan adjusted the fuel-ratio and listened for further hints of trouble as they ploughed through the deluge above the jungle. Little Isabel mimicked her mother by muttering something about hating the rain and then fell asleep like her sister.

Half-an-hour out from Bogotá the engine sputtered twice before quitting altogether. Juan frantically checked the gauges. No warning signs, no indicators of the problem. Frustrated, he tapped each of the dials and warning lights, hoping to shake up a loose connection in time to find a fix. When he tapped the oil pressure gauge, he got his answer. The needle immediately dropped to zero, and the warning lamp and buzzer went into full alert. He looked over at Consuelo and the girls, but they slept. Juan quickly kissed the crucifix hanging on the rosary around his neck and looked for a flat surface for an emergency landing.

The altimeter dropped quickly as the plane lost power. Juan was confident he could glide them down safely if he could only find a road or a field until a bolt of lightning punched a hole through the port wing and the semi-controlled glide became a slow, inevitable spiral down into the Colombian jungle. The ground rushed up at them, and he unclipped his harness to reach around and hold his babies one last time.

The aftershock rattled the bus windows and tested the springs of the nearly retired Blue Bird school bus but Juan's brain was still reliving the crash five years ago. He closed his eyes again, took a deep breath and slapped himself hard across the face. The crash of the Cessna in Colombia was once again banished back to the world of his nightmares, but the slap set up a feedback loop through Juan's hearing aid. He tapped the aid. When that didn't work, he worked the on-off switch to reset it.

This was his sixth hearing aid since the crash that killed him, Consuelo, and the girls. Unfortunately he hadn't stayed dead, thanks to the old cocoa farmer who pulled him from the wreck a moment before the fuel ignited and the Cessna blew apart. With a combination of CPR and prayer, Juan was dragged back from the land of the dead badly burned, completely deaf in one ear, half-deaf in the other, and with a strange, wobbly limp. The day he left the hospital he changed his name to Miguel and left both flying and Colombia behind for Chile and a bus.

"Yo, Miguel! We just about ready to get this show back on the road?"

The young American preacher, Father Charles, stood in the doorway of the bus, having decided their roadside piss break was over and done. Juan looked at his watch. He'd only been asleep for two minutes, though it had felt like another lifetime within his nightmare.

"That was the second aftershock since we stopped so let's get moving and get to those quake-made orphans in Coronel where we can do God's good work."

He laughed at the last bit, and a dire chill ran down Juan's spine despite the midday heat on the Chilean back roads.

"Si, Padre. We can go as soon as everyone is loaded back up."

He looked around and noticed few of the twenty International aid workers had actually gone more than a few steps from the bus. The aftershocks tended to send people running for cover or at least holding onto something a little more solid, but every one of this group stood around taking slow drags on American cigarettes without much concern for the ground shimmying beneath them.

While his passengers butted out and loaded up, he walked around his bus, making a quick circle check, looking for loose bolts, leaks, or any one of the dozens of things that could spell disaster in an instant. One of the pretty young German nurses approached and in near-perfect Spanish purred, *"How much further, Miguel?"* She put one slender, tanned, manicured hand on his scarred forearm, and his head nearly exploded with screams.

Papa! Don't go! Stay! Don't go with them!

Evil, Papa! Evil!

His knees weakened, and his belly clenched up. The voices he heard were little Isabel's and Giselle's. He looked around for his babies but saw only the tall blonde nurse looking nonplussed as if she hadn't heard the screams at all. The screams of the dead, the screams of the dying—the screams of his daughters!

He yanked his arm back, and the nurse's handprint on his old scars quickly faded from a new, ripe, red burn to white scar tissue. The new mark disappeared altogether, leaving only his old, puckered, scarred skin. The screams stopped when the contact was broken. Even though the tactile terror faded fast, his arm still burned. After a moment all was normal again, though the nurse watched Juan closely, her head tilted a little to the right.

"Que pasa, Miguel? Are you okay?"

Juan forced a smile. "I am fine, senorita."

"Okay, but you still did not answer my question. How long?"

"Uh, we just passed Talca, senorita, so maybe five or six hours, if we're lucky. Probably closer to eight. Reports coming from the coast are saying the further west we go, the worse shape the highway is in. This quake was bad."

"Sixth largest ever recorded by a seismograph, handsome. It looks like 2010 is off to a fast start." She boarded the bus, sidling down the aisle to her seat.

Juan yanked his dirty red bandana out of his pocket and wiped his arm where she'd touched him. The effort didn't rid him of the dirty feeling nesting in his soul. He got back in his seat, wondering what the hell was going on.

The American preacher rounded up the last of the group and followed them onto the bus. "Could have been there a lot faster if we'd flown, Miguel."

Juan nodded and started the bus. "Si, that is true, but I do not fly and neither does Esperanza, my bus." If he'd been completely honest with his customers he would have said he didn't fly any more. If he were completely honest, he wouldn't be pretending to be a Chilean named Miguel, even though he was now probably more Miguel the half-deaf, crippled Chilean bachelor than Juan, the divorced, child-killing Colombian pilot.

"Well, just so long as we get there before midnight. I'd like to get to work with those poor souls while the moon is full and ripe."

Sporadic laughter came from around the bus, but Juan gave all of his attention to getting off the soft gravel shoulder and back on the road.

A little more than an hour later, Juan heard a voice just behind him and looked over his shoulder at the speaker, one of the three elderly nuns. She spoke so softly he couldn't hear her. "Uno momento." He reached behind his ear and turned the hearing aid volume up as high as it would go. "Si, Sister?" He kept his eyes on the road but leaned toward her to hear her better.

Her low voice sounded strong and clear. "I asked if you would care for a bottle of water, my son. I noticed you finished yours a few miles back." She held up a plastic bottle from one of the many cases the group had brought with them. "It's not cold, but it is refreshing."

"Muchas gracias, Sister." Juan reached up and opened his hand, not wanting to take his attention away from the trio of crashed and burned out transport trucks they were passing. The bottle was placed firmly in his hand. "Thank you." He quickly placed the bottle in the wire cup holder bolted to the dashboard and got both hands back on the steering wheel to get them around the mess of buckled and rough road.

"My pleasure, my son."

Holding on to the seat backs, the nun made her way back to her seat. Other than her shuffling footsteps, the bus was eerily silent as they rolled along. Juan looked up at the cabin-view mirror wondering if his passengers were rubbernecking at the accident but someone had tilted the mirror up so that it pointed at the roof and not at the seats. Not wanting to spare a hand to unbuckle his seat belt and reach up to fix it while he drove, he left it in the odd position for the time being.

As they left the third wrecked truck behind them, Juan heard a low, beastly growl followed by a chuckle coming from the seats. What in God's name?!

That growl was answered with another. With a quick, worried glance over his shoulder, Juan saw his twenty passengers looking out the various dusty windows. There was another growl. He concentrated on the sound and could eventually distinguish words within the guttural utterance.

"All dead. Gone. Out of our reach."

Juan was confused. Who was out of reach?

"Yes, but be patient. The quake orphans are waiting. Amdusias has been busy gathering them from the surrounding ruined countryside."

Amdusias? Where had Juan heard that name before?

"King Amdusias? You trust him not to start without us?"

"I didn't say he hadn't. I told him one in twenty was his, just so long as his total for us topped one hundred and twenty."

"Will he find that many?"

"He was at two hundred and eleven when we last spoke. He's been up and down the coast gathering together the lost, the broken, and the disenfranchised. He wanted to use his legions, but I reminded him we're not to draw attention to ourselves."

"If he's done this much on his own then he's welcome to his five percent."

"I'm sure his majesty will be so pleased he has your approval, Belial."

A deep chuckle followed before the two voices went silent.

Juan kept driving, trying to make sense of the strange conversation. Amdusias and Belial? He knew those names, but couldn't remember from where. The voices were those of his passengers, but at the same time, they weren't. He thought it was like having one of those United Nations translators repeating the Yugoslavian or French representative's words into Spanish a moment after they were spoken in their native tongue. Or was it all in his head? Were the heat and the thin mountain air messing with his mind? He shook it off and drove on.

A few miles down the road another bus lay twisted and shattered in the ditch where it had been tossed by the earthquake. A row of broken bodies lay next to the road. At least three people worked to retrieve more corpses from the wreck. Nearby, a turkey vulture rocked from foot to foot, waiting for a rescuer to turn his back so it could hop in and feed. Two of the rescuers lifted the body of a young girl out through a shattered window. All Juan could think of was his own dead babies and his role in their deaths. For five years he'd been berating and cursing himself for not finishing his pre-flight inspection, his circle check. He also cursed himself daily for allowing Consuelo to bully him into taking the easy way. He was sure he would have found the oil leak and either fixed it or postponed the flight and to hell with the stupid third wedding of a mean cow whose husbands would rather die of heart attacks than live another day with her.

"Earthquakes are the best."

He blinked away his self-pity at the sound of the comment growled behind him. The *best*?

"I used to like floods, but the pickings are too thin for the effort it takes."

"What about hurricanes?"

"Only if we can get there before the cleanup progresses too far. New Orleans was a mess. It was great. Enough suffering for all of us."

Enough suffering?

"January 23, 1556. Shaanxi Province, China."

"700,000."

"830,000 was our final total."

"Now *that* was a feast."

"I didn't feed like that again until the Calcutta cyclone in 1737."

"You were there? Me, too!"

Juan reached up and turned off his hearing aid. Who or what in God's name was he hearing? After a moment he turned his hearing aid on again, though he was terrified of what he was going to hear next.

"Why does that not surprise me, Dajjal?"

"Says she who never misses a meal. I'm surprised you weren't here during the actual quake, Lamashtu."

Lamashtu? Another name he'd heard once before? When he was young?

"There was an odd spike in the birth rate in Northern Africa, and I was needed to thin things out."

"Infants? Lucky you."

Stunned, disoriented, and nauseated by what he heard, Juan slowed the bus and pulled over on the shoulder. He needed air and silence. Dammit, he needed the voices to stop, wherever they were coming from.

"Hey, Miguel, que pasa?"

"Sorry. My, um, turn to piss. Maybe a good time for a smoke, too." He pushed on the metal handle and swung the door open, swapping the stifling heat of the bus for a little of the slightly cooler mountain air. As he stood, he nudged the cabin-view mirror down with his elbow until he was sure it would give him a good view of his passengers when he reclaimed his seat. Maybe if his eyes could see the lips moving with the words he heard it would all make sense.

"Did I hear smoke break?" The German nurse was right on Juan's heels when he stumbled down the steps.

He limped around the front of the bus. Out of sight, he removed his hearing aid, bent over, and poured water over his head. He rubbed the warm wetness into his face and washed away the sweat salt and road grime, and then put his hearing aid back in.

"You okay, Miguel?"

He should have known he wouldn't be alone with this group. "The thin mountain air and no lunch, Padre."

"Well, my friend, that won't do at all. I'm sure between the twenty of us we can round up a little sustenance for our good driver."

"I'm fine, Padre, really. Much better now that I've had a

little fresh air." He was damn sure he didn't want to share what passed for food with this group.

"Nonsense! I insist. As a matter of fact, I'm sure I have an apple you're welcome to."

"Padre ..." He knew he was losing the argument.

"You need to eat, and a nice juicy Granny Smith will hit the spot. Don't tell me you're not at least a little bit tempted, Miguel." Father Charles stepped back into the bus, and Juan's hearing aid picked up the preacher's low, growly whisper clearly through the open window.

"We have to keep the driver strong and lucid. We may need him to get us past any road blocks the military set up to keep the curious away from the worst areas. I need a Granny Smith apple and something substantial, like a sandwich."

Even Juan's faulty hearing aid couldn't clarify the following exchange of low growls, but a moment later Father Charles stuck his head out of the door. "Load up, people! We're over halfway there."

When Juan dropped down into the driver's seat the preacher handed him the promised apple, a plastic-wrapped sandwich, and a warm juice box drink.

"Hopefully this will help, my friend."

"Gracias. I am feeling much better now and will get us back on the road before I eat." Juan forced himself to accept the offered food and placed it down to the left of his seat.

"I don't want you distracted while you drive, Miguel. We can take a few more minutes here."

"Nonsense, Padre. If I cannot eat and drive at the same time, I would not be able to call myself a bus driver."

"Well, if you insist."

"I do, Padre. And thank the people who shared. I am blessed by their generosity."

"Think nothing of it."

Juan cranked the door closed, released the parking break, shifted Esperanza into gear, and was a little less gentle as he got his beloved bus back onto the black-top. The preacher returned to his seat.

Juan felt something bump his left foot and looked down quickly to see the apple rolling around. No way was he going to eat anything from the hands of these people. He crushed the apple under his heel to keep it from rolling around. He glanced up at the newly adjusted mirror to see if anyone had noticed his disdainful treatment of their gift. A horn honk on his left side yanked his attention back to the road before he could focus on their faces in the vibrating mirror.

Once the old Ford passed them and sped on, Juan shot a glance at the mirror and nearly screamed at what he saw. It could not possibly be what he thought. He blinked, rubbed his eyes quickly, and reached for the bottle of water. He might indeed be suffering from heat stroke for in that brief look into the mirror he was sure his passengers had all donned bizarre, horrific, Halloween masks.

He quickly looked back over his shoulder to confirm or deny the sight, but the faces looking out the windows or down into books and magazines were human faces. They were tired and hot and probably a bit hungry themselves, but they were human.

Remembering the conversations he'd been overhearing, he forced his eyes to look back up at the mirror. Madre de Dios! Clamping his jaw shut so he didn't utter the words out loud, he drove on, his hands shaking. As the miles rolled past, he stole occasional glances up at the mirror and his mind cleared, his resolve strengthened, and his hands eventually steadied. They were beasts!

Demons, Papa!

Isabel? Yes! And she was right. He looked at demons! Near the back was a handsome man—with bat wings! Where the German nurse had been sat a hideous, human-sized viper. In the front seat an angel with the head of a lion read Jennifer Rahn's *Wicked Initiations*, the book he'd seen the Padre with. A bump in the road got Juan's attention for a moment, but his eyes flickered straight back to the mirror. He was certain of it. Sangre de Cristo, they were demons! It could be the only explanation! These were not masks he was looking at. Not a hallucination. It was ... what? A vision? A sending? A glimpse into another reality? Was he dead? Was this Hell? Why him?

"You really should keep your eyes on the road, my friend. I moved that mirror up so you wouldn't get distracted by silly ideas."

"I ... you ..." He looked directly at the speaker. Father Charles crouched next to him, a very human Father Charles. He had neither lion's head nor angel's wings. He sweated and smiled, though the smile didn't reach his eyes.

"What? What are you thinking, Miguel? Or should I call you Juan? See, we all have our little secrets that aren't really secrets after all, my friend."

Juan shivered and stole a look at the mirror. A demon squatted beside him. "I'm not going to let you ..." His brain tripped over itself as it tried to adjust to the information it received.

"Let us what, Juan? You'll do nothing. There is nothing you can do, so just shut up and drive." The tires on the right side of Esperanza grabbed at gravel, and the preacher gently placed his overly warm hand on Juan's head, turning his attention back to the road. "Maybe you should forget your loco notions and just do what you've been paid to do—take us to the earthquake survivors. You accepted my silver so you really have no choice."

Demons, Papa!

Juan kept his eyes front as Father Charles straightened from his crouched position, tore the mirror off its mount, and smashed it with his fist. "Problem solved, Juan. No more delusions, illusions, or hallucinations. Let's just get to those poor orphans and render them all the succor we possibly can."

A dark, evil hunger stained the words, and Juan truly knew terror for the first time in a very long time. Not for himself, but terror for the children those creatures would find at the end of this journey. Horror for their innocent souls and the souls of anyone who would keep those beasts from their meals, or harvests, or whatever the Hell they planned to do.

Gripping the wheel until his knuckles nearly cracked, he guided Esperanza down the mountain road as it steepened and the curves became more pronounced. He slowed reflexively, not wanting to break an axle in a hole or skid into the rock face. His brain spun, lost in the enormity of it all.

A growly whisper came from the middle of the demonic pack he chauffeured. "There's nothing quite like the taste of a five-year-old girl's soul when she looks into my eyes and thinks she sees love while I drain her essence. Mmm hmm."

The highway edged close to the drop-off. Without a second thought, Juan, who had already died once in this lifetime, shifted his good foot from the brake pedal to the throttle and guided his Esperanza, his 'Hope', through a quake-made rift in the guardrail and off the precipice.

Amidst the anguished screams and wailing fury of the demons behind him, the former pilot smiled peacefully and spoke his last thought aloud to no one in particular. "I really have missed flying."

TIM REYNOLDS is a proud IFWit twistorian, bending and twisting history into fictional shapes for sheer entertainment. His published stories range from lighthearted fantasy to turn-on-the-damned-lights-now horror, and can be found in various anthologies around the world or all in his first collection, *The Death of God & Other Stories*. His first published novel, *The Broken Shield*, was an urban fantasy with pixies, Sasquatch, the Holy Grail, a smartphone app, and Lucifer himself. His latest novel, *Waking Anastasia* (Tyche Books), tells the story of a man who accidentally awakens the mischievous ghost of Anastasia Romanov. Find Tim at: www.tgmreynolds.com.

EARTH AND FLAME

By Susan Forest

Kaolin coalesced from earth and smoke in a dry summer wood.

She filled her lungs with a glory of scents—juniper, heather, sage, a dozen more—and wandered, wondering, among gnarled old-woman trees. Delighted by silky heat, rough bark and spongy moss, she slipped through the half-light of dawn, drawn by a hunger, a prickle beneath her skin, a restlessness, toward the gurgle of water on stone.

Where the emaciated stream trickled into an aqueduct, a man with knotted muscles and thick, dark hair dug with a bronze shovel. At the rustle of her presence, he rose like a lion, his strong, sensual hands smeared to the elbows with yellow-brown clay.

Hands.

Kaolin marveled. She had no hands, only arms that tapered to delicate points.

This man—this was the source of her thirst, the yearning that lured her to earth. His gaze caught Kaolin in a gasp of recognition and he stilled, amazed, as though movement would break the spell between them.

She lifted her wings of gossamer and stretched in sultry

welcome, smoke trailing from her feathers' fanned tips to disappear among the woody shadows.

In thrall, the man took a step toward her.

She turned, a languid movement, and her form twisted into the shape of a young olive tree, wings branching to become narrow leaves, toes rooting into cool soil.

He approached her, mud-smeared, taking in her guise, her scent, the sigh of her leaves, her beauty.

He stretched an exquisite finger to caress her cheek, and she caught her breath as sudden pleasure raced across her skin and into her core. Who was this man, this beautiful being of earth and water?

A breeze sprang up, hot and harsh, plucking at her branches.

"Gaius?"

The man turned, and the withdrawal of his touch left Kaolin bereft.

The wind raised a choking dust.

A woman, clothed in colorless rags that seethed in the turbulent air, materialized on the far bank of the river. Her pale hair writhed about pallid eyes and skin, translucent in the growing dawn.

"Aeola." Gaius splashed through the creek to her side.

Aeola laughed a tinkling laugh and catching his hand, tugged. "The fish is smoked. Come and eat. Who knows what we'll eat tomorrow."

The hot wind rose, tossing Kaolin's branches, tumbling twigs.

Gaius heaved a goatskin bag to his shoulder. "I found wonderful fine-grained clay, Aeola. And I had a vision of the amphora I'll make."

The wind threw Gaius' words to the sky.

"Wonderful!" Aeola gamboled ahead of him down the dry, shrubby hillside.

Gaius paused an instant to look back at Kaolin, and again, heat smoldered in her chest.

"Gaius!"

Gaius shook his head with a smile of wonderment, and turned to trudge down the hill.

When Kaolin faded from the world to her home of crystalline light, she ached with joy and grief, and a tiny blemish scarred her cheek.

Kaolin danced for him, flame.

Through the drought of summer, she returned again and again, appearing in the downy petal of an orchid, the blush of sunset, the sweep of a valley. She came, too, in abundance of grain, in the spring of a baby goat, in the lines of an old man's face. She smiled in the shine of Aeola's eyes.

She came, always, as beauty.

Gaius returned her gifts. For her, he adorned pots and plates and vessels and ewers. Here he painted her as he'd first seen her, a wind-tossed olive tree. Here she was as a pregnant goat, a bowl of figs, a sleeping child.

At first, they trifled, toyed, teased. But as they grew close, their play became urgent, a craving, a thirst. Gaius cast clay on his wheel in fever, eyes closed, disregarding hunger and fading light. Kaolin infused the clay, caressing his hands as he caressed her. She led his hunt among the rocky hills for pigments of copper and cobalt and zirconium. She pushed him to find her beauty in the brilliance of smoky glazes, in the shapes of ewers, in adornment etched by twig and ash and leaf. Gaius pushed Kaolin to show him pulsing color and line and shape.

They stumbled upon moments of ecstasy approaching godliness, and finding them, were drawn back to each other, to hunt again.

"You work too hard, you know." Nomos, the village baker, stopped in the dust by Gaius' kiln. "A pot of red clay serves as well as one of white. A plain ewer pours as well as one decorated with men at harvest."

The autumn wind whipped across the village square and flickered Kaolin's fiery dance below the kiln and she wished this intruder gone.

Gaius knelt in the dirt and his exquisite hands fed her twigs and sticks. A low table stood nearby with bisque bowls dipped and daubed in glaze. "We paint antelope on the boulders."

"That's different." Nomos settled bony thighs on Gaius' stool. "We show the antelope it is safe to come here and share our goats' pathetic graze." He spread his hands and grinned. "There are no hunters hiding in the brush!"

The wind gusted, clattering sand against the kiln, and Kaolin ducked.

"I paint fat grain for the same reason." Gaius stacked bricks to break the wind. "To show the Gods our need."

Nomos leaned two palms on his knees. "Show the Gods our river overflowing, then. Show them our aqueduct gushing, if you want to help. That's why our babies die. That's why our old men sit and mumble. The Gods ignore our prayers for water." He shook his head in disgust. "I don't know what we've done to anger them."

Kaolin, flame, pirouetted above the embers and rose to flick her wings against the brick above her, sharing her fever with the kiln.

"The Gods love beauty." Gaius nudged a log under Kaolin to feed her. "Beauty will draw their attention."

"Eh." Nomos shook his head. "Well, if it's beauty you want, look over there."

Gaius looked where Nomos pointed. "Oh…"

The inconstant wind spun about, flattening Kaolin.

Aeola frolicked with a handful of other young women, tossing grain into the air to let it fall on a blanket, letting the breeze carry away the chaff.

Gaius pulled his paddles from beneath the table and opened the kiln. He lifted an unembellished serving bowl to the table.

Kaolin lifted her flames, feebly battling the gusts.

"No schools of fish?" Nomos asked, eyeing the plain dish. "No pregnant goats?"

"Aeola wanted it that way. It's for her." Gaius gave the paddles to Nomos. "Will you watch the kiln? It needs to cool."

Kaolin cried out a choking crackle that was lost in the laughter of the wind.

"Go!" Nomos encouraged Gaius, pulling down the windbreak and kicking the fire apart. Kaolin tumbled to ash.

Kaolin began to vanish.

Within, her love and pain grew unabated, but outwardly she became like reflection on water: smoke, more than flame; pentimento, more than earth.

Techne cradled Kaolin in his arms, as she'd done for her sisters and brothers who'd faded to dreams. Like Kaolin, each of her kind was complete, but for a single flaw. One sister had no voice. A brother had no eyes; another, no words; another, no ears. Techne had no legs. And those who'd ventured into the world, given of themselves, too weak to resist the desire to approach the Gods, had suffered. One sister's wing was shattered. Another had a shard broken from her face. Kaolin carried burns from every touch of Gaius' fingers.

But Techne was young. He had never left their home of globed light. He asked the questions Kaolin once had asked. "Does it hurt?"

"Yes."

"Will it happen to me?"

"If you are very, very lucky."

Her younger brother pondered this with doubt in his eyes, and she pressed her cheek against his hand in reassurance.

"You must remain in our world, then," Techne said. "You can't go back to him."

"I must."

"To have your feet burned to ash? To have your body scarred? To have your bones and skin and hair blow away like dust in the wind?"

"He also bears the scars of loving me."

"Gaius no longer sees you, even when you go to him," the young one protested. "He forgets you, and his forgetting starves you."

Kaolin was silent. Techne was wrong. Gaius still saw beauty. She knew he did. The beauty of practical things. Of muscles hardened by labor. Of seeds gathered and spread. Of pots, thick-walled and serviceable. And Gaius still gave of himself. He gave respite to a thin wife, delicate as air, easily burned by the sun, inconstant as the wind.

"I've been gone too long."

"You can't go back!"

The boy was untried. He could not know. Gaius was Kaolin's life and breath. He was her conduit to the Gods. She would not leave him.

One last time, she took in Techne's face and form, achingly beautiful but for his missing legs; and the globe of crystal light that was her home, where she'd never had the slightest want.

Then she closed her eyes and slipped into the world.

Summer heat pulsed the air, fragrant with night-scented stalks. The thin moon flicked in and out of a troubled sky.

Kaolin crept into his hut, silent with the breath of two sleepers. Gaius, her Gaius, Gaius of the beautiful hands, lay on his back, one arm thrown over his head, lashes locked, a thin-woven cover pushed away. Beside him, cocooned, lay Aeola, his wife.

Kaolin slid between Gaius' arms, aching with the remembrance of him, of their forgotten intimacy.

Gaius shifted in his sleep.

Do you remember, Gaius?

His strength made her real.

The nightingale's song?

Joy in his touch melted her flesh.

The down on a crocus? The ripple of brightness on running water?

He moaned and held her to him.

Do you remember beauty? For its own sake? Divine, soul-satisfying, Elysian…

She infused herself into his strong, slender hands, became his hands. *These hands. That build. That make. That create homage to beauty, homage to the Gods…*

He woke, caressing her ephemeral body.

She turned in his arms. *The Gods, Gaius. The givers of life, of water—*

"Water," he whispered into her hair.

Kaolin crept from the bed and turning that he might look on her face, took his hand. "Come."

He saw her, then, and his countenance solidified with remembrance.

"Come."

He followed her through the silky heat into the moonlight.

Build.

With the fever of passion, he drew his tools, his clay, his water. Shunning the wheel, he kneaded the soft earth. Kaolin warmed the clay, became pain, became one with his hands, his art, his vision. Together they worked, together—

"Gaius?"

Gaius turned, startled.

"What are you doing out here?" Aeola's voice from the doorway, querulous. "It's the middle of the night."

"Hush," he whispered. Kaolin writhed in his hands, slippery, her passion an overpowering fever. "Go back to bed. I couldn't sleep."

The woman shuffled forward heavily, and a breeze sprang up. "What are you making? We need no more pots."

Kaolin moaned, caressed his palms. *Water*...

"Its—it's for the aqueduct," Gaius said.

Aeola approached him, thin and big-bellied. She frowned, her unbound hair whipping about her face. "A figurine? What use—"

"It's you," Gaius showed her the form in his hands, Kaolin in his hands.

"That's not me."

Kaolin turned in the wetness of his fingers. The hot wind cooled them, rattled straw on the village rooftops.

Gaius indicated the large belly on the statue. "It will grace the spout of the aqueduct. To show the Gods why we need water—"

Aeola laughed and the gale swirled stinging dust around them. "The Gods need your sweat in the fields, not in your trinkets. How can you work when you've been up half the night? Come to bed!"

Kaolin arched, filling his hands, becoming his arms, shoulders, neck, heart.

"No."

Aeola flinched.

The sirocco howled.

Kaolin throbbed with the beat of Gaius' pulse, wild ecstasy flooding her limbs. *Build! Make! Create!*

"Please," Gaius cried against the storm. "Go in. I'll come when I can." He turned back to Kaolin and stroked the figurine, shaping, refining, opening his soul.

"No!" Weeping, Aeola fell to her knees by his side, hair and rags billowing in the blast. "I am your wife! I bear your child—I need your strength. Your child needs your teaching. The village needs the food from your labor. You cannot *waste*—"

Gaius turned on his wife. "This work is my life and breath, my conduit to eternity—" Kaolin's fever filled him, blinding Gaius to the woman at his feet. "Aeola, I love you, but I cannot leave my work. Go, now. Please! I will return to you by and by."

Kaolin infused his belly, his legs—

"You choose fire over the very air you need to live?" Aeola's shriek rose to join the tempest. She lifted her hands and the poles on the huts shook, tools clattered from the benches, branches tumbled about the square.

Gaius held the figurine, held Kaolin, up to the Gods. She was perfection, now leather-dry, and hard, and strong.

Fire.

No! Aeola withered to dust, whirled into storm, shrilled and snatched at them, spitting sand.

Gaius and Kaolin laid the figurine in the kiln and Kaolin ran down Gaius' arms and burst into flame, slashed by the sandstorm's erratic blasts. Kaolin scorched the kiln, blistering its base, igniting the air within, fusing the clay.

Aeola pummeled Gaius with choking dust and stones and branches, battered the kiln, throttled Kaolin, snatching away her breath.

Now!

Kaolin returned to Gaius' body—his heart, his mind—and together they burned as one flame. Together they drew the masterwork from the fiery womb. Kaolin Gaius rooted into the earth, kiln embraced in the pyre of their arms.

Aeola screeched in wrath and agony.

But Kaolin Gaius rose up against the wind and spoke in one voice. "Aeola! You will not have me. My path is not the toil of the earth, but the immortality of the Gods." Gaius Kaolin flung fiery hands out to the sky and the kiln burst, its blast a wall striking the wind, driving the gale upon itself. With a final screech, Aeola fell back to the maelstrom of her beginnings.

Shock and silence filled the village square.

In the stillness, shards of the shattered kiln showered onto the dry earth. Aeola, the wind, was gone.

Gaius Kaolin cradled the figurine in the breathless calm, bereft of wife, lover, child...pain and hollowness. The years ahead would be companionless. Childless and celibate.

A waiting, a hush, filled the skittering of kiln shards striking the earth.

What was done, was done.

Gaius Kaolin brought the figure—full with child and beautiful beyond understanding—to the spout of the aqueduct and fastened it there.

Kaolin Gaius knelt and raised the masterwork to the gray Heavens. *Please, Gods, accept this gift.*

A pock.

A sign? The ways of the village and the word of the Gods would live in clay figures and painted pots.

Another.

A pitter.

See our need. Bring us water that we might live and prosper, to glorify you.

Raindrops. Pattering on stony ground. Presage to a dry lightning storm? Or rain, real rain?

The figurine blushed, a pulse of rose giving life to porcelain cheeks.

The thrumming of rain on earth intensified.

And the skies opened. Gentle, nourishing moisture soaked the thirsty soil. The aqueduct trickled, surged, gushed, washing away all trace of dust and wind.

Gaius Kaolin rejoiced in the rain. She was, he was, water and smoldering earth. He was, she was, flame, epiphany.

Three-time Aurora Award finalist, SUSAN FOREST is a writer of science fiction, fantasy and horror, and a freelance fiction editor. Her stories have appeared in *Asimov's*, *Analog*, *Beneath Ceaseless Skies*, *Tesseracts*, *OnSPEC* and her collection, *Immunity to Strange Tales*, among others. Susan has judged the Endeavour Award, and Robin Herrington Memorial Short Story Contest and contributes to Calgary's annual literary festival, When Words Collide. Susan is secretary for the Science Fiction and Fantasy Writers of America (SFWA), teaches creative writing at the Alexandra Centre, and has appeared at numerous local and international writing conventions.

BIDING TIME

By Robert J. Sawyer

Ernie Gargalian was fat—"Gargantuan Gargalian," some called him. Fortunately, like me, he lived on Mars; it was a lot easier to carry extra weight here. He must have massed a hundred and fifty kilos, but it felt like a third of what it would have on Earth.

Ironically, Gargalian was one of the few people on Mars wealthy enough to fly back to Earth as often as he wanted to, but he never did; I don't think he planned to ever set foot on the mother planet again, even though it was where all his rich clients were. Gargalian was a dealer in Martian fossils: he brokered the transactions between those lucky prospectors who found good specimens and wealthy collectors back on Earth, taking the same oversize slice of the financial pie as he would have of a real one.

His shop was in the innermost circle—appropriately; he knew *everyone*. The main door was transparent alloquartz with his business name and trading hours laser-etched into it; not quite carved in stone, but still a degree of permanence suitable to a dealer in prehistoric relics. The business's name was Ye Olde Fossil Shoppe—as if there were any other kind.

The shoppe's ye olde door slid aside as I approached—

somewhat noisily, I thought. Well, Martian dust gets everywhere, even inside our protective dome; some of it was probably gumming up the works.

Gargalian, seated by a long worktable covered with hunks of rock, was in the middle of a transaction. A prospector—grizzled, with a deeply lined face; he could have been sent over from Central Casting—was standing next to Gargantuan (okay, I was one of those who called him that, too). Both of them were looking at a monitor, showing a close-up of a thizomorph fossil. *"Aresthera weingartenii,"* Gargalian said, with satisfaction; he had a clipped Lebanese accent and a deep, booming voice. "A juvenile, too—we don't see many at this particular stage of development. And see that rainbow sheen? Lovely. It's been permineralized with silicates. This will fetch a nice price—a nice price indeed."

The prospector's voice was rough. Those of us who passed most of our time under the dome had enough troubles with dry air; those who spent half their lives in surface suits, breathing bottled atmosphere, sounded particularly raspy. "How nice?" he said, his eyes narrowing.

Gargantuan frowned while he considered. "I can sell this quickly for perhaps eleven million ... or, if you give me longer, I can probably get thirteen. I have some clients who specialize in *A. weingartenii* who will pay top coin, but they are slow in making up their minds."

"I want the money fast," said the prospector. "This old body of mine might not hold out much longer."

Gargalian turned his gaze from the monitor to appraise the prospector, and he caught sight of me as he did so. He nodded in my direction, and raised a single finger—the finger that indicated "one minute," not the other finger, although I got that often enough when I entered places, too. He nodded at the prospector, apparently agreeing that the guy wasn't long for this or any other world, and said, "A speedy resolution, then. Let me give you a receipt for the fossil ..."

I waited for Gargalian to finish his business, and then he came over to where I was standing. "Hey, Ernie," I said.

"Mr. Double-X himself!" declared Gargalian, bushy eyebrows rising above his round, flabby face. He liked to call me that because both my first and last names—Alex Lomax—ended in that letter.

I pulled my datapad out of my pocket and showed him a picture of a seventy-year-old woman, with gray hair cut in sensible bangs above a crabapple visage. "Recognize her?"

Gargantuan nodded, and his jowls shook as he did so. "Sure. Megan Delacourt, Delany, something like that, right?"

"Delahunt," I said.

"Right. What's up? She your client?"

"She's *nobody's* client," I said. "The old dear is pushing up daisies."

I saw Gargalian narrow his eyes for a second. Knowing him, he was trying to calculate whether he'd owed her money or she'd owed him money. "Sorry to hear that," he said with the kind of regret that was merely polite, presumably meaning that at least he hadn't lost anything. "She was pretty old."

"'Was' is the operative word," I said. "She'd transferred."

He nodded, not surprised. "Just like that old guy wants to." He indicated the door the prospector had now exited through. It was a common-enough scenario. People come to Mars in their youth, looking to make their fortunes by finding fossils here. The lucky ones stumble across a valuable specimen early on; the unlucky ones keep on searching and searching, getting older in the process. If they ever do find a decent specimen, first thing they do is transfer before it's too late. "So, what is it?" asked Gargalian. "A product-liability case? Next of kin suing NewYou?"

I shook my head. "Nah, the transfer went fine. But somebody killed the uploaded version shortly after the transfer was completed."

Gargalian's bushy eyebrows went up. "Can you do that? I thought transfers were immortal."

I knew from bitter recent experience that a transfer could be killed with equipment specifically designed for that purpose, but the only broadband disrupter here on Mars was safely in the hands of the New Klondike constabulary. Still, I'd seen the most amazing suicide a while ago, committed by a transfer.

But this time the death had been simple. "She was lured down to the shipyards, or so it appears, and ended up standing between the engine cone of a big rocketship, which was lying on its belly, and a brick wall. Someone fired the engine, and she did a Margaret Hamilton."

Gargalian shared my fondness for old films; he got the reference and winced. "Still, there's your answer, no? It must have been one of the rocket's crew—someone who had access to the engine controls."

I shook my head. "No. The cockpit was broken into."

Ernie frowned. "Well, maybe it was one of the crew, trying to make it look like it *wasn't* one of the crew."

God save me from amateur detectives. "I checked. They all had alibis—and none of them had a motive, of course."

Gargantuan made a harrumphing sound. "What about the original version of Megan?" he asked.

"Already gone. They normally euthanize the biological original immediately after making the copy; can't have two versions of the same person running around, after all."

"Why would anyone kill someone after they transferred?" asked Gargalian. "I mean, if you wanted the person dead, it's got to be easier to off them while they're still biological, no?"

"I imagine so."

"And it's still murder, killing a transfer, right? I mean, I can't recall it ever happening, but that's the way the law reads, isn't it?"

"Yeah, it's still murder," I said. "The penalty is life imprisonment—down on Earth, of course." With any sentence longer than two mears—two Mars years—it was cheaper to ship the criminal down to Earth, where air is free, than to incarcerate him or her here.

Gargantuan shook his head, and his jowls, again. "She seemed a nice old lady," he said. "Can't imagine why someone would want her dead."

"The 'why' is bugging me, too," I said. "I know she came in here a couple of weeks ago with some fossil specimens to sell; I found a receipt recorded in her datapad."

Gargalian motioned toward his desktop computer, and we walked over to it. He spoke to the machine, and some pictures of fossils appeared on the same monitor he'd been looking at earlier. "She brought me three pentapeds. One was junk, but the other two were very nice specimens."

"You sold them?"

"That's what I do."

"And gave her her share of the proceeds?"

"Yes."

"How much did it come to?"

He spoke to the computer again, and pointed at the displayed figure. "Total, nine million solars."

I frowned. "NewYou charges 7.5 million for their basic service. There can't have been enough cash left over after she transferred to be worth killing her for, unless ..." I peered at the images of the fossils she'd brought in, but I was hardly a great judge of quality. "You said two of the specimens were really nice." 'Nice' was Gargantuan's favorite adjective; he'd apparently never taken a creative-writing course.

He nodded.

"*How* nice?"

He laughed, getting my point at once. "You think she'd found the alpha?"

I lifted my shoulders a bit. "Why not? If she knew where it was, that'd be worth killing her for."

The alpha deposit was where Simon Weingarten and Denny O'Reilly—the two private explorers who first found fossils on Mars—had collected their original specimens. That discovery had brought all the other fortune-seekers from Earth. Weingarten and O'Reilly had died twenty mears ago—their heat shield had torn off while re-entering Earth's atmosphere after their third trip here—and the location of the alpha died with them. All anyone knew was that it was somewhere here in the Isidis Planitia basin; whoever found it would be rich beyond even Gargantuan Gargalian's dreams.

"I told you, one of the specimens was junk," said Ernie. "No way it came from the alpha. The rocks of the alpha are extremely fine-grained—the preservation quality is as good as that from Earth's Burgess Shale."

"And the other two?" I said.

He frowned, then replied almost grudgingly, "They were good."

"Alpha good?"

His eyes narrowed. "Maybe."

"She could have thrown in the junk piece just to disguise where the others had come from," I said.

"Well, even junk fossils are hard to come by."

That much was true. In my own desultory collecting days, I'd never found so much as a fragment. Still, there had to be a reason why someone would kill an old woman just after she'd transferred her consciousness into an artificial body.

And if I could find that reason, I'd be able to find her killer.

My client was Megan Delahunt's ex-husband—and he'd been ex for a dozen mears, not just since Megan had died. Jersey Delahunt had come into my little office at about half-past ten that morning. He was shrunken with age, but looked as though he'd been broad-shouldered in his day. A few wisps of white hair were all that was left on his liver-spotted head. "Megan struck it rich," he'd told me.

I'd regarded him from my swivel chair, hands interlocked behind my head, feet up on my battered desk. "And you couldn't be happier for her."

"You're being sarcastic, Mr. Lomax," he said, but his tone wasn't bitter. "I don't blame you. Sure, I'd been hunting fossils for thirty-six Earth years, too. Megan and me, we'd come here to Mars together, right at the beginning of the rush, hoping to make our fortunes. It hadn't lasted though—our marriage, I mean; the dream of getting rich lasted, of course."

"Of course," I said. "Are you still named in her will?"

Jersey's old, rheumy eyes regarded me. "Suspicious, too, aren't you?"

"That's what they pay me the medium-sized bucks for."

He had a small mouth, surrounded by wrinkles; it did the best it could to work up a smile. "The answer is no, I'm not in her will. She left everything to our son Ralph. Not that there was much left over after she spent the money to upload, but whatever there was, he got—or will get, once her will is probated."

"And how old is Ralph?"

"Thirty-four." Age was always expressed in Earth years.

"So he was born after you came to Mars? Does he still live here?"

"Yes. Always has."

"Is he a prospector, too?"

"No. He's an engineer. Works for the water-recycling authority."

I nodded. Not rich, then. "And Megan's money is still there, in her bank account?"

"So says the lawyer, yes."

"If all the money is going to Ralph, what's your interest in the matter?"

"My interest, Mr. Lomax, is that I once loved this woman very much. I left Earth to come here to Mars because it's what she wanted to do. We lived together for ten mears, had children together, and—"

"Children," I repeated. "But you said all the money was left to your *child,* singular, this Ralph."

"My daughter is dead," Jersey said, his voice soft.

It was hard to sound contrite in my current posture—I was still leaning back with feet up on the desk. But I tried. "Oh. Um. I'm ... ah ..."

"You're sorry, Mr. Lomax. Everybody is. I've heard it a million times. But it wasn't your fault. It wasn't anyone's fault, although ..."

"Yes?"

"Although Megan blamed herself, of course. What mother wouldn't?"

"I'm not following."

"Our daughter JoBeth died thirty years ago, when she was two months old." Jersey was staring out my office's single window, at one of the arches supporting the habitat dome. "She smothered in her sleep." He turned to look at me, and his eyes were red as Martian sand. "The doctor said that sort of thing happens sometimes—not often, but from time to time." His face was almost unbearably sad. "Right up till the end, Megan would cry whenever she thought of JoBeth. It was heartbreaking. She couldn't get over it."

I nodded, because that was all I could think of to do. Jersey didn't seem inclined to say anything else, so, after a moment, I went on. "Surely the police have investigated your ex-wife's death."

"Yes, of course," Jersey replied. "But I'm not satisfied that they tried hard enough."

This was a story I'd heard often. I nodded again, and he continued to speak: "I mean, the detective I talked to said the killer was probably off-planet now, headed to Earth."

"That *is* possible, you know," I replied. "Well, at least it is if a ship has left here in the interim."

"Two have," said Jersey, "or so the detective told me."

"Including the one whose firing engine, ah, did the deed?"

"No, that one's still there. *Lennick's Folly*, it's called. It was supposed to head back to Earth, but it's been impounded."

"Because of Megan's death?"

"No. Something to do with unpaid taxes."

I nodded. With NewYou's consciousness-uploading technology, not even death was certain anymore—but taxes were. "Which detective were you dealing with?"

"Some Scottish guy."

"Dougal McCrae," I said. Mac wasn't the laziest man I'd ever met—and he'd saved my life recently when another case had gone bad, so I tried not to think uncharitable thoughts about him. But if there was a poster boy for complacent policing, well, Mac wouldn't be it; he wouldn't bother to get out from behind his desk to show up for the photo shoot. "All right," I said. "I'll take the case."

"Thank you," said Jersey. "I brought along Megan's datapad; the police gave it back to me after copying its contents." He handed me the little tablet. "It's got her appointment schedule and her address book. I thought maybe it would help you find the killer."

I motioned for him to put the device on my desk. "It probably will, at that. Now, about my fee ..."

Since Mars no longer had seas, it was all one landmass: you could literally walk anywhere on the planet. Still, on this whole rotten globe, there was only one settlement—our domed city of New Klondike, three kilometers in diameter. The city had a circular layout: nine concentric rings of buildings, cut into blocks by twelve radial roadways. The NewYou franchise—the only place you could go for uploading on Mars—was just off Third Avenue in the Fifth Ring. According to her datapad, Megan Delahunt's last appointment at NewYou had been three days ago, when her transfer had actually been done. I headed there after leaving Ye Olde Fossil Shoppe.

The NewYou franchise was under new management since the last time I'd visited. The rather tacky showroom was at ground level; the brain-scanning equipment was on the second floor. The basement—quite rare on Mars, since the permafrost was so hard to dig through—was mostly used for storage.

"Mr. Lomax!" declared Horatio Fernandez, the new owner; I'd met him previously when he'd just been an employee here. I'd forgotten what a beefy guy he was—arms as big around as Gargalian's, but his bulk was all muscle.

"Hello," I said. "Sorry to bother you, but—"

"Let me guess," said Fernandez. "The Megan Delahunt murder."

"Bingo."

He shook his head. "She was really pleasant."

"So people keep telling me."

"It's true. She was a real lady, that one. Cultured, you know? Lots of people here, spending their lives splitting rocks, they get a rough edge. But not her; she was all 'please' and 'thank you.' Of course, she was pretty long in the tooth ..."

"Did she have any special transfer requests?" I asked.

"Nah. Just wanted her new body to look the way she had fifty Earth years ago, when she was twenty—which was easy enough."

"What about mods for outside work?" Lots of transfers had special equipment installed in their new bodies so that they could operate more easily on the surface of Mars.

"Nah, nothing. She said her fossil-hunting days were over. She was looking forward to a nice long future, reading all the great books she'd never had time for before."

If she'd found the alpha, she'd probably have wanted to work it herself, at least for a while—if you're planning on living forever, and you had a way to become super-rich, you'd take advantage of it. "Hmmph," I said. "Did she mention any titles?"

"Yeah," said Fernandez. "She said she was going to start with *Remembrance of Things Past.*"

I nodded, impressed at her ambition. "Anybody else come by to ask about her since she was killed?"

"Well, Detective McCrae called."

"Mac came here?"

"No, he *called.* On the phone."

I smiled. "That's Mac."

I headed over to Gully's Gym, since it was on the way to my next stop, and did my daily workout—treadmill, bench press, and so on. I worked up quite a sweat, but a sonic shower cleaned me up. Then it was off to the shipyards. Mostly, this dingy area between Eighth and Ninth Avenue was a grave for abandoned ships, left over from the early fossil-rush days when people were coming to Mars in droves. Now only a small amount of maintenance work was done here. My last visit to the shipyards had been quite unpleasant—but I suppose it hadn't been as bad as Megan Delahunt's last visit.

I found *Lennick's Folly* easily enough. It was a tapered spindle, maybe a hundred meters long, lying on its side. The bow had a couple of square windows, and the stern had a giant engine cone attached. There was a gap of only a few meters between the cone and a brick firewall, which was now covered with soot. Whatever had been left of Megan's shiny new body had already been removed.

The lock on the cockpit door hadn't been repaired, so I had no trouble getting in. Once inside the cramped space, I got to work.

There were times when a private detective could accomplish things a public one couldn't. Mac had to worry about privacy laws, which were as tight here on Mars as they were back down on Earth—and a good thing, too, for those, like me, who had come here to escape our pasts. Oh, Mac doubtless had collected DNA samples here—gathering them at a crime scene was legal—but he couldn't take DNA from a suspect to match against specimens from here without a court order, and to get that, he'd have to show good reason up front for why the suspect might be guilty—which, of course, was a catch-22. Fortunately, the only catch-22 I had to deal with was the safety on my trusty old Smith & Wesson .22.

I used a GeneSeq 109, about the size of a hockey puck. It collected even small fragments of DNA in a nanotrap, and could easily compare sequences from any number of sources. I did a particularly thorough collecting job on the control panel that operated the engine. Of course, I looked for fingerprints, too, but there weren't any recent ones, and the older ones had been smudged either by someone operating the controls with gloved hands, which is what I suspected, or,

I suppose, by artificial hands—a transfer offing a transfer; that'd be a first.

Of course, Mac knew as well as I did that family members commit most murders. I'd surreptitiously taken a sample from Jersey Delahunt when he'd visited my office; I sample everyone who comes there. But my GeneSeq reported that the DNA collected here didn't match Jersey's. That wasn't too surprising: I'd been hired by guilty parties before, but it was hardly the norm—or, at least, the kind of people who hired me usually weren't guilty of the particular crime they wanted me to investigate.

And so I headed off to find the one surviving child of Megan and Jersey Delahunt.

Jersey had said his son Ralph had been born shortly after he and Megan had come to Mars thirty-six Earth years ago. Ralph certainly showed all the signs of having been born here: he was 210 centimeters if he was an inch; growing up in Mars's low gravity had that effect. And he was a skinny thing, with rubbery, tubular limbs—Gumby in an olive-green business suit. Most of us here had been born on Earth, and it still showed in our musculature, but Ralph was Martian, through and through.

His office at the water works was much bigger than mine, but, then, he didn't personally pay the rent on it. I had a DNA collector in my palm when I shook his hand, and while he was getting us both coffee from a maker on his credenza, I transferred the sample to the GeneSeq, and set it to comparing his genetic code to the samples from the rocket's cockpit.

"I want to thank you, Mr. Lomax," Ralph said, handing me a steaming mug. "My father called to say he'd hired you. I'm delighted. Absolutely delighted." He had a thin, reedy voice, matching his thin, reedy body. "How anyone could do such a thing to my mother ..."

I smiled, sat down, and took a sip. "I understand she was a sweet old lady."

"That she was," said Ralph, taking his own seat on the other side of a glass-and-steel desk. "That she was."

The GeneSeq bleeped softly three times, each bleep higher pitched than the one before—the signal for a match. "Then why did you kill her?" I said.

He had his coffee cup halfway to his lips, but suddenly he slammed it down, splashing double-double, which fell to the glass desktop in Martian slo-mo. "Mr. Lomax, if that's your idea of a joke, it's in very poor taste. The funeral service for my mother is tomorrow, and—"

"And you'll be there, putting on an act, just like the one you're putting on now."

"Have you no decency, sir? My mother ..."

"Was killed. By someone she trusted—someone who she would follow to the shipyards, someone who told her to wait in a specific spot while he—what? Nipped off to have a private word with a ship's pilot? Went into the shadows to take a leak? Of course, a professional engineer could get the manual for a spaceship's controls easily enough, and understand it well enough to figure out how to fire the engine."

Ralph's flimsy form was quaking with rage, or a good simulation of it. "Get out. Get out now. I think I speak for my father when I say, you're fired."

I didn't get up. "It was damn-near a perfect crime," I said my voice rock-steady. "*Lennick's Folly* should have headed back to Earth, taking any evidence of who'd been in its cockpit with her; indeed, you probably hoped it'd be gone long before the melted lump that once was your mother was found. But you can't fire engines under the dome without consuming a lot of oxygen—and somebody has to pay for that. It doesn't grow on trees, you know—well, down on Earth it does, sort of. But not here. And so the ship is hanging around, like the tell-tale heart, like an albatross, like"—I sought a third allusion, just for style's sake, and one came to me: "like the sword of Damocles."

Ralph looked left and right. There was no way out, of

course; I was seated between him and the door, and my Smith & Wesson was now in my hand. He might have done a sloppy job, but I never do. "I ... I don't know what you're talking about," he said.

I made what I hoped was an ironic smile. "Guess that's another advantage of uploading, no? No more DNA being left behind. It's almost impossible to tell if a specific transfer has been in a specific room, but it's child's play to determine what biologicals have gone in and out of somewhere. Did you know that cells slough off the alveoli of your lungs and are exhaled with each breath? Oh, only two or three—but today's scanners have no trouble finding them, and reading the DNA in them. No, it's open-and-shut that you were the murderer: you were in the cockpit of *Lennick's Folly,* you touched the engine controls. Yeah, you were bright enough to wear gloves—but not bright enough to hold your breath."

He got to his feet and started to come around from behind his funky desk. I undid the safety on my gun, and he froze.

"I frown on murder," I said, "but I'm all for killing in self-defense—so I'd advise you to stand perfectly still." I waited to make sure he was doing just that, then went on. "I know *that* you did it, but I still don't know why. And I'm an old-fashioned guy—grew up reading Agatha Christie and Peter Robinson. In the good old days, before DNA and all that, detectives wanted three things to make a case: method, motive, and opportunity. The method is obvious, and you clearly had opportunity. But I'm still in the dark on the motive, and, for my own interest, I'd like to know what it was."

"You can't prove any of this," sneered Ralph. "Even if you have a DNA match, it's inadmissible."

"Dougal McCrae is lazy but he's not stupid. If I tip him off that you definitely did it, he'll find a way to get the warrant. Your only chance now is to tell me *why* you did it. Hell, I'm a reasonable man. If your justification was good enough, well, I've turned a blind eye before. So, tell me: why wait until your mother uploaded to kill her? If you had some beef with her, why didn't you off her earlier?" I narrowed my eyes. "Or had she done something recently? She'd struck it rich, and that sometimes changes people—but ..." I paused, and after a few moments, I found myself nodding. "Ah, of course. She struck it rich, and she was old. You'd thought, hey, she's going to drop off soon, and you'll inherit her newfound fortune. But when she squandered it on herself, spending most of it on uploading, you were furious." I shook my head in disgust. "Greed. Oldest motivation there is."

"You really are a smug bastard, Lomax," said Ralph. "And you don't know *anything* about me. Do you think I care about money?" He snorted. "I've never wanted money—as long as I've got enough to pay my life-support tax, I'm content."

"People who are indifferent to thousands often change their ways when millions are at stake."

"Oh, now you're a philosopher, too, eh? I was born here on Mars, Lomax. My whole life I've been surrounded by people who spend all their time looking for paleontological pay dirt. My parents both did that. It was bad enough that I had to compete with things that have been dead for billions of years, but ..."

I narrowed my eyes. "But what?"

He shook his head. "Nothing. You wouldn't understand."

"No? Why not?"

He paused, then: "You got brothers? Sisters?"

"A sister," I said. "Back on Earth."

"Older or younger?"

"Older, by two years."

"No," he said. "You couldn't possibly understand."

"Why not? What's that got—" And then it hit me. I'd encountered lots of scum in my life: crooks, swindlers, people who'd killed for a twenty-solar coin. But nothing like this. That Ralph had a scarecrow's form was obvious, but, unlike the one from Oz, he clearly *did* have a brain. And although his mother had been the tin man, so to speak, after she'd uploaded, I now knew it was Ralph who'd been lacking a heart.

"JoBeth," I said softly.

Ralph staggered backward as if I'd hit him. His eyes, defiant till now, could no longer meet my own.

"Christ," I said. "How could you? How could anyone ...?"

"It's not like that," he said, spreading his arms like a praying mantis. "I was four years old, for God's sake. I—I didn't mean—"

"You killed your own baby sister."

He looked at the carpeted office floor. "My parents had little enough time for me as it was, what with spending twelve hours a day looking for the goddamned alpha."

I nodded. "And when JoBeth came along, suddenly you were getting no attention at all. And so you smothered her in her sleep."

"You can't prove that. Nobody can."

"Maybe. Maybe not."

"She was cremated, and her ashes were scattered outside the dome thirty years ago. The doctor said she died of natural causes, and you can't prove otherwise."

I shook my head, still trying to fathom it all. "You didn't count on how much it would hurt your mother—or that the hurt would go on and on, mear after mear."

He said nothing, and that was as damning as any words could be.

"She couldn't get over it, of course," I said. "But you thought, you know, eventually ..."

He nodded, almost imperceptibly—perhaps he wasn't even aware that he'd done so. I went on, "You thought eventually she would die, and then you wouldn't have to face her anymore. At some point, she'd be gone, and her pain would be over, and you could finally be free of the guilt. You were biding your time, waiting for her to pass on."

He was still looking at the carpet, so I couldn't see his face. But his narrow shoulders were quivering. I continued. "You're still young—thirty-four, isn't it? Oh, sure, your mother might have been good for another ten or twenty years, but *eventually* ..."

Acid was crawling its way up my throat. I swallowed hard, fighting it down. "Eventually," I continued, "you would be free—or so you thought. But then your mother struck it rich, and uploaded her consciousness, and was going to live for centuries if not forever, and you couldn't take that, could you? You couldn't take her always being around, always crying over something that you had done so long ago." I lifted my eyebrows, and made no effort to keep the contempt out of my voice. "Well, they say the first murder is the hardest."

"You can't prove any of this. Even if you have DNA specimens from the cockpit, the police still don't have any probable cause to justify taking a specimen from me."

"They'll find it. Dougal McCrae is lazy—but he's also a father, with a baby girl of his own. He'll dig into this like a bulldog, and won't let go until he's got what he needs to nail you, you—"

I stopped. I wanted to call him a son of a bitch—but he wasn't; he was the son of a gentle, loving woman who had deserved so much better. "One way or another, you're going down," I said. And then it hit me, and I started to feel that maybe there was a little justice in the universe after all. "And that's exactly right: you're going down, to Earth."

Ralph at last did look up, and his thin face was ashen. *"What?"*

"That's what they do with anyone whose jail sentence is longer than two mears. It's too expensive in terms of life-support costs to house criminals here for years on end."

"I—I can't go to Earth."

"You won't have any choice."

"But—but I was *born* here. I'm Martian, born and raised. On Earth, I'd weigh...what? Twice what I'm used to ..."

"Three times, actually. A stick-insect like you, you'll hardly be able to walk there. You should have been doing what I do. Every morning, I work out at Gully's Gym, over by the shipyards. But you ..."

"My ... my heart ..."

"Yeah, it'll be quite a strain, won't it? Too bad ..."

His voice was soft and small. "It'll kill me, all that gravity."

"It might at that," I said, smiling mirthlessly. "At the very least, you'll be bed-ridden until the end of your sorry days—helpless as a baby in a crib."

ROBERT J. SAWYER won the best-novel Hugo Award for *Hominids*, and has twelve other Hugo nominations to his credit. He's also won the Nebula Award (for *The Terminal Experiment*), the John W. Campbell Memorial Award (for *Mindscan*), and the Audio Publishers Association's Audie Award for Best SF Audiobook of the Year (for *Calculating God*), plus Canada's Aurora Award (a record-setting fourteen times), Japan's best-foreign-novel Seiun Award (three times), and China's Galaxy Award. In 2014, he was one of the initial nine inductees into the Canadian Science Fiction and Fantasy Hall of Fame. The ABC TV series *FlashForward* was based on his novel of the same name.

THE PHOENIX OF BURGESS

By David Worsick

Arnold stood in line, gazing out the window at the thick snow and bare poplar trees, waiting in the crowd for the exhibit to open. Other professors and lecturers in the line were talking about the recent daylight firebombing of a history department on the east coast. He listened. And another history department halfway across the continent attacked two days later.

That's not just an angry student, he thought. *How could someone get a Molotov cocktail on top of a twelve-story building? All universities have high fences and guarded entrances. A medieval trebuchet on a pickup truck?*

Josef, from the history department, entered the line after Arnold. Josef took his wool hat off his blond head and asked, "Mind if I join you?"

"Sure, Josef."

Josef would know about trebuchets, thought Arnold.

"You are good at problem solving, I was told," said Josef, very quietly.

Arnold whispered back, "In ancient history? Do you need a robot to crawl down tunnels in pyramids? I've designed that before."

"Not that. We have brought in something dangerous."

Arnold stared at Josef. "So that's why we're whispering. Now, don't tell me there's a curse on the mummy."

"I am a late Roman professor, *nicht*, I mean, not near-prehistoric, Arnold."

"Okay, it's not mummies. What is it?"

"What we have attracts arsonists."

"What?"

Nearby, other people in line turned toward them.

Josef said, even more softly, "Parchments we found in the desert. One and a half millennia old. These parchments may challenge the beliefs of very fanatical people. They already tried twice to destroy these things."

"Something that old and crumbly? Josef, what are they full of?"

"Truth that can cause problems."

"How did the dean let you bring that in? You know what a politically attuned nanny he is."

Josef sighed and said, "I saw that within weeks of starting here."

"So young and yet so cynical."

"I am just two years younger than you, Arnold."

"True, your cynical side has much room to grow. Nevertheless, how did you get the dean's permission?"

"We never told him. Besides, we thought nobody would know where those parchments were. But soon after we moved them from one university, its history building was bombed. At the university we were planning to take them to, that department was fire-bombed next. We brought them here, secretly. Now we need to protect them."

"But all universities ban weapons. You bring a gun on campus and it's an immediate firing."

"Of course we would not fire it unless… Oh. You mean job termination."

Arnold shook his head. "Well, the dean's predecessor would have gleefully taken the risk of these artifacts, but not our poor current dean. You'd better move the parchments next week. Rent a storage unit somewhere Tuesday. It's too late today; they close early on the Family Day Friday. It's a good thing he's off at a conference."

"So, it's true, is it? We've been hearing rumors about forbidden parchments," said a mathematician behind them. Others in the line shook their heads in agreement.

Arnold looked around and then stared at Josef, saying, "You're not very good at this smuggling thing, are you? It seems everybody but me knew already."

"Sorry, I thought nobody knew."

The exhibit doors opened and a young woman came out.

"Hi, guys," she said.

Arnold smiled, admiring her ample brown hair. "So, Barrietta, is everything ready? I heard your group of paleontologists did a magnificent job on my toys."

"Well, thank you, Arnold! Okay, everybody come in!"

The line of professors and university staff entered a large basement room of boxes filled with bubble wrapped stuff. Ahead was a massive aquarium.

Barrietta said, "Welcome to the Cambrian, folks."

Arnold said, "Isn't Cambrian a geological time? The first time creatures grew shells?"

"Pretty good geology for a robotics engineer," Barrietta said, smiling.

"Thanks, now let's see this project using my machinery. Josef, this should take your mind off your problem."

"You study these creatures?" asked Josef.

Arnold replied, "No, I just designed the armature and framework. What geologists cover them with is their own business."

Josef walked to the massive aquarium and said, "There are corals in there but no water!"

"It's not a real aquarium and those are plastic and rubber models," said Barrietta.

"But they swim in there, no, they fly! I see now!" Josef said, pointing.

Indeed, Arnold thought, but he expected that. What he

wasn't expecting was how life-like the end results were. The Paleontologists' concept for this display was working. Looking closely, he could barely see the tiny, clear blades that carried the oddities through the make-believe ocean.

"Gentlemen and ladies," said Barrietta, "welcome to the most realistic Burgess Shale recreation in the world."

"Ah, they're drones," said Josef. "But their fins and limbs move. And the floor creatures are crawling!"

"Well, those are really rolling on small wheels, but we make the limbs move so people assume they're crawling," she said. "Here we have trilobites made from laser-cut steel and plastic legs."

"What is that little turtle covered in paring knives?"

"That, Josef, is *Wiwaxia*, and it's more of a slug, we think," Barrietta said, beaming.

Arnold thought the slug looked more like half a pine cone given a Mohawk haircut made of daggers.

More people from every department were coming in, at least three dozen. This really was popular. Mrs. Weighman from Computer Science was there bragging to her programmer colleagues about the insect-brain coding she used in these models. Arnold now noticed that the flying drones didn't run into each other or into walls. And the crawlers weren't doing a demolition derby. *Shame,* he thought, *'cause crashing, smashing trilobites sounded like fun.*

"Do they have some sort of sight or radar?" a geologist asked.

Barrietta said, "They have working eyes, simple things. We can even set up chases, like carnivores hunting prey."

Somebody asked, "How advanced is this technology?"

Arnold finally had a chance to show off.

"It sprang out of our proprietary project. It involves arthropodic programming, carbon nanotubules and non-von Neumann architecture. The rock hounds were designing this exhibit and wanted the creatures to swim without endlessly looping like toy trains. We realized that this was the perfect lab for our own studies and, see, we were right."

"They can see?" an historian asked.

"Yes, but black and white motion using compound optic fibers, like bug eyes but simpler. The larger ones also have micro cameras with normal focus broadcasting to a phone. That's so we can make one swim around and greet visitors," said Arnold.

Now he really wanted one himself, just to greet department heads.

Barrietta then pointed out a two-inch flying shrimp carrying two clam shells on its back. On top was a tiny frame holding four clear propellers. Underneath were many little claws.

On the fake sea floor below was a four-inch chubby worm with a dozen stubby legs, even a pair on its butt. Its mouth looked like an old cannon, with a ring of tiny bayonets facing out.

Barrietta then brought out a box of models. An engineer reached into it and yelled as one of these worms wrapped around his fingers.

"Please don't do that. It's triggered to wrap around coral branches." She pulled it off and brought out a different model. "*Hallucigenia*!"

The Hallo Genny worm was an inch-long bolt with two rows of spikes, two rows of legs and a flat head. It looked like a medieval club.

The box also contained tiny flying pitchforks covered with fuzz and dragging long antennae like curly moustaches.

"This is *Leancholia*," Barrietta said, gesturing to a larger creature.

This Melancholia beast was well equipped, with six short whips in front of its football body of rings. Kinky.

A four-inch long creature, *Sanctacaris*—though Arnold decided he'd call it Santa Cars—had rows of heavy plates, clusters of hooks by its mouth and a head with ear flaps.

"Drones!" Josef suddenly yelled. "They use drones with gasoline bombs!"

"What?" said Arnold.

"What do you mean?" asked Barrietta.

"How the terrorists bomb the universities! You cannot buy rocket fuel, you cannot get through the gates without being searched, but a drone can carry a Molotov cocktail. That is just gasoline and bottles, all legal. You can hardly hear drones and it was overcast for each attack, so they are difficult to see. That is how they attack!"

Now everybody talked at the same time. Arnold looked around at the numerous boxes.

"Barrietta, you mentioned that you were selling models to other institutions, didn't you? Exactly how many exhibits?"

Barrietta said, "When we found out that every fossil-loving institution wanted one of these dioramas, we made sales to fifty-three universities and museums."

Arnold said, "That's a lot of fossil-loving institutions. Barrietta, how could you make money on things this complicated?"

"They're unique. Dinosaurs are popular too but far too big. These things are small and weird. With 3D printing, vacuum molding and computerized assembly, they're cheaper than you'd expect. We found a firm that can create hundreds of CPUs at a good price. We now have a few hundreds of these crawling and flying models."

"All ready to use?"

"Yes, we were going to ship them after the grand opening next week. Why?"

"All nicely packed?"

"Yes, Arnold, but what are you getting at?" asked Barrietta.

"An air force, that's what."

The crowd shut up and turned toward him. Finally, he thought. People are listening to an engineer.

"An aerial force of Cambrian critters. We'll chase away any terrorists with creepy crawlies. How many can be flown by remote control?"

"The large ones. Some *Opabinia* and a few others. I think we have about thirty that can be piloted."

She brought out a monster with six propellers. It had odd flaps on its side, two eyes on stalks and two things that looked like jumbo shrimp curving out from under its head.

"Bloody hell, that's more than two feet long!" said one historian.

"This is *Anomalocaris*, the largest animal we found from five hundred million years ago. And you'd be right to be afraid of this. It was a vicious hunter."

Arnold noticed a large, toothy hole underneath. He took the model from Barrietta and raised it high, saying, "Welcome to the Tyrannosaurus Rex of the Cambrian age, people. All hail Anomaly Carrot! If drones attack, this will be our Tiger Tank. Oh, do the claws grab?"

"Yes," said Barrietta, "and the mouth chomps so we could feed it clay trilobites in demonstrations."

"Really? Well, ladies and gentlemen, we have our air force."

A middle-aged woman said, "How would these little things stop drones? Fire sling shots? The average drone is at least a foot long."

"Swarming," said a biologist, "You have the numbers."

"Yes, we programmed them so we can easily move them all together, in case of a fire," said Mrs. Weighman. "It wouldn't take much coding to make them gang up on anything large."

"So, you can have a vast fleet of extinct flying invertebrates?" asked Josef.

"Yes, why not? It's not like their descendants will sue us for copyright infringement," said Barrietta. "I think it's a good idea."

Yes! thought Arnold.

Josef approached the Anomaly Carrot. "My great-great-grandfather flew a tri-plane."

"*My god, he's channeling his inner von Richthofen.*"

A graduate student of something obscure said, "This is very good, but we might not have time to stop them."

Arnold replied. "We'll have time. We've already installed

cameras all over the place, even the forest. They work really well."

"When did you do that?" a man asked.

Arnold continued, "The university did it, three years ago, a couple of years after they put up the fencing. It was just for general security, but the cameras would easily see drones."

"Who's watching all these cameras?" asked Barrietta.

Arnold replied, "They're programmed to detect motion, alert us and start recording. You know, catch vandals? Now we probably won't have to ever use your toys, but can we get all the batteries charged up? Just in case?"

A flurry of geoscientists volunteered.

"And we'll need a handful of pilots. Any more volunteers?"

Many offered, including Josef, no surprise there, and Arnold himself. Mrs. Weighman would handle the overriding controls for the autonomous ones. Arnold knew he was going to forget all the names, except for his favourite Anomaly Carrot and Hallo Genny. To remember the Opa name, he just imagined the five-eyed beast carrying a glass of ouzo in its one claw.

The group trained the entire afternoon and, indeed, Josef was darn good at flying extinct life forms.

Being single, Arnold stayed late. He spent that Friday evening modifying some of the models. Tomorrow there were no classes, but Arnold was still coming in. It might all be unnecessary, but how often did an untenured assistant professor get to be part of something this potentially wild?

Next morning, a surprising number of professors and graduate students showed up at the Geoscience building, even from the Athletics department. Arnold looked over at the History building across the snow-covered plaza. It was unlikely that the terrorists knew of the parchments' new location, despite everybody here knowing. However, true to his training in safety margins, Arnold had asked a few students to monitor the security cameras over this weekend. The students had his cellphone number, so he played Snoopy and the Red Baron with one of the tank-like Anomalies. With his phone attached to a game controller, Arnold got good at maneuvering the beast, watching through its mini-cam. The phone rang. He took it off the controller and answered it. His toy hovered nearby.

"Hi, you see anything, Carol?"

He listened for the few seconds it took Carol to report. Then he yelled out, "Everybody, get these things outside! I think we have attackers coming!"

With so many people, the defending drones were ready in a hurry. Some athletes sprinted back to their building while others carried the heavier boxes. An astrophysicist phoned her department and told them to hurry over with scopes. Arnold noticed that she carried binoculars. *Good grief, is everybody here already prepared for this?* Even Arnold had brought his old slingshot and lead balls, and his own pair of binoculars, of course. He put on his coat and toque, grabbed his new toy and ran toward the Department of History.

"On top of the building," yelled Josef. "We need the full all-round view!"

An odd cloud formed above the trees to the east. Arnold took his binoculars out from their case and peered through the auto- adjusting lenses. Drones, maybe forty of them. Big cargo carriers, most of them, at least two feet long, some even bigger. Many carried bottles. Not good, he thought, we only outnumber them by a factor of six.

He ran into the History building, accidentally scaring one coed with his big toy. On the top floor, he went up the stairs to the roof, now crowded with drones and their pilots.

Arnold returned his phone to the receiving channel for his big, brave defender.

Mrs. Weighman had a laptop with a Wifi extender, a folding chair and thin gloves for her hands. She yelled, "I've got control of the drones. Now, stuff the bombers with their worms."

"Worms?" said Arnold. He saw people picking up both spiked and coral-hugging worms.

He sent his own toy into the sky. Around him, it looked like Barrietta had turned groups of academia into trained pit crews. They crammed ancient sea worms into the claws of both autonomous drones and piloted drones. Down on the parking lot his fellow engineers filled the tractor-treaded carriers Arnold had designed. These moving trunks were tiny versions of the Navy Higgins boats, meant to carry little police robots on land instead of big marines over water. The engineers were loading them with piles of trilobites and knife-studded Wee Waxies. Several hard-hat men had remote controls. As if it wasn't weird enough already.

The astrophysicists had finished setting up telescopes and binoculars on the roof. He hurried over to the star gazers and the other pilots.

"What happens if they set the building on fire? Can we get down fast enough?" someone from the Law school asked.

"*Nein*, nobody's going to set any fires, not with me here," said Josef, in a leather pilot's cap, goggles, a long scarf and a leather jacket. "The Athletics department will guard the roof and floors with fire extinguishers, bats and hockey sticks."

"But they're way over on the other side of the campus," said Arnold, feeling worried.

"They are athletes. They can run."

It was a good thing Barrietta had insisted that everybody train using gloves, because Arnold certainly didn't want to stay out here with bare fingers in this cold. He noticed that Josef flew a three-prop, one-clawed, three-inch Opah-Binny, with a tiny leather helmet and a teensy scarf on its little head. Really! Where on earth did he get those things on such short notice?

Barrietta, in her pink jacket, had just lofted a Santa Car, its claws carrying fuzzy pitchforks. Flower decals were stuck on the creature. Now a great cloud of fossils flew up toward the foes.

"The drones are carrying either bottles or steel balls, grenades I think. At least one has what looks like an air gun," said a star gazer.

To break through the windows, thought Arnold. Big balls and a big gun never went well with big bottles. His cell phone was fixed at the top of his gaming controls. The wide-angle mini-camera worked well enough but he was still glad he could see his drone from the roof.

He asked Mrs. Weighman, "How did they find out so quickly?"

She answered, not even looking away from her screen, "Social media, likely. They must be using a search bot looking for talk about arson and parchment. People just don't think when they twitter."

The two forces met. The hulking drones of the terrorists wove among the little fossils of the geeks. Giant mechanical zombies versus clever little pseudo-bugs. Mrs. Weighman flew her robots toward the attackers. The fossils attacked, bombing with worms or shredding with claws. Arnold dove his Anomaly down on a four-rotor drone and used his claws to grab its middle. He hit Bite Mode. The attacker broke apart, exploding in flames. The terrorist drones were mostly plastic. Why spend money on expendable tools? Arnold's drone dodged to the left without any orders. A window breaker sped by, missing it by inches. So even the piloted fossils had automatic programming!

Someone yelled out, "My monster just ripped that drone in half!"

"I replaced the claws with steel-backed carbide blades last night," Arnold called back. *Better brag now, I might not get another chance, eh?*

Now for the next moronic thug of a brainless machine. *I've got a semi-smart fossil and you don't*, Arnold thought. The entire roof was a din of warnings, encouragements and swearing. Beyond them were multiple bonfires in the snow. He went back to viewing through his phone. Next to his drone, another Anomaly Carrot threw its steely head into a drone's rotor. The drone dropped its grenades and spun prop over landing gear into the snow. Its own cargo blasted it to shreds. *Now, how'd they get grenades?* Arnold wondered.

Through his camera, he saw Josef's tiny Opa grab onto a propeller shaft and snap it. The drone turned upside down and plummeted. Through the minicam Arnold saw another Anomaly get punched by a window breaker. Its body broke in half.

The window breaker was suddenly attacked by worms dropped by a Santa Car. Hallo Gennies jammed pitchforks into it and two worms wrapped themselves around a rotor. The air gun flipped and fell. A fuzzy pitchfork flew into another drone, fatally wrapping its antennae around the propellers.

Now Arnold went after the next drone. He stopped his fossil. The enemy drone was carrying neither bottles nor grenades. It had vertically spinning buzz saws at its side and it was charging. His drone jumped out of the way by itself. *Pay attention, man! Don't freeze!*

Josef's drone zoomed in. It jabbed the buzz saw's camera and climbed, ripping the camera off. It then dropped the camera on the front propeller, breaking it. The buzz saw banked, sliced through another invader and crashed into a tree, shredding bark everywhere. Arnold made his fossil scan around. Another damn window breaker was charging him from the rear. He dodged the air piston, hitting the drone's propellers with his steel body instead. The window breaker did ice skater flips and attacked the snowy ground. He rotated his view back to Josef's Opa. Beyond the Opa, an automated pitchfork rammed itself into a Molotov cocktail bottle that exploded into flames. The Opa now dove into a drone's motor. It pulled away with split wires falling from its claws. *Good Lord of Theory, Josef had really sharpened those claws!* The drone's propellers stopped.

Through his own drone's mini-cam, Arnold could see the piloted fossils dropping springy and spiky worms on invaders. Other prehistoric drones rammed the horde. The Melancholia's Kevlar whips were particularly good against propellers. He could see more little pitchforks playing kamikaze. Meanwhile, the Opa swooped and cut plastic props and power cords. Behind him he heard whoops of victory. Beside him, Mrs. Weighman was dancing. *Give them the tools*, Arnold thought, *and they'll get the job done.*

He finished off another drone with his arthropod robot and then noticed the land boats unloading dozens of trilobites on the road through the trees. He hovered his drone and looked through his binoculars, seeing four trucks surrounded by angry men. Little black things and little spiky things motored around and under the trucks. The men were desperately trying to stay away from the crawlers.

Back to the battle. Arnold spun his view around. Some attackers had slipped by the fossil army and were now rushing the building, flying over scattered fires and shattered flyers in the deserted parking lot. He spun his own drone around to return, but it couldn't fly fast enough. Then a small cloud rose behind him. *We have a second wave?* Mrs. Weighman furiously typed away on her laptop, her face grimmer than he had ever seen before. At her feet was a broken buzz saw drone and her left leg was bleeding.

Drones full of flammables and explosives passed over the parking lot. Cambrian carnivores grasped with their claws. Molotov cocktails scorched sidewalks, garden beds and stone walls. Students dumped barrels of sand on the bonfires and splashed water on the flames burning the window sills.

Arnold heard a scream. Spinning around, he saw five buzz saws. Arnold's drone was still too far away. Barrietta dropped her controls and ran. The attackers swooped down and suddenly two young men in t-shirts, Hachamura and n'Bolo of the Phys. Ed. department, jumped up and swung dumbbell handles like staffs. N'Bolo caught a drone from underneath, breaking the frame so the propellers now pointed out. The rearranged attacker fluttered pathetically as its props tried to pull it apart. They succeeded. More buzzers and bombers bit the gravel roof. Several Molotov tossers evaded the defenders and flew toward them. Three more bombs hit the roof. Arnold felled a drone with his slingshot, but it crashed in a roaring blaze. Students ran to every conflagration, spraying foam, dumping sand and laying down fire blankets.

Finally, only fossils remained in the air.

Arnold heard sirens approaching. *The neighbors must have seen the blazes.* He set his model on hover, turned toward the forest and spotted the vehicles in the distance. Using his binoculars, he saw a truck in the woods driving through crawling fossils. A hooded man with an assault rifle rode in the back. With its wheels skidding on top of flittering fake trilobites, the truck crashed into a tree, popping the hood. A furry pitchfork flew into the engine and smoke rose up.

"Good little ancient arthropod," he yelled.

Another of the trucks stranded on the shoulder, its wheels shredded. *Must have hit those Wee Waxies.* As he watched, little drones smashed into the second truck's windows and fenders and tore off the side mirror, the radio antenna and the windshield wipers. The men inside screamed. Then an Opa rose from the back of the truck with a grenade, its claw holding the weapon by the pin. The riders burst out of the cab. The grenade dropped off its pin. The truck rose up in a blaze of explosives and gasoline.

Another truck nearby caught fire and the entire road was ablaze, except for one more truck stuck in the middle, its wheels also shredded. The terrorists hid underneath that one, pushing trilobites away. He could sense their panic even from where he was.

Arnold lowered his binoculars. A complete success, thanks to everybody. Now they just had to clean up the battle site. But he heard crying behind him. He turned and saw Barrietta weeping. She said softly, "I didn't want anyone to get hurt," over and over again. He hadn't seen anybody seriously injured, not even the terrorists, but he had been rather distracted. He went over and hugged her.

The police and the Fire Department arrived shortly after. The attackers surrendered without a shot, their rifles scorched and their nerves broken by Cambrian fakes. When the defenders tallied up the destroyed and damaged drones, it had taken two worms and two drones for every attacker. They still had enough for some customers.

The local web news rushed reporters to the university, but none of the staff came forward. No one mentioned parchments. All that the world had were neighboring witnesses, large tracts of melted snow, blackened pavement, the remains of the trucks, scorched illegal rifles, considerable drone wreckage, a cluster of surrendered men, a few snippets on social media about old, forbidden writings, and seven movies taken by neighbors and passers-by, showing the dogfights.

The grand official opening of the Burgess display went on as planned on the holiday Monday, pleasing massive crowds. The Geoscience department shipped some drone orders out by courier and the dean returned from the conference.

Five days later, the dean called Arnold into his office. When Arnold returned to his own office, one of the tenured history professors came to visit. The professor said, "Josef's gone. The dean fired him for breaking regulations. I thought you should know."

"Would the Board of Directors let the dean do that?"

"They're a useless board of directors. They don't oppose, they rubberstamp and collect their pay. Oh, he also had the parchments shipped back to the country of origin, so we'll never see or hear of them again."

"That's terrible. Josef was my friend," said Arnold. "And those parchments were extremely important to history. Even an engineer like me knows that."

"The dean's the dean. He might not be able to bully old geezers like me but he can do whatever he wants to untenured kids like Josef and Barrietta."

"Barrietta?"

"Yes, she's gone too, for unauthorized use of other departments' resources. He's also shut down their Burgess project. Not part of the university's mandate, apparently. Mind you, I wouldn't worry about the parchments," the old man said.

"Why not?"

"Well, when you've seen as much garbage as I have, you learn to take precautions. I had every inch of those parchments photographed, with teams working day and night. We shall take over that history project and there's no dean or director we won't stand up to. We have tenure and we have friends who are big donors. I guess you'll carry on your miniaturization project."

"No, I'm not. I've been sacked too. My work on the fossils is an unbudgeted and unapproved expense."

A janitor dropped a large envelope and several cardboard boxes at Arnold's door and left, chuckling.

The historian looked like he was thinking deeply about something. He then said, "Wait, that uncle of yours, call him."

"My lawyer uncle?" Arnold asked.

"Yes, call him now, before you sign anything in that envelope. And make sure you take a copy of every important memorandum you sent or got."

"I don't know about this."

"I do, Arnold, and I'm not leaving until you phone him. And use your cellphone instead of the office phone."

So Arnold called his uncle and explained mostly everything while the professor waited. When Arnold finished, the patient professor smiled.

"Arnold, you gave him my number!"

"He specifically asked for it. He wanted inside information."

"Excellent. What else did your uncle say?"

"That the Anomaly Carrot's teeth are nowhere as sharp as his and the dean and his board of directors will have to face the fire. I guess we're going to fight this."

"Even better. I'll round up supporters here and in other universities. You'd be amazed how well we fossils can fight when we gang up."

DAVID WORSICK is a technical writer from Calgary, Canada. Several decades ago, he wrote the children's book: "Henry's Gift, The Magic Eye" and evaded fame. Now he expects to evade fame again.

SLAYER'S REVENGE

By Chris M. Jessop

The *Hafgya* glided silently through the fog, and I could see nothing, not even the water below. That was the only way to hunt dragons. If the dragon saw us coming, we'd be dinner for the fishes.

I pulled my crystal porpoise from under my shirt and kissed it. Wouldn't do to forget the goddess even if I'd always given my ships one of her names. I patted the wooden quarter-deck fife rail.

The ghost of a port broad wind only just filled our sprits'l and main. If that new mother's boy of a wizard, who was now leaning against the mizzen mast three feet away, lived up to his patter and reputation, the wind would remain just so and the fog would hold.

The wizard stepped forward to the navigation table and whispered, "Captain Edilon, sir, I can see the dragon." He marked the dragon and our position on the chart.

By the goddess! I took two steps to the whipstaff and whispered "Hard to starboard."

As the steersman obeyed, the ship creaked around and sailors ran to trim the sails before they could flap. A towering rock loomed out of the fog like a ghost and slipped astern.

"Steer north by east."

This dragon's lair was three-hundred ship-lengths away perched on the cliff-shore, perhaps thirty fathoms up. Two years ago, the monster had cast a spell to lift the fog. Why, I'll never know. There were natural fogs enough on these dismal shores. I'd sworn that I'd get the bugger, and this time I wasn't going to let him take my ship, my hand and most of my misbegotten crew. Curse that demon-spawned dragon.

A sailor stomped up the high sterncastle ladder. I cursed the clumsy oaf silently and promised that I'd flog the man later if the dragon hadn't heard.

As the *Hafgya* slid forward, I squinted and gathered up my spit and phlegm in my mouth, then swallowed it. Tasted vile but no stupid noises now. What would this dragon's parts be worth? Twenty-thousand crowns? Maybe thirty? My missing hand itched.

The wizard crumpled to the deck. His cloaking and fog spells must have drained him. Wuss! At least the pathetic wimp had the sense to pass out silently.

A wave slapped the side of the ship. The cloaking spells were dissipating!

"Fourth hell," I cursed. "Hard starboard about."

The sailors ran to obey, but I still could see nothing even though the blasted fog was breaking. The mains'l blocked the view forward but the quarter deck was the command deck. I could not leave.

Ghostly cliffs appeared and high above us a dragon shrieked, a noise like ripping steel. Was that darkness in the fog the span of leathery wings?

The ballista crew let loose, and the marker-buoy chain ran out with a noisy rattle. Idiots. I clenched my remaining hand. I'd made them train hard but shooting at ghosts would doom us all.

The dragon screamed again, and wings churned the remaining mist into shreds. It leapt into the sky, its size blotting out the weak sun. Had they hit it? Had the steel bolt penetrated the hell-spawn's massive armor? The monster was enormous, the largest I'd ever seen. Would it smash the wooden ship with its spiked tail like last time?

My heart stopped.

So did the dragon. Its wings splayed and folded.

A piercing scream ripped the sky apart, and a pulse of magic flashed so strong that even my simple eyes saw the coruscating indigo light. Then the monster hit the ocean, as if one of the moons had fallen from the sky. A pillar of water erupted taller than the main-mast.

Damn! That was close.

"All hands brace for—"

The crashing wave hit.

As large as the *Hafgya* was, she bucked like a horse, skewing sideways and heaving as if the mother of all storms had broken. Salty spray sheeted down, soaking the sails, the decks and even the high sterncastle. Waves crashed over the midship gunnels and swamped the scuppers.

Those that hadn't grabbed masts, belaying anchors or the capstan were thrown. Two men screamed as they slammed into the fo'c'sle gunnel. One fell back to the deck in a spray of blood while the other cartwheeled into the ocean.

The upper foremast stays snapped. Wood, rope and heavy canvas slammed into the deck and the ocean.

The *Hafgya* was a sturdy ship, and the tempest passed.

I strode forward from the stern and climbed down ladders while shouting, "Re-load the ballista! Where's the buoy? Tell me that you useless louts haven't lost sight of the buoy. First mate, stay the foremast! You two to the pumps!"

For half a glass, chaos ruled the decks, but my commands had the sailors running and returned some order. The ship's momentum carried us to the floating buoy, and with every available sailor manning the capstan, they winched the sunken carcass to the surface. Even if the *Hafgya* was a three-hundred ton carrack, there was no chance of getting this one on the deck. Its wings made the *Hafgya* look like a rowboat.

I smartly slapped on my leathers and readied my axes, saws and crowbars. The sun glinted on the black armor of the monster and the gray cliffs not fifty ship lengths away. We'd have to be right smart before the wind picked up. If the wind didn't shift, we'd be on the lee shore. Those cliffs would shatter any ship. The sailors were already repairing the foremast, but until we jettisoned the unusable bulk of the black dragon, we would be vulnerable.

I was just going over the port gunnel when a sailor screamed, "Dragon off starboard quarter!"

I whipped around. Another dragon hovered on the other side of the sterncastle. The ballista crew earned their keep. The weapon slewed around, and even with no chain and buoy to mark where the dragon fell, the ten pound razor-tipped steel shaft flew straight, fast and true.

And with an audible clang, stopped dead twenty feet from the dragon. It splashed into the ocean.

We were dead. This dragon wasn't as big, its wingspan still easily five times longer than the *Hafgya*. We had no chance. Would it burn us to a crisp with its breath? Or use its overwhelming magic? I didn't enjoy the idea of going slowly mad. As beautiful as the monster was with shimmering light blue and purple scales, dark blue and gold antennae and tufts, it was a killer, a man-eater.

Any moment now we would all die. Might as well go smartly as slowly, so I ran up the ladders to the quarter-deck, towards the monster.

It hovered unnaturally in the sky, its deep-blue leathery wings beating slowly. What the hell? Was it toying with us?

I shouted, "Get on with it, you hell-spawn!"

Still the dragon hovered.

Another bolt flew from the ballista. Good for them! Yet again the bolt slammed into the invisible wall and splashed into the ocean. Those bolts could shatter stone!

The dragon flicked its wing and the ballista shattered, the snapping sinews cracking like a lightning bolt. Its crew collapsed to the deck, wounded by flying steel and wood.

Still the dragon just slowly flapped its wings.

A golden light appeared in its chest so bright that when I

threw up my right arm, I could see through my flesh.

When the gold dimmed and I could see again, no dragon flapped its wings. A tall maiden with long blond hair and a mottled sea-green gown hovered in a nimbus of light.

What was this? She—

An angry voice filled the sky and she stabbed her finger at me. “Why do you kill my companions?”

What?

Half the crew huddled behind cover, the others staring in wonder at the woman. I said nothing as I hid behind the gunnel.

“Speak to me or I will call more dragons to my side.”

She had been a dragon and dragons were intelligent. Everyone knew that. They also didn’t lie, couldn’t lie. The hell-spawn monsters could deceive though. They were magical, very magical, and that was why we hunted them, to sell their parts to wizards.

Two specks appeared in the sky and grew as the dragons approached.

I stood and touched my dolphin with my hand. “I’m not scared of you, demon-spawn. I’m loyal to the Queen of the Oceans, and you can’t touch our souls.”

She laughed. “No! You are not. I am Hafgya. You named your ship after me, yet you hunt and kill my warriors and companions. You are not one of mine.”

Oh my goddess.

I threw myself down onto the deck. “I’m sorry!”

“Stand up.”

I stood, trembling.

“You’re sorry, are you? Sorry that you were caught? Sorry that you made hundreds of thousands of crowns selling dragon parts? Sorry that you killed my companions?”

All of those were correct. The goddess’s companions! I had worshipped her all my life, ever since I first sailed on my father’s ship. What was money? Security. Power. What was power if you died because the gods and goddesses withheld their protection?

"I'm sorry I killed your dragons! Please, I didn't know. Yes, I did it for money. I promise to never do it again."

She clenched her hands. "What to do with you?"

"I promise. Please, you can let us go. Mercy!"

"No. I must make an example of you."

I fell to my knees and clasped my hands. "Oh wondrous Hafgya, Queen of the Oceans, please hear my prayer. I will atone for the killing of your dragons. I will give my fortunes to poor and needy sailors' wives. Please spare us from your wrath."

Since nothing happened, I looked up. The black and red dragons now hovered in the sky beside her.

"I can't let you go. Others will follow your successes."

"I will atone!"

She glowered. "Yes, you will."

The goddess's green skirt and long hair snapped with the wind from the dragons' wings.

"I pronounce your doom. Tell your men to man the longboats."

I turned and shouted the commands. They didn't need to be told twice. Half a glass later, the two boats were hanging over the sides. The men scrambled in, dragging their wounded comrades with them, and the still unconscious wizard.

I waited to follow. I was the captain.

"Not you."

So be it. My life was the price? Sailors always knew that any voyage might be the last. If the goddess said it must be, who was I to argue.

I signalled the men. They lowered the boats to the ocean.

"Before I enact your doom, I will say this: you slander dragons with your stories. They do not rape and eat young virgins. They do not slaughter villages and steal gold. What would dragons want with virgins and gold? Your kind does that. Not dragons. Mark my words well, you men in the boats."

Once the boats pulled away, Hafgya gestured to the dragons.

They swept forward, one on the starboard side and one above the ship, and breathed, drenching the bows with mucus. Fire ignited in front of each dragon, engulfed the forecastle and poured down onto the main deck. The dragons took another breath and sprayed flame over the waist and the sterncastle. Fire dripped over the hull down into the water.

Sails, ropes and spars ignited into a roar of flame. When the heat reached me, I felt my skin crisp from the scorching flames.

It was searing agony and I crumpled against the burning gunnels. I tried to stand, to throw myself into the water, but I couldn't get to my feet. I stopped trying. There was no way to escape dragon fire.

The pain stopped. The ship still burned. My flesh burned. The sticky muck from the dragons covered my arms and chest in flame, but I felt nothing. I could hear the fire, the splitting of the timbers, the hissing of the sea water. Pitch in the deck bubbled and smoke rose to the sky, a pillar marking our doom.

Once the whole ship was aflame, the dragons flew away.

The mainmast cracked and fell away into the ocean, still burning as it sank. Yet, its shadowy outline still stood where the wood, canvas and rope had been.

I could hear the goddess over the roaring fire. "You will sail the seas undying, unliving, until you save one dragon's life for each that you have taken. Only then will your spirit join the dead. Until that time you will wander the world, alone, and you will never leave the sound of the ocean."

I looked at the nearest overcrowded longboat.

"They will survive to spread the story of your doom to the lands. Your wife and children will have to console themselves with your money."

She shimmered back into the blue and purple dragon that dwarfed the now almost transparent *Hafgya* and plunged into the ocean. Only a few lingering parts of the keel still burned.

I'd killed eleven dragons in the past twenty years. How long would it take to save eleven dragons? And how could any mere human save any dragon? Had the goddess thought of that?

Would I be able to work out how? Or was my real doom that I couldn't?

I had until the gods blew the Raven Horn at their final battle to find out.

CHRIS JESSOP has worn many hats including astrophysicist, software and web-site designer/consultant, and dancer. He is the happiest when creating something (solid, intangible or ephemeral) or when exploring a character, an idea, ruins, nature or history. These influences shape all his fiction whether it is science fiction or fantasy.

A MURDER AT CARLETON HOUSE

By Chris Patrick Carolan

An explosion marked the unsuccessful end of Experiment 242—a small one as far explosions went—resulting in little more than a fizzle and a pop, barely loud enough to be heard above the tiny death cry of a wispy zephyr. The Technomancer's Guild taught that invention was the end result of a series of botched attempts to solve a problem, but even a minor failure such as this irked Isaac Barrow.

He scratched his bestubbled chin as he waited for the small cloud of acrid smoke to clear, trying to think what might have gone wrong. He had painstakingly followed every step; by all rights, the elemental bonding should've taken hold. Instead, the thin, silver ring he had inset into the frame of the glider was marred by a sticky black residue, all that remained of the scorched zephyr. "The damned thing wasn't exactly easy to capture, either," he muttered as he inspected the glider's wings.

The machine itself seemed to have survived the zephyr's immolation, though one section of oiled canvas on the left wing had been singed. "That can be replaced easily enough. Far from a total loss, then," he said aloud to no one in particular, thinking about how best to unbind the zephyr's remains and reattempt the procedure.

The chime rang just then, alerting him to a caller at the door to his streetside office. He knew he had flipped the sign in the window to CLOSED before making his way downstairs to work on the glider. If there was anything he found more vexing than failure, it was being interrupted as he worked. Annoyed, he turned down the gas lamps and headed for the stairs.

He unbolted and threw open the heavy door to the street, ready to dispatch whomever was waiting on the other side. Instead, the irritated glare of Inspector Jonathan Eddings of the Halifax Constabulary caught him short.

"Well then, where the hell have you been?" the inspector demanded in his blustering Mancunian brogue without so much as a *how-do-you-do*. "Need I remind you, Isaac, that we were to be dining at Carleton House tonight? My personal thanks for your assistance with the Halliday case?"

"Was that ... Is today not Sunday?"

Eddings smacked his forehead. "It's Tuesday bloody night, Barrow," he exclaimed, "and by the smell of you, you've been locked away in that rathole you call a workshop all week. It's time you came outside and got some fresh air. Past time, actually. Whatever you're playing at down there can wait."

Barrow's face lit up. "It's actually a rather fascinating experiment, Jonathan."

"Tell me about it over dinner if you must, Barrow," Eddings cut him off. "Right now we're going to march you home for a wash up, a shave, and a clean suit." He eyed the scruffy technomancer. "If you have one, that is."

"God save the Queen!" Inspector Eddings boomed as he hoisted a glass into the air, his third of the evening. He had paused mid-tirade only to toast Victoria with each drink as it arrived. The Dominion of Canada had been independent of

British rule for well over a decade, but the Queen was still widely revered, and even moreso on this, the celebration of her birth.

Lollygaggers and gadabouts, Barrow thought cagily as he regarded the well-dressed revelers around him. The Carleton House Men's Social Club catered to established gentlemen and the *nouveau riche* alike. Barrow, as a rule, had little use for either group. As a novelty for the occasion, the club had trotted out a small army of automatons to serve as bussers for the evening. He tried his best to appear indifferent as he watched the mechanical men go about their menial tasks. *A miracle of modern engineering walks in your midst, and you popinjays have them clearing away your empty glassware.*

The remnants of his own meal sat in front of him. He hadn't realized quite how ravenous he was, and had devoured the meat with a haste which would've made the arbiters of propriety recoil in horror. He noted that Inspector Eddings, in contrast, had barely touched his own plate while he upbraided Barrow at length for his absentminded nature. *For a man who was so upset to be kept waiting for dinner, he certainly is taking his time eating it now.*

"And why would anyone want to go flying about up in the air like a daffy old seagull anyway?" the inspector demanded, his lecture apparently reaching its climax.

A scathing response died on Barrow's lips at the crash of a chair hitting the floor accompanied by a cry of horror from the far side of the room. Barrow and Eddings were on their feet in an instant. "Make way, damn it," Eddings bellowed as he shouldered past several dapper fellows, Barrow trailing a pace behind. "Halifax Constabulary!"

At the center of the throng, a man lay sprawled on his back, his seat knocked violently aside as he had tumbled. Bloody froth, still bubbling from his mouth and nose, streaked down the front of his white shirt. Spatters of blood also stained the tablecloth where he had sat dining just moments ago. An automaton in a crisp black suit had already set to the task of straightening up the disarrayed table setting.

"Don't you touch one blasted thing!" Eddings shouted at it. The knife and fork the automaton held dropped to the table with a clatter. The mechanical man assumed the dutiful posture of a gentleman's valet, standing stock-still in place to await further instructions.

Two of the fellows the fallen man had been dining with stood gawping nearby. A third crouched at his side, clasping his wrist to track his pulse. He looked up and shook his head somberly. The man on the floor was dead, his face ashen and his lips already turning an unwholesome blue.

"What happened?" Eddings demanded, dropping to one knee on the other side of the body.

"He seemed fine until he began coughing into his handkerchief," the dead man's crouching friend explained. "When he pulled it away from his face, it was full of blood. He looked at it for a moment and muttered something I couldn't make out, then he started to convulse. Blood just ... erupted from his nose and mouth. I've never seen anything like it."

"No, you wouldn't have," Barrow said, regarding the scene dispassionately from where he stood, a few feet back, working his fingers into a pair of white cotton gloves. "There aren't many spells which burn up a man's lungs from the inside like that."

Inspector Eddings sat puffing a cigar behind his desk, his eyes tracked with red. His office, like the rest of the Constabulary Headquarters in the basement of Halifax City Hall, was cramped, damp, and dimly lit, the cloying smoke from his cigar making it feel all the more claustrophobic. Barrow couldn't tell whether it was the cigar smoke or simple exhaustion that stung at the inspector's eyes. He doubted Eddings had slept much if at all the night before; even once his constables had arrived, the onerous task of taking down witness statements from every man present at Carleton House had dragged on well into the early morning hours.

"Doctor Brookfield is welcome to waste his time performing the Marsh test if he chooses," Barrow said, settling into the seat on the other side of the desk. He hadn't lingered at the horrific scene quite as late as his friend, instead heading home for a few hours rest before rejoining the inspector at his office. "I can already tell you he won't find the slightest trace of arsenic in Edward Osgood's body."

"And what makes you so bloody sure of that, Barrow?"

"The symptoms don't quite fit." Barrow stated with a shrug. "Arsenic poisoning begins to manifest as much as a week before lethality, Jonathan. Diarrhea, vomiting, and convulsions often start days before the major organs begin to shut down, and even then Osgood's hemoptysis was well beyond what you would expect to see in even a severe case of arsenical poisoning."

"Hemo-whatsis?" Eddings interrupted.

"Coughing up blood," Barrow explained. "Besides which, his friends all say he seemed perfectly healthy right up until the moment he started coughing into his napkin."

"It was his handkerchief, but go on."

"Let's not get tripped up on irrelevancies," Barrow chided his friend, waving the inspector's correction and a thick coil of cigar smoke aside. "The fact is Edward Osgood was a healthy young man, who went from the smiling picture of health at dinner to drowning on the floor as his lungs filled with his own blood in a matter of seconds."

"And you think someone put a hex on him."

Barrow nodded.

Eddings took another long draw on his cigar, exhaling slowly. "Isaac, you know what the chief constable is going to say if I tell him that Osgood was killed by an evil wizard."

"You know how I hate that word, Jonathan," Barrow said with a wince. "Such a childish, utterly ridiculous term. Anyway, like it or not, whoever killed this man did so without the use of any earthly poison. I'm certain of it."

"Fair enough. You're more often right about these things than not. I'll let Doctor Brookfield run his tests, though. It'll give me something to tell the chief inspector and buy us some time to figure out this load of hokery-pokery you've dropped in my lap," Eddings declared, drawing another cringe from Barrow. "So who could have done it?"

Barrow frowned. "Anyone could have, but almost no one would. There's a very good reason you don't often see spells of bane used to murder people, Jonathan. Their use is proscribed by explicit writ of the Triune Congress. People already hate and fear magicians enough as it is without deadly curses being thrown around."

"Bloody hell, Barrow. Whoever wanted Edward Osgood dead must've had a damned good reason, then."

"Indeed. What do you know about the men he was dining with?"

"Not many leads there, I'm afraid. The three of them barely knew him, as it turns out. The man who checked him for a pulse when he keeled over was Robert Farland, a coworker at the Union Bank. He did say Osgood had been seeing a young woman, a Miss Anna Ross, but he didn't know much more about it than that. We'll be speaking with her, of course."

"A jilted paramour, perhaps?"

"We won't know until we interview her," Eddings shrugged. "The other two blokes were college chums of Farland's who hadn't met Osgood until an hour before he dropped dead. Hard to think they'd be behind it. But it had to have been someone who was at Carleton House last night, hadn't it?"

Barrow shook his head. "Not necessarily. Spells of bane can be effected over a considerable distance, and many are rather slow in killing. Several hours or even days might have passed between when the spell was cast and when it finally caught up with Osgood."

"So you're telling me that our murderer might've been anywhere in the city at the time Osgood up and died?" The inspector sighed and shook his head. "Barrow, you do have a way of making these things complicated."

Barrow simply grinned.

Eddings shot him a venomous glare. "Very well. Miss Ross works at the Dominion Cotton mill. I'm headed there now, if you'd like to sit in on the interview. I'll have some of the constables head down to the bank where Osgood worked to get the scope of things down there." He stubbed out what was left of his cigar, then rose and snatched up his overcoat and walking stick on his way out the door.

The thunderous beat of machinery could be heard through the walls of the small office on the third floor of the Dominion Cotton Mills factory. Barrow stood near a window overlooking the production floor, admiring the massive spinning and weaving machines as they processed bales of raw cotton into yarns and cloth. Some would be shipped inland to Montreal, Toronto, and other Canadian cities, but much of the factory's output was bound for more lucrative American and European markets.

Inspector Eddings sat on the far side of a broad table, drumming his fingers against the wood. Barrow could tell the inspector wanted to get on with the business of interviewing Anna Ross, just as soon as the girl could be brought up from her spot on the production line downstairs. No more than ten minutes had passed since the gaffer had gone to fetch her, but the inspector was not known as a patient man.

Finally, the door opened and Miss Ross followed the gaffer into the room. The fellow made his introductions and fled, leaving her alone with Barrow and Eddings. She was dressed quite plainly and wore her chestnut hair pinned up at the back, a few strands on each side hanging loose against her cheeks. Despite her tousled appearance, she held her head high. It was easy to see she was quite pretty underneath the grunge of factory labor.

"Have a seat, Miss Ross," Eddings said. "This shouldn't take very long, and then you can get back to work. What is it you do here?"

"I run one of the spooler machines, twisting threads from sixteen bobbins into four separate lengths of yarn," she said, a bemused expression on her face. "But you didn't have the gaffer pull me away from the floor to ask me about how yarn is made."

Barrow couldn't help but smile at her forthrightness.

"Ah, no, Miss Ross," Eddings said, caught somewhat by surprise at her candor. "In fact, Mister Barrow and I are investigating a murder. Did you happen to know a fellow by the name of Edward Osgood?"

"Edward is dead?"

"I'm afraid so," Eddings said gently. "He died last night while dining at Carleton House. I understand the two of you were quite close."

One of her eyebrows quirked upward. "Who told you that?"

"One of his friends," Barrow interjected, curious at the young woman's mild response. "Robert Farland?"

"Well, then I suppose Edward hadn't quite told Robert everything. It's true that Edward and I had been seeing each other, but it was all over between us."

"And why was that?" Eddings asked.

She sighed and shook her head sadly. "We were friends in Toronto. We'd known each other since we were teenagers, and studied at Queen's together, but we were never romantically involved back then. We wrote to each other after I left for Halifax a little over a year ago. When Edward finished school and took the job here at the Union Bank...well, I suppose I was homesick for Toronto, and I fell for someone I shouldn't have."

"Why shouldn't you?" Eddings pressed. "He was a handsome young fellow, one with a good job."

"He was also a notorious tomcat, Inspector Eddings," Anna replied with a shrug. "He always was, even when I knew him in Toronto. I thought perhaps he may have grown out of it in the last few years, but it seems I was wrong."

"So you ended things."

"Oh no, Inspector. He ended things between us when he took up with some strumpet typist. I just had to do the hard part of telling him to get out of my sight and waste no time doing it!"

"How is it that a woman who studied at Queen's University has come to be working in a cotton mill in Halifax?" Barrow asked.

"I trained as a schoolteacher, Mister Barrow." She straightened one of the stray wisps of hair that had fallen across her cheek. "The job I came here to take had disappeared by the time I got off the train. The mill was the only work I could find at the time, and a girl needs to eat. I'm only here until I can save enough to return to Toronto."

Eddings leaned back in his chair and drummed his fingers on the table once more, pausing thoughtfully before he answered. "We may need to speak with you again, Miss Ross. Please don't leave Halifax in the meantime."

Barrow and Eddings walked the long corridor that ran down the middle of the constabulary headquarters, heading for the interrogation room. "Do you think the girl's good for it, Barrow?"

"I don't know, Jonathan. I imagine the girl was upset, but was she angry enough to kill Osgood with dark magic? They had only been involved for a few weeks."

"Hell hath no fury, Isaac," the inspector quipped as a constable handed him a folder. He flipped open the cover and scanned the report inside.

"Who is he?"

"Thomas Norton, one of the other juniors at Union Bank," Eddings said, peering into the interrogation room through the screened window separating it from the corridor.

"The bank where Edward Osgood worked."

"The same," Eddings nodded. "Of the lot of them down there, he's apparently the only one with any sort of grievance against Osgood, though he declined to tell the constables what had provoked their falling out."

"Well, shall we see what he can tell us?" Barrow asked, heading for the door.

Thomas Norton was a small, tidy man nearing middle age. His hair and mustache were neatly trimmed, and while his tweed suit wasn't the most fashionable choice, neither was it shabby enough to draw notice. Indeed, he seemed a most unremarkable sort of fellow.

Eddings took the seat opposite Norton while Barrow stood nearby. "I hope you won't mind Mister Barrow sitting in on this. He's something of a special consultant working with us on this investigation."

Norton glanced up at Barrow. He said nothing, but his expression was icy.

"So, Mister Norton, my constables tell me you work at the Union Bank, is that so?"

Norton regarded the inspector with something approaching mild indifference. "Correct," he answered, wasting no words.

"Did you know a Mister Edward Osgood who recently started work at the bank?"

Norton nodded, once. "I did."

Another exceedingly concise response, Barrow noted.

"Did you know Mister Osgood was murdered the other night?"

"I'm not one for engaging in the office gossip, Inspector Eddings, so I hadn't heard about it until your constables came to the bank this afternoon. Arsenic, was it not?"

"The coroner is looking into that," Eddings said. It was, after all, not exactly a lie.

"From the sound of it, his death was a frightful thing, but I'll shed no tears at his passing."

"That's rather cold of you to say, Mister Norton," Eddings said. "I understand you had something of a personal grudge against Osgood. What was that about? Did his coming to work at Union Bank cost you a promotion?"

"If you're asking if I had any reason to poison Edward

Osgood, I can assure you I had neither the motive nor the means," Norton said, now sounding smug. "If anything, Edward would've wished me dead."

"Now, that is very interesting," Eddings said slowly, one eyebrow arching sharply upwards. "And just why might that've been?"

"Because he knew I was about to denounce him as a wizard."

Barrow bristled.

"Why would you do that?" Eddings interjected before Barrow could speak. "Even if it were so, it's no crime under the law, and no concern of yours what any man does on his own time. What was there to gain by it?"

"I looked for no gain in it, Inspector," Norton said with a shrug. "The man was an abomination, in consort with Satan himself. I would've been doing God's work."

That was too much for Barrow. "And who are you to decide the will of God, Mister Norton?" he demanded, slamming one clenched fist down on the table, his outburst startling both Norton and Inspector Eddings. "By what arrogance do you think it's your place to spread your own hatred and fear in His name?"

"Suffer not the witch to live," Norton replied in measured tone, leveling an unflinching gaze at Barrow. "Nor the wizard. Is that not what the Bible says? The law of man—the law you speak of, Inspector Eddings—is not the law of God, more's the pity."

Barrow took a step towards him, but Eddings was already on his feet and caught the technomancer by the arm. "Steady yourself, Isaac," he said under his breath. Regaining his composure, Barrow nodded and Eddings released his grip. "Mister Norton," said the inspector, "I thank you for your time, but I think it might be best if you leave. Now."

Norton gathered up his hat and coat, heading for the door. He paused, looking over at Barrow. "It's too late for Edward Osgood, Mister Barrow. May God have mercy on his soul. There is time yet, however, for other sinners to seek redemption."

At that, Eddings threw open the door and roughly hustled Norton out into the hallway. "Get this man out of here," he barked at a passing constable. "See that he wastes no time in clearing out!"

Barrow stood at the end of the table, leaning heavily on both fists. His knuckles were white as he pushed against the polished wood. "I'm fine, Jonathan," he said after a long moment, looking up at the inspector. "Do you know where Edward Osgood was staying?"

Eddings nodded carefully. "A boarding house, over on Dresden Row."

Barrow jotted the address down in a small notebook. "I'll need to see his room."

"You go on ahead, then. I have to meet with the coroner before he knocks off in an hour or so," Eddings said. "I can have one of the constables go with you, if you like?"

"I don't think that will be necessary," Barrow said, glancing at his watch. The afternoon had all but slipped away. "I'll meet you back here at the station, first thing tomorrow morning."

Edward Osgood's room at the boarding house was much as Barrow had expected it would be. Having only arrived from Toronto eight weeks earlier, he had not quite settled in before being struck down by the spell that had killed him. A few shirts and suits hung in the wardrobe, and his undergarments were folded neatly away in the drawers below. A handful of books lined a shelf above a small writing desk, but he had apparently had little time to accumulate much else in the way of those small personal items that turn a rented room into any sort of home.

It has to be here somewhere, Barrow thought as he pulled open a drawer on the writing desk. Aside from a few pencils and a small writing pad, the drawer was empty. He tapped his fingers on the underside panel of the drawer then repeated this with the two remaining drawers. "No false bottoms, then," he muttered.

He similarly checked the wardrobe drawers, finding nothing out of the ordinary. That left only the bed. He dropped to his hands and knees to peer under the bed, but all he found there were a few dead insects and some swirling clumps of gathering dust. *The housekeeper must've had the month off*, he thought sardonically. Undeterred, he ran his fingers along the inside of the bed's side rails, then the front, but again he came up empty-handed. He finally turned his attention to the simple, utilitarian headboard.

Pulling the headboard slightly out from the wall, he heard something drop to the floor with a slight *clink*. Reaching under the bed, he pulled out a small brown leather case. It was well-worn and about half the size of a normal briefcase. Unbuttoning and opening the case, he smiled.

"You were right about at least one thing, Barrow. Doctor Brookfield found no trace of arsenic in Edward Osgood's body."

Barrow hung his coat and hat on one of the hooks near the door in the inspector's office. "Of course he didn't, Jonathan," he said mildly, as though the possibility he might be mistaken had never occurred to him. He settled into a chair and placed the leather case he had discovered in Osgood's room on the inspector's desk. "Tell me, do you have Edward Osgood's personal effects here at the station? The things he had on him when he died, I mean?"

"Of course, down in the evidence room. Hang on a minute." Eddings poked his head out into the corridor. "Oi! Fetch me Edward Osgood's things. Case number eleven-nineteen."

Several minutes later, the constabulary's single automaton clanked into the inspector's office carrying the requested file box. Unlike the flashy machines clad in the latest finery at Carleton House, the constabulary's unit wore no uniform at all, its gleaming brass and steel skin plating on view for all to see. It set the box on the desk and stood in place to await further instruction.

Eddings seemed to take little notice of the automaton as he pulled the lid off the box and removed the articles within. "Well then, be off with you!" he finally barked at it. The machine sketched a rough military salute and trundled off towards the hallway. Eddings shook his head. "Bloody thing. Well, what are we looking for here, then?"

"Anything that might hold a reserve of magical energy," Barrow said as he rummaged through the items. There wasn't much in the box; Osgood's clothing, a small case containing a pair of eyeglasses, an expensive-looking jeweled tie pin. He rifled through Osgood's billfold, but found only banknotes and a few calling cards within, then pulled Osgood's bloodstained waistcoat out of the box and went through the pockets. "Ah, here we go!" He held up a golden watch on a chain.

Eddings eyed the piece skeptically. "His pocket watch?"

"Just so," Barrow said absently as he examined it. "Jonathan, do you remember the experiment you interrupted when you called at my door the other night?"

"Something about, what was it ... Element blending, wasn't it?"

"*Elemental bonding.* As I was about to explain to you when Mister Osgood died, it's a relatively new alchemical process by which mechanical devices are augmented by merging them with the vital essence of a metaphysical entity."

"Interesting enough, I suppose," the inspector shrugged, "but what's it got to do with the price of beans?"

"Elemental bonding can be a costly and difficult procedure, but it's a good way to enhance the functionality or efficiency of a machine." Barrow turned the watch over to show the inspector a thin silver ring inlaid on the backside of the gold casing. Several tiny symbols were inscribed within the silver circle. "Edward Osgood's pocket watch, for example, has been bonded with a minor horological spirit. This watch will never lose time, and will never need winding."

"Get to the bloody point, Isaac," Eddings replied, snatching the watch from his hand to examine it himself.

"You'll remember that I told you spells of bane are proscribed by the Triune Congress? Well, it's because they can be deadly for the one casting them, too. A small error on the spellcaster's part, or any outside interference present at time of casting, could cause a spell of bane to backfire."

"I ... wait, so you mean to say that ..." Eddings regarded the timepiece in his hand with renewed interest and, Barrow thought, something approaching horror. "Bloody hell!"

"Just so, Jonathan. Anyone with a modicum of inborn ability can learn a few spells. Even the dangerous ones, if he has access to the right codices." He unbuttoned and laid open the scuffed brown leather case from Osgood's room to show the inspector several small glass phials and tiny amber specimen bottles, none large enough to hold more than an ounce or two. "Osgood had the beginnings of a very rudimentary sorcerer's apothecary. Henbane oil, myrrh, powdered crab shell. Everything one might need for a series of very simple conjurations, or," he paused as he pulled a small, battered booklet from the case and handed it over to Eddings, "any number of deadly curses."

"It's in Latin," the inspector said, scratching his chin as he read the worn cover. "*Maledicta Devotatio* ... Does that mean what I think it does?"

Barrow nodded. "Edward Osgood had sorcerous talent, sure enough, but he was untrained and not half as clever as he thought he was. He lashed out—I suppose we'll never know whether at Anna Ross in anger or at Thomas Norton in fear—but he didn't realize the magical energy concentrated within his pocket watch would direct his own hex back at him." Barrow shook his head sadly. "It's likely he didn't even realize anything had gone wrong until he started coughing up blood."

"And by then it was too late," Eddings finished for him, snapping the pocket watch shut. "Right then, shall we say next Tuesday evening at eight o'clock?"

Barrow regarded the inspector for a moment, bewildered.

"It's very simple, Barrow," Eddings chuckled. "Between

solving yet another case for us, and the meal that was interrupted the other night, I still owe you a dinner!"

CHRIS PATRICK CAROLAN has never traveled by hovercraft or eaten an ostrich, but by becoming a published writer has achieved at least one of the goals he set for himself in his Grade 11 Career and Life Management class workbook. His music journalism has appeared in publications including *BeatRoute* and *Comatose Rose* magazine, and he currently contributes front page content to Allspark.com, a pop culture website with over 10,000 registered users. Born in Glasgow, Scotland, he now lives in Calgary, Alberta, where he is working on his first novel, a paranormal mystery set in 1880s Halifax.

THE NIGHT OF THE FIRE

By Colin Maheu

Zoe would have enjoyed watching the place burn to a pile of blackened rubble. Two weeks of living in a room with ugly cream-yellow wallpaper on concrete was enough to make her wish she had set the fire herself. It burned in a room on the third floor of the hotel and, for a while, the smoke and flames appeared fearsome enough to spread and engulf the rest of the building. It was something to see—she could give it that. *If I have to evacuate in the middle of the night and stand here shivering in the street, I should at least get a show out of it.* But the firemen got there quickly, and soon the fading plume rising from the broken window was all that remained.

She and the other girls sent to Calgary for flight attendant training were all assigned rooms on the twenty-sixth floor, just to ensure that they never got a break from each other.

Thankfully, they would be spared smoke damage. Didn't really matter either way. Zoe's purse and phone—the only things she had in Calgary worth saving—were with her.

"They say the guy in the room set the fire trying to kill himself," Ashley whispered into her ear.

Who says? And why would they tell you? She made a dismayed noise and waited for Ashley to go whisper the rumor to someone else.

It still made her cringe a little when Ashley talked to her. The unlucky girl was the cousin of Zoe's ex-boyfriend, Brad. It was excruciatingly awkward.

Recognizing her from Facebook upon their first meeting, there was nothing to do but blurt, "Hi, I'm Zoe. I dated your cousin." She had no doubt that word of her new life performing CPR on plastic dummies would be trickling back to Brad by now.

Zoe pictured him with some faceless blonde, in bed with the computer, laughing at pictures of her with messed up makeup, sloppy and drunk. Ashley had a way of photographing her at the worst moments, and at the worst angles, and always seemed to post them and tag her immediately. There was no way to stay ahead of it.

Living well was supposed to be the best revenge, but Zoe couldn't think of how to spin the way she felt into a success story, even for the audience of "friends" that she had accumulated in her travels. She posted less and less, and now only looked at Facebook to make sure she wasn't tagged in any particularly heinous photos. And to compulsively creep people, of course.

Maybe living well is the best revenge, but wanting revenge means he still has a hold on me. He wins.

Ashley and Soo were posing for a selfie in front of the firetruck and joking about what to hashtag it. Ash had been sneaking pictures of the firefighters all night, captioning them 'Enjoying the view!! *#hotfiremen*" with a heart-eyes emoji to hammer home the point. Zoe's Instagram feed was, at this point, flooded with pictures of things that were still going on in front of her. Still, she scrolled, if only to make sure there were no pics of her braless, shivering in her pjs.

And the *#hotfiremen* were pretty poor specimens too. *Nothing like the calendars,* she thought to herself with a wry smile.

Zoe's excitement had long since died down, and it was

freezing out. She was about ready to go back inside and get what little sleep she could.

"You look cold," said a voice behind her.

"What was your first hint?"

She turned around and saw a handsome young man in a wool overcoat with a briefcase and a travelling blanket, which he held out to her.

She didn't particularly feel like striking up a conversation with a stranger at 2 a.m. outside a burning building, but she was in no position to turn down the blanket. In the rush to secure her valuables, she had neglected to dress for the weather.

"Thank you. I'm Zoe."

"Sean," he replied, holding out his hand for her to shake. "Where are you from?"

"Vancouver." How was his hand so warm out in the cold?

"Here on business?"

"Yeah, basically."

There was little in the world that she wanted less than to talk about flight attendant school with this guy who looked for all the world like the dumb young businessmen who flew first class and thought every young stewardess was into them.

"How about you?" Best let him talk about himself.

"I'm in chemical engineering. Here from Edmonton. My company—"

Zoe tuned out and imagined being back in bed. She kept half an ear on what Sean was saying, waiting for a pause, then said, "Oh, sounds like interesting work."

A silence fell. Zoe hated silences. The whole point of pretending she was interested was to avoid them. Brad had always let the long silences hang. Staring her down. She began to feel tight across the chest—

"I heard a guy tried to kill himself," she blurted.

"Which guy?"

"The guy who set the fire."

He shook his head. "People don't set fires to kill

themselves."

She found his dismissiveness annoying. "People set fires for all kinds of reasons," she argued.

"No, people *make* fires for a lot of reasons. You can cook, you can cast and smelt metals, bake clay—which are all the same thing, by the way."

Zoe didn't understand what he was trying to say, but she recognized when she was being talked down to. This guy had the classic snotty tone of someone who needed everyone to know how smart he was. Unless he was joking? She was bad at reading irony and dry humor, at least while shivering in the middle of the night.

"People set fires to destroy things," she pointed out, not sure why she was still engaging with him. "The guy just wanted to destroy himself."

"Matter can neither be created nor destroyed. Pretty basic physics."

Zoe was about ready to give the blanket back and invite Sean to get lost.

"In Hawai'i they worship Pele, the goddess of fire. They call her 'the eater of the land,'" she blurted, not sure what it had to do with anything.

Sean turned and stared at her, eyebrows raised, mouth open. Had she said something dumb? She scanned his eyes. He was waiting for her to keep talking.

"I'm a flight attendant out of Vancouver. I have a lot of Hawai'i layovers."

He nodded.

"Uh, yeah. There's a lot of stuff about fire in the mythology. You know, the volcanoes. But a lot of it was lost after the missionaries came."

Sean looked back up at the building, at the gaping hole on the third floor. "It does look like something an avenging god would do, doesn't it? There's power there."

"The Hawai'ians believed there were spirits who could capture the souls of the living and bend them to their will," Zoe said. *See, I know things too, mister.* "One time, an old woman told me about the night marchers—the spirits of dead warriors. They go around carrying torches."

"Oh yeah?" He seemed fixated on what she was saying.

"Yeah. And if you look them in the eye, they'll take you with them, and you'll be forced to march on and on forever."

His eyes narrowed a bit. "Spooky."

He looked kind of cute the way he was hanging on her every word.

"Right?" Zoe smiled. "Maybe one of them dropped his torch on the third floor after taking someone off to the spirit world."

He looked like he was about to say something else when one of the firemen spoke into a megaphone.

"Folks, I want to thank you for your patience. In a few minutes we expect the building to be cleared for re-entry."

The crowd on the sidewalk applauded a bit. Zoe waited for Sean to talk.

But he didn't pick the conversation up. She felt like she was back in the living room with Brad again, watching him smirk over an uncomfortable pause.

"Zoe, come get in the picture," Danielle called out. She and Ashley were gathering a bunch of people in front of a ladder truck, with the firefighters in the middle.

Zoe turned. "Wanna be in the picture too?"

Sean smiled. He didn't seem like a snarky know-it-all when he smiled. She must have had it wrong. His grin was boyish and sincere, and, for a moment at least, she decided she liked him.

They bunched in against everyone to fit into the frame, with Zoe to the far left of the back row.

"A little more to the right, Zoe," Danielle said, motioning with her free hand. "Okay, good."

Sean reached his left arm out and put it around her shoulder. She had missed that feeling.

"Okay, everyone say '*fire!*'" shouted Danielle. "Three, two, one—"

"*Fire!*" they repeated in unison as the LED flash strobed.

"I guess we can thank the goddess Pele," Sean said as the group broke apart, taking his arm back.

She waited for more. He let his words hang, as if waiting for her to praise his wit. If anyone ever asked her why she talked so much when she was nervous, she would blame it on jerks who throw out vague nonsense to draw people into conversations they don't want to have in the first place. She could see in his eyes that Mr. Chemical Engineer thought he was terribly enigmatic.

"What do you mean?" She didn't want to, but she asked anyway.

"The transforming fire," he explained. "Iron becomes steel, clay becomes pottery, meat and vegetables become a meal—" he took her by the hand and drew her in close to him, forcing her to crane her neck upward to keep eye contact—"and strangers become friends?"

There was something about his voice. That smile. Or was it his shoulders? His arms? She had been so lonely since Brad. Like an old spinster lady. She pulled a WestJet pen and an old receipt out of her purse and scribbled her number on it.

"Give me a call if you're gonna be in town awhile," she said, as if she didn't really give a damn either way.

He took the paper between his middle and fore fingers and smiled that same perfect grin.

"Good night, Zoe."

The next day dragged by in an eternity of exhaustion. Ashley, Soo, Danielle, and the other girls seemed to have no problem working on four hours of sleep or talking tirelessly about the night before.

Ashley had given her phone number to one of the firemen and was checking her phone every two seconds. Zoe did much the same, but tried not to let it show. If the other girls found out about her chemical engineer, the news wouldn't take very long to make its way back to Brad. She didn't want him to know. It made her feel absurdly guilty.

As the day went on and on and no message arrived, she got irritated, then silently furious. *He might have at least texted, "Good morning," just so I'd have his number too.*

She knew she shouldn't have given him her number. Guys didn't like that. Guys liked to be the ones to ask. But it was stupid to dwell on it. So why was she?

That night they all decided to study together in the hotel lounge so that no one would fall asleep early. There was too much material to memorize.

"I'll sleep when I'm certified," Ashley vowed, taking a shot of espresso as if it were tequila.

Zoe, for her part, was eating chocolate-covered coffee beans like they were peanuts. Her eye twitched—a good sign that they were working.

She positioned herself in the lounge so she could keep one eye on the bank of elevators out in the lobby. *What am I gonna do if he comes through? Run up and jump on him like a golden retriever?* And why did she seem to care so much? She vaguely remembered how annoying he was, but mostly pictured his smile. It stuck in her head like a bad song. She had to admit though, something about his grin just seemed full of light.

Incandescent. That was the word. All the awkward silences she'd have to sit through didn't seem so terrible when she thought about Sean's smile.

"Shh! Shut up, guys. Look." Danielle elbowed the girls to either side of her.

"A fire at a hotel in downtown Calgary early this morning," said the voice-over as the footage of the firetrucks and billows of smoke played on the TV. The *maitre d'* pulled a remote control from behind the bar and turned the volume up.

"None injured. The police have not been able to rule out arson," the anchor continued.

Rzzzzzzzzzz! Zoe's phone buzzed in the pocket of her jeans. She leapt up and ran into the lobby to answer it.

Once she reached a suitable corner, she took a deep breath and swiped the phone open.

"Hello?"

"Hey, Zoe."

Oh no.

"How… Brad, how did you get this number?" But she knew.

"When I heard there was a fire I just wanted to—"

"I'm fine. Ashley could have told you that. I don't think you should be calling me."

"I just …"

He let the silence hang, like he always did. She hated how much she had missed the sound of his voice, how it cooled her down, slowed her breathing, and made her stomach unclench. Her mouth hung open. Silence was agony.

"Goodbye, Brad." She bit her lip to stop herself from whispering "I love you," as she had always done so freely before.

She crumpled into one of the chairs in the lobby and took the deepest breath she could without letting out a sob.

Scumbag. So transparent. If he thought he was going to catch her in a vulnerable moment—that she would fall into his arms because of a damn fire—

"Now there's a face I can't forget."

She opened her eyes. Sean stood over her, his face almost glowing. His eyes seemed even more boyish and kind than they had in the middle of the night. She couldn't let him see how flustered she was. She smiled, but then remembered she was annoyed with him.

"Why didn't you call me?"

He pulled a brown napkin out of the flap of his briefcase and handed it to her, leaning in close. "Should we get out of here?"

There was something absurd about uttering that line in the lobby of a hotel, and it was too much, on top of everything else. Her laugh came out choked.

Zoe wiped her hot tears away. He took her by the hand and they went to the elevators.

"I thought we were getting out of here." She frowned at

him.

"We will," he promised, pulling her onto the elevator. He pressed the button for the fifth floor. When they got off, he led her toward the stairwell instead of to a room. She could smell smoke. They went down the stairs, and the smell got more intense, until it was almost nauseating.

And then they were in front of Room 301. There was no door. Whether it burned up or had been broken down and thrown away, Zoe couldn't tell. The inside of the room was black and grey, ashes and debris. Cold air blew in through the shattered windows. She shivered as she looked in from behind the caution tape that blocked the doorway.

"We're not supposed to be here, are we?" she whispered.

"Just look for a minute."

"It gives me the creeps. Everything all charred and destroyed..."

"Mmm," Sean murmured, as if words were not necessary. He moved in behind her and put his arms around her waist.

"It turns out the guy didn't kill himself," she said, still whispering, "and no one was hurt." She couldn't think of anything else to say.

He pulled her around toward him, gently, but firmly, and kissed her. It was the weirdest kiss of her life, but she felt that bitter, angry place inside her cooling and dissipating, like running a burn under cold water. She had missed being touched so much. She thought of Brad, and the way his kisses had always been slow and passionate. Sean was different. He kissed her so hard, she felt like he was about to lift her off her feet. Zoe put her hand behind his head and gripped him by his hair. His hand snaked around her waist and pulled her into him.

She could have knocked him on his back and done it right there, in the pile of ashes and charred furniture. She would sear away the thought of Brad and his embraces until they were nothing but dust, like the Room 301 of her mind.

Sean pulled back from her and held her face in his hands. She smiled, leaning in to kiss him again, but he held her back.

"Zoe, have you ever met someone and felt like they were the only one who could really see you?"

"I guess, yeah." She couldn't see what he was trying to get at. For a guy who didn't bother to call or text he sure came on strong.

"Hello? Is someone there?"

They pulled apart. The voice came from the stairwell.

"Oh, god," she hissed.

"Run for the east stairwell," said Sean, "I'll distract him."

"That's stupid. Just come with me."

"I'll meet back up with you," he promised.

"Room 2605. Make sure none of the other girls see you."

He grinned again. "They won't."

Footsteps echoed down the stairwell, getting louder. There was no time to argue. She ran down the hall for the stairs on the other side.

"Hey! I can hear you running. Get back here," the guard's voice called. He sounded old. Maybe he wouldn't be able to keep up with her.

How had Sean gotten away from him? She heard the voice yelling out, following her. Could that jerk have slipped back into the room, using her as a decoy so he could slip out behind the guard? She would have words with him about that, the no-good …

She waited an hour. Then two. The kiss with Sean hadn't satisfied her hunger. Not even close. She paced the room waiting for his knock. *Where the hell is he?* Like hunger, her need for him reached an unbearable pitch, then blunted itself. It wasn't as acute, but it was there beneath the surface. She wanted to devour him.

So she paced. Bit her nails. Tore apart an old coffee cup, tiny piece by tiny piece until it was confetti. She took the book of matches with the name of the hotel on it and lit the whole thing at once. It sizzled as it caught flame, then ate away at the paper until it licked at her fingertips. She opened the sliding door and threw it down on the concrete balcony. It curled, glowing red, and then white, until it blew out.

There was a knock on the door. Zoe leaped to answer it, but found only Ashley there.

"Hey," she said, "you left your books and ran off. I wanted to see if you were okay. I texted, but…"

Zoe pulled out her phone. The screen was black and dead.

"Uh, yeah. Sorry, I didn't see them."

"Are you—"

"Yeah, I'm good."

Ashley's lips pursed to one side of her mouth and her brow tightened with concern. "Did he… Did he call you? I told him you were okay, but he—"

"Yeah. He—"

"I'm sorry, Zoe, I shouldn't have given him your number. He just seemed so worried about you. You haven't seemed…" She moved her lips but the words didn't come. "I just wanted…"

"It's okay."

Zoe felt jumpy, like when she was on the phone and had to go pee. She needed this conversation to be over. Sean might be there any minute. And she didn't want to think about Brad for another second. She wanted Sean to kiss her again, she wanted to feel…

Full of light.

She took her books back.

"Are you really okay?"

Zoe made herself smile apologetically. "I'm just tired, really." *The best lies are true.*

Ashley looked like there was more she wanted to say, but Zoe closed the door. She bolted over to the bedside table where her phone charger was plugged in, wondering if Sean had tried to call her, and hated herself for caring so much. Her breath was shallow and she could feel herself panicking. It was *her* fault. He probably tried to call her, and she was too dumb to check that her phone was on.

She thought of Room 301. Black and twisted, gray ashes blowing in the wind. Then she remembered the blaze at its highest. Even from ground level, across the street, it had been so bright, fighting so hard to stay lit. It had flared, crackled, raged against its own quenching. Zoe wanted to be like that. No one would be able to put her out.

Where was Sean? She wanted him so bad; she wanted to burn herself away, from the inside out, until the thought of Brad and the sound of his voice made her feel nothing at all. She'd be someone else entirely.

She shook her phone. *How long can this useless thing take to charge?* The battery icon flashed—a little sliver of red. She put it down on the bedside and tried to take a deep breath.

Zoe started so hard she almost fell off the bed as the strident, impossibly loud electric ring of the room phone filled her head. She grabbed the receiver.

"Hello?"

"Hey, it's me."

"For god's sake, Sean." Her heart was pounding.

"Meet me back at our spot."

She was furious. "No, damn it, don't make me go back there. My room. Now. I'm not going to just wait around for you," she said, trying to sound as if she meant it.

She took a deep breath and slammed the receiver down, praying it would work.

Please. I need this.

She picked up her cellphone. It finally started. Notifications popped up all at once.

"Jeff, Anna, Blake and 42 others like a photo you're tagged in."

She swiped the screen open and waited for Facebook to load. Ashley's photo was captioned, "This party's on #*fire*!"

She tapped, opening it fullscreen. Maybe her mom would get a kick out of it. Might as well screengrab and send it.

Zoe squinted at the photo. There were about forty people, all bunched together in front of the ladder truck. She zoomed in, looking for herself at the far edge of the photo.

Her stomach clenched.

There she was on the far left, with only empty space between her and the edge of the frame. Sean wasn't there.

Her head jerked up as three soft knocks landed on the door. She froze. Closed her eyes. Three more knocks, harder, more insistent this time.

Zoe stood and walked over, reaching for the knob. She paused, set her lips, and swung the door open.

He stood there, smiling all the anger out of her. She turned her back on him wordlessly and made for the bed.

"You're not a chemical engineer, are you?" she said as she picked her phone up and held it out toward him.

He sighed as he looked at the picture. "I really did hope it was all a dream."

"I'm starting to hope that too," she snapped, grabbing the phone back. "What the hell, Sean?"

"When you turned to me when I spoke to you on the night of the fire, I thought it all must have been a weird nightmare."

"What was all a weird nightmare?"

He held up his arms and waved them at the room. "This. All of it. All I can remember is walking around this hotel trying to talk to people. Everyone looks right through me. Except you."

None of this was right. This wasn't what was supposed to happen. She was supposed to meet someone new and forget Brad. Zoe pressed her face into her pillow. The sobs were silent, racking her body until she came up gasping for air.

Before she knew it his arm was around her. The other stroked her hair. He whispered but she wasn't listening. Soon he was kissing her again and she still wanted him to. As badly as before. Worse.

Something stabbed into Zoe's side as she rolled onto her back. *What the…*

She wasn't on the bed anymore; she was on the floor and a sharp edge dug into her side. She sat up and saw it belonged to a scorched metal bed frame that lay to her right. They were back in the burnt out room.

"How did we get here?" she asked.

Sean sat on the debris and rested his head in his hands. "I don't know, Zoe. It's like this place keeps drawing me back. I just don't want to be alone anymore."

She stood up and looked out into the black sky, all but the brightest few stars obscured by the city lights. They seemed to reach out to one another across the empty expanse of the night.

Zoe decided not to ask him any more questions. The way his face twisted as he tried to make sense… It wouldn't do. She liked it when he smiled.

She took him by the hand and looked into his eyes. "You're not alone. I'm here."

Forgetting about all the eyes that had watched her through uncomfortable silences, she let the smell of smoke fill every fragment of her consciousness and no longer felt the cold.

COLIN MAHEU is a writer of fantasy and speculative fiction currently finishing his first novel and writing short stories about Zoe the flight attendant. Now based in Calgary, he grew up in Ottawa and also lived for several years in South Korea. He wishes to thank *Enigma Front: Burnt* for being the first publication to put his fiction in print. He can be reached at @colinlovesbirds on Twitter.

CRASH

By Ron S. Friedman

N*ear Saturn, January 16th, 2097*

Ying Sun tapped the rusty control panel. The fuel indicator needle sat near zero. She turned off the *Rolling Stones* music and brought up the *Zheng He*'s schematics on the main display. Her finger slid over the scroll wheel, switching the image to the planned trajectory through Saturn's rings.

"Looking at the fuel indicator for the thousandth time won't change our propellant level," the voice of Zhulong, the ship's A.I., came through the vessel's speakers. "Forget it, missy. We don't have enough fuel to attempt an alternate maneuver. Your time would better be spent preparing the landing gear or fixing the leak in compartment C24." Zhulong's snakelike image appeared on the monitor. "We don't want another engine failure now, do we?" He grinned.

"Shut up, Zhulong! You're pretty annoying for a computer." She wished the spacecraft had a simple autopilot nav system, and an off button for this irritating Artificial Intelligence. But it wasn't like she had a choice in this matter. As the only survivor of the People's Liberation Army Inner Mongolia detachment, she was lucky to find this piece of junk vessel in an abandoned test facility. All things considered, being alone in space with an irksome virtual talking dragon was far better than being hunted down by brainwashed gamers in the scorching Gobi desert.

"You're one to talk," a smirking Zhulong retorted and faded, leaving Ying staring at her own reflection.

She looked older than her thirty-year-old self. Dark circles surrounded her eyes and, in the zero-gravity environment, her unwashed hair was a mess. "Motherless goat of all motherless goats," she yelled and kicked the base of the panel. Being reminded of the grime and sweat of two weeks without a shower made her itch.

Ying looked through the window as the *Zheng He* got closer to the gas giant's rings. Saturn grew bigger. She drifted to the command chair and buckled in. The *Zheng He* was a thirty-year-old warship, a relic of the Chinese Space Force. With all the leaks, corrosion, broken systems and shortages of air, water, propellant and … well, of just about everything, she had to wear her EVA suit at all times. Ying ignored the helmet beside her. She didn't want to put it on; her own body odor was just too strong.

The *Zheng He* was now close enough in its approach that Ying could see the rings' meteoroids. Most of them were smaller than a tennis ball, but some were as big as a house. She felt an urge to bite her fingernails, if not for her gloves.

A wail of alarm and the beeps of priority signals broke the silence.

"Proximity alert!" Zhulong announced.

"Oh shit, oh shit, oh shit!" Ying gripped her seat tight. She stared out the front window with her eyes wide open. It didn't matter how many times Zhulong had told her that the gap between the F and G rings was statistically safe, she still hated the idea of passing through it. The fact that the *Cassini-Huygens* spacecraft had plunged through the gap more than ninety years ago with no issues didn't mean squat. *Cassini-*

Huygens had been a tiny, unmanned vessel, unlike the two-thousand-ton Chinese space cruiser she was in. Ying hoped her ship had sufficient fuel to attempt a safer slowing maneuver.

The external cameras displayed little puffs of plasma, as thousands of dust particles collided with her ship at twenty kilometers per second.

She held her breath, wondering how many meteoroids sped pass the spacecraft's bow.

A few seconds passed, and the *Zheng He* cleared the ring.

Ying threw her hands in the air. "We've made it, Zhulong. I shouldn't have doubted you." She wished he was flesh and blood so she could hug and kiss the annoying A.I.

BANG! The side panel blew up. Debris flew through the air in a dangerous shower of sparks. A fireball engulfed the bridge. The walls, the control panel, and her own chair burst into an inferno.

Ying screamed in agony. The flames consumed everything in their path. Her EVA suit blocked most of the heat, but she wasn't wearing her helmet. She covered her eyes, trying to stay conscious amid the firestorm. But the pain … "Ahhh!" She could smell her own skin burning.

A cold spatting of liquid covered her blisters as a hiss filled the bridge. She thanked her ancestors and the Three Star Gods that the fire suppression mechanism was one of the few systems that remained operational.

"What's wrong? Are we hit? Did we lose the engine?" The words coming out of her mouth sounded weird, as if she'd had her entire mouth numbed at the dentist. With all the smoke and the steam, she couldn't see the monitor. She untied herself and searched for the first-aid kit.

"Zhulong?" The A.I didn't respond. The monitor, covered in melted aluminum, was dead.

"Please, please, please. Not now." Ying frantically checked for loose cables. She mashed the power button. Nothing.

The low pressure alarm howled. There was no time to diagnose Zhulong or worry about personal first-aid. "Sorry, friend." Ying grabbed her helmet and put it on.

Titan appeared in the front window. Saturn's largest moon was still nearly 1.2 million kilometers away. Ying wondered if the Titan colony, her goal, had survived. The colony hadn't responded to her long range transmissions. Would she be able to make contact with the settlers once she was in orbit? She had no fuel, her ship was breaking apart. It's not like she had other alternatives. She adjusted the controls on the mostly undamaged panel and switched on a small microphone.

"Mayday! Mayday!" she shouted in English into the microphone. The pain was unbearable. She struggled not to faint. "Can anyone hear me? Mayday!" She forced herself to speak.

Nothing but static. Not that she had much hope, given that no one had responded to her long range radio calls since she'd fled Earth.

"Mayday! Mayday! This is Ying Sun from the Chinese cruiser *Zheng He*." Ying breathed heavily. "My vessel is damaged and I require immediate assistance."

"I can't hear …" A woman's faint voice came through the speakers. "My name is Lora … from the Titan colo… shortwave … you."

Ying nearly jumped in joy. Someone was alive on Titan.

She tried to re-establish communication. But no additional response came.

She stared out the window as Titan slid across the sky. Her ship was slowly spinning out of control, and her A.I. was dead. She would have to make her approach manually. She pulled out a paper-thin tablet and swiped through the screens until she found the trajectory simulation. At sixteen kilometers per second, it would take her twenty hours to reach Titan.

Ying cleared the ashes off the pressure gauge. Great, zero atmosphere. She sighed. Twenty additional hours with her stinky helmet on and no access to a first aid kit or washroom.

Ying was exhausted and so was the ship's fuel. With her and the *Zheng He* both running on vapors. She had managed to crash-land the *Zheng He* on a snow-covered mountain ridge, about a hundred and fifty kilometers from the location of the *Huygens* habitat.

She initiated a self-diagnosis. The results were off the scale. The only bright spot was that she had sustained no bone injuries and only superficial damage to her EVA suit. She released a sigh of relief and made a mental note to give a generous offering to her ancestors.

"Zhulong, are you there?" After twenty hours of numbness, she was able to talk with slightly less pain. "If you can hear me, just be aware that we've made it."

No answer came. During her voyage from Earth, she'd gotten used to the maddening A.I. But now when it went dead, she realized he was her only friend.

Burnt debris covered the floor and the panels. Ying thought Earth was bad, a place she had desperately fled, but at least it had breathable air. Now, unless she could contact the colony, she'd be marooned on a frozen, unhospitable moon with her virtually dead ship. She unbuckled herself, and tried to walk around. It wasn't anything like weightlessness, but she felt extremely light. It was going to take her time to learn to walk here. For now, she would have to hop around like a slow-motion kangaroo.

Her EVA suit stank of urine, sweat and burnt skin. The facial burns were extremely tender. Since she couldn't remove her helmet to inspect the damage, she decided to check on Zhulong.

The lights went off.

"Really?" Ying slapped her hip, questioning the wisdom of the universe. "Now the batteries are dead? What have I done to deserve this? Did I offend someone?"

Ying turned on a small, helmet-mounted flashlight. She jumped to the control panel, opened a hatch and typed.

"Speak to me, buddy. For the last two weeks I could never get you to shut up. Now, that I need you, you decide to go quiet?" She punched Zhulong's monitor in frustration, stirring aluminum dust. The monitor remained offline.

"I'm going to die, alone." Tears flowed down her burnt cheeks.

"Get a hold of yourself, Ying," she spoke aloud. "You're the commander of this damn ship. Now calm down! That's an order!" She slowly sank to the floor. "I know where I am. I'm not too far from the *Huygens* habitat. Even exhausted, I should be able to cover the distance in a few hours. Also, before I crashed I spoke with someone on the radio. As far as I know, a rescue mission is on its way. Now, Ying Sun, what's next on the agenda?"

She looked around the devastated bridge. "Radio. I must power the radio."

A few more clicks, and she manually kick-started the backup generator. Bright light flooded the bridge. Now she was able to see the full extent of the damage. The radio and the microphone had been smashed. A giant metal plate that fell from the ceiling had shattered it. Ying stared at the crushed radio with her mouth wide open.

The terrain was covered with a thick layer of methane snow, which Ying managed to walk on without sinking in. Thank the gods for Titan's low gravity. When she reached the summit, she turned and stared down at the *Zheng He.* Her ship rested on the side of the mountain, perhaps five hundred meters below her.

"Poor girl." Ying said to her spacecraft, as if the ship could hear her. "You're not going to fly anytime soon." Her mind lingered on the virtual dragon, the dead heart and soul of the old ship.

To the north, Ying could see a dark methane lake. To her east, a second mountain ridge blocked her view. She stared at the ridge for a long moment.

"Hello." She shouted, ignoring the pain. "Can anyone hear me?"

Nothing but the echo in her helmet and the howling wind.

"Figures." She shrugged.

Ying kneeled and took out her folded tablet from a pouch attached to her leg. With Zhulong's breakdown, this device was the only Titan map at her disposal. She unfolded the paper-thin tablet, laid it on her hip, and moved her gloved finger along the center until she found the location of the *Huygens* habitat. Ying stood and flipped the tablet, holding it upside down, examining the lake and the ridge. She shook her head and sighed. The distance was way too far.

Suddenly, a strong gust snapped the lightweight tablet out of her hands. The flexible material fluttered and flew into the air.

"No, no, no, no!" Ying cried in panic.

She jumped and missed the tablet by a centimeter. She fell down on the slope, leaving a mark in the snow. The tablet flew up and away at an increasing speed.

"No, no, no. Don't!"

A few seconds later, the tablet disappeared into one of the whiskey colored clouds.

Ying fell to her knees and cried.

The *Zheng He*'s external door opened. With her EVA suit covered by a thick layer of snow, Ying dragged herself through the airlock.

She walked to the command panel, turned the media server on and cranked up the speakers. Rolling Stones music flooded the bridge.

She stared at the shattered radio, and kicked it. Then she sat on the icy floor as she burst into laughter. She saluted the dead monitor. "If I could take my helmet off, I would have a drink in your honor, my friend. See you in the realm of the dead … soon."

The howling wind lashed against the metal hull.

"Zhulong, how much time do you think I have before I run out of water, air, heat or whatever? How long before I die?"

No reply came.

"Screw you, Zhulong. Stay dead. See if I care."

Ying crawled on all four to the communication panel. She looked over the smashed radio.

She made herself stand, opened a drawer and pulled out an obsolete paper binder that read 'Ship Schematics'. She flipped the pages until she reached the radio diagram. The comparison to the broken radio was not promising.

"Where in the middle of Titan can I find multi-zpx negators? Dammit."

She continued to flip through the pages. "Not even a walkie-talkie? What a piece of shit spacecraft."

She threw the binder in frustration. It exploded and the papers scattered across the floor. One page settled near her feet. She picked it up and read through the schematics.

She laughed. "The emergency beacon. Yes!"

Adrenaline revived her exhausted body. With new strength, she hopped to the engine room.

The five hours that had passed since Ying activated the beacon were the longest period she'd ever experienced.

She heard banging on the external pressure hull. Someone, or something, was outside.

She opened the airlock and found two figures in crude iron EVA suits attached to massive looking wings. One of the figures was standing, tinkering with the backpack of the other, which was on its knees. They both turned and stared at her.

Ying was confused and, in the absence of any known protocol, she decided to salute. "My name is Ying Sun," she spoke English, remembering that the habitat had been a NASA project. "I've come from Earth."

"Earth?" the standing iron-clad astronaut said in a

masculine voice. He let go of the other figure, folded his wings and stepped forward. "I'll be damned. After thirty years? We lost all hope of ever seeing a Terran ship again. How is it possible?"

"You must help me." Ying pointed desperately to the inside of her vessel. "My partner … um … an A.I system, is dead. I need a technician."

The kneeling figure raised its head. "Ying?" She exhaled. "Did you say Ying Sun?"

Ying looked to the figure, her eyes wide open.

"I'm Lora Morel." The kneeling astronaut stood up, leaning on her comrade. "I spoke with you on the radio." She paused and took a deep breath. "We came as soon as I detected your distress beacon. We are all safe now." She stared at her male partner for a long moment. "Right, wiseguy?"

"You betcha!" The guy pointed at the *Zheng He*.

Then he turned to Ying. "Let's take your A.I. friend's module to the habitat. I'm sure we can find someone who is able to fix it. That is, if we can find compatible parts."

Through their helmet visors, Ying could see that Lora was smiling. In spite of her aching burns, she smiled back.

RON S. FRIEDMAN is a finalist in the 2016 Aurora Awards, Best Short Fiction category. His stories have appeared in Galaxy's Edge, Daily Science Fiction, as well as in a number of anthologies. Ron received six Honorable Mentions in Writers of the Future Contest. Ron Co-edited Enigma Front and Enigma Front: Burnt anthologies, and he appeared as a panelist / presenter at WWC, Calgary Comic Expo, Con-version, and VCON. For more details, please visit Ron's website: https://ronsfriedman.wordpress.com.

THE GEARS OF JUSTICE

By Brent Nichols

V*ancouver, 1888*

The piercing blast of a steam whistle brought Kim Jensen's head snapping up. She rose from her seat in the parlor of McClane Mansion, one of the Vancouver area's grandest estate homes and secret headquarters of Team Justice, and ran to the secret panel on the back wall. She pressed the nose of a small bronze satyr and a section of the wall slid back to reveal a hidden room with none of the lavish decoration of the rest of the house.

Inside, Henry McClane, known to the world as the Harpoonist, sat peering intently at a telegraph set clicking away on the table before him. The rest of the team rushed in, Wu pushing Dan "Crusher" Carter in his wheelchair. Kim joined them, and they watched impatiently until the telegraph fell silent and McClane looked up.

"Bank robbery," he said crisply, "on Water Street. A gang has taken hostages. The coppers have them surrounded. It's a standoff for now. Looks like a job for us."

"Right," said Carter, "let's go." He was the team's leader, in spite of legs that had been withered by polio. With more active pursuits denied to him, he'd turned to science as an outlet for his considerable energies. He was the mastermind behind the tools that made Team Justice what it was.

Kim led the way down a short secret passage leading to the stables behind the mansion. She hopped into the cab of the Justice Wagon, a steam-powered carriage that was the talk of the west coast. She grabbed a lever beside the driver's seat, dragged down hard, and heard a rumble as lumps of coal tumbled into the banked boiler fire.

A familiar anxiety rose within her as the fire grew. Not three feet behind her, hungry flames lapped at the coal and flickered upward to heat the Wagon's boiler. She told herself for the thousandth time that she was perfectly safe, but the old scars on her back seemed to pucker as the flames behind her rose.

Wu clambered up into the cab beside her. His Typhoon costume, a leather mask and a long, loose-fitting black coat, were already in place. He was the only member of the team to disdain the power of steam. He could do things with his hands and feet that should have been impossible. When Kim demanded to know how he did it, he would smile and explain that "chi" was his steam.

Carter and McClane thumped around in the back of the carriage. A knock on the back of the cab told her they were ready to move.

She glanced at the steam gauge on her dash. Nearly there. This was always the hardest part. Before dashing pell-mell into danger and adventure there was a frustrating period of sitting idle, waiting for the steam pressure to build.

Kim pulled her own mask into place. It was all the costume she needed, since her role was to drive the Wagon, staying always in the cab. Most of the world didn't even realize Team Justice had a fourth member.

The three men were misfits, made redundant by changing technology. Their secret war against the underworld was their way of putting meaning back into their lives. Kim helped them because they'd saved her on the night her world burned.

She didn't care about the war on crime. She cared about Team Justice. She would do anything for them.

At last the needle touched the red line and Kim pushed forward on the drive lever. The Justice Wagon slid smoothly into motion, the stable's spring-loaded doors swinging open as the Wagon pushed its way through, then snapping shut behind them.

She watched the mirrors mounted over the estate's front gate as she rolled up. No traffic was in sight, as was usual in this quiet stretch of road on the outskirts of the city. Someone in the neighborhood had to suspect that Team Justice was headquartered nearby, but so far their lair was more or less secret.

They rolled out onto the road, Kim turning expertly with tugs on the steering levers. As pressure built in the boiler she was able to increase speed. They moved into the streets of Vancouver and traffic made way for them. She rarely had to pull on the cord for the steam whistle.

She took in the details as she drove, because Vancouver changed each time she saw it. Every building was brand new. It was two years since the Great Vancouver Fire, and the good people of Vancouver were rebuilding at an astonishing rate. Almost no evidence remained of the conflagration. The last of the rubble was long since cleared away, and new construction was everywhere.

Kim liked to think of it as a good omen. Like Vancouver itself, her life had been destroyed utterly by the fire. Like the city, her life was going through dizzying growth and change. Unlike the city, though, her personal scars lingered.

Almost every aspect of Vancouver was changing with bewildering speed, and Team Justice was a product of that change. It was only three years since the national railroad had been abandoned and an airship terminal had linked Vancouver to the rest of the country. The sleepy coastal town had become a major hub linking Asia to the rest of North America. Vancouver was already eclipsing Victoria as the most important port in Western Canada. The city was growing exponentially, explosively, faster than anyone could keep up.

Vancouver had only had its own police force for two years, and already the original force had been disbanded and replaced by provincial special constables. The civic fathers adjusted as quickly as they could, but the criminal underworld reacted even more quickly, turning Vancouver into a hotbed of smuggling and vice. Team Justice fought on the front lines of the battle to keep organized crime from conquering the city completely.

And the battle was heating up. An explosion tore the air as they turned onto Water Street, and Kim caught a brief glimpse of a fireball roiling into the air somewhere ahead. Then the Bank of British Columbia came into view. She could see police stumbling back from the bank or crouching behind whatever cover they could find.

Three men burst from the bank's front doors. Bandanas covered their faces. One man held a shotgun; the others carried pistols. Taking advantage of the confusion in police ranks, they sprinted down Water Street, running directly away from the Justice Wagon.

Kim grinned wolfishly and gave the engine more steam. A fit, motivated man could outrun the Wagon for a short time, but the steam engine never got tired.

The Wagon raced along the street at a break-neck pace, Kim fighting the urge to whoop, and the fleeing bandits glanced back over their shoulders. Kim was closing the distance when they cut sharply to the left, dashing down a side street toward the waterfront.

She took the corner at high speed, wincing as she heard sounds of sliding and thumping in the back of the Wagon. She hoped Carter was in his suit already. He would be having a hard time of it, otherwise.

They were nearly to the waterfront. There wasn't much street left in front of them, and Kim moved her hand to the brake lever. But the bandits swerved to the right and dashed into a dilapidated warehouse.

The Justice Wagon roared into the warehouse behind them, Kim hauling on the brake lever, and the Wagon shuddered to a halt. Kim's adrenalin rush started to fade. From here on she would be a spectator, locked in the cab watching while her teammates rounded up the bad guys.

The bank robbers were nowhere in sight, but they couldn't have gone far. Typhoon gave her a grin, threw open the door, and sprang out. She heard a thump as the back door of the Wagon dropped open, then the steady thud of massive footsteps as Crusher came lumbering out.

The three of them gathered in front of the Wagon. Typhoon in his long black coat and dark leather mask was the least prepossessing one, but quite possibly the most dangerous. The Harpoonist made a dashing form beside him, with burgundy trousers tucked into tall boots, and a burgundy jacket flaring around his hips. A harness on his back held two metal cylinders, tanks of compressed air stored at fantastic pressures. A bandolier across his chest held a selection of steel harpoons, and a hose ran from one of the pressurized tanks to a harpoon gun in his hands.

Crusher, however, was the show-stopper of the group. In his powered suit McClane was able to stand upright. His entire body was encased in a framework of copper and steel. He weighed nearly as much as the Justice Wagon. Six strong men couldn't have lifted his suit, but he could move in it, and wield tremendous force.

The boiler built into the back of the suit was the secret to his abilities. Crusher stood only a bit taller than a normal man, with metal plates under the soles of his feet and a curved steel framework over his head, but his steel body was strangely thick, to allow for a firebox, water tank, condenser, and insulation.

Kim wanted to cringe every time she looked at him. So much heat, so much fire, only inches from his skin! It seemed horribly dangerous to her, and she didn't like to even be near him when he was in costume.

The three men gazed around, then looked at each other

and started forward, peering into the gloom. The warehouse was mostly empty, with a few scattered crates or piles of debris cluttering the floor. The only light came from small, grimy windows high on the walls.

They spread out, Crusher walking down the middle of the floor, no doubt because he found it difficult to turn. Typhoon moved to the right wall, the Harpoonist to the left.

Something stirred in the rafters of the warehouse, all three men turned their heads to look, and something fell from the darkness. At the same time the floor seemed to heave around Typhoon. A cargo net a dozen feet wide shot into the air as another net, filled with rubble to act as a counterweight, tumbled from the ceiling. The first net closed around Typhoon in an instant and yanked him fifteen feet into the air.

Crusher began the ponderous process of turning his metal suit. In a moment he was lumbering toward Typhoon. The Harpoonist moved to the centre of the warehouse, his head turning as he scanned the darkness on every side.

"No," Kim murmured, shaking her head. "Don't you see it's a trap? Stop following their plan!"

It frustrated her endlessly that no one on the team would think strategically. When she told them as much, they would chuckle and tell her that her habit of thinking in elaborate circles was no good for an action hero. When you were fighting for your life you had to make snap decisions, guided by your instincts.

Still, a bit of strategy wouldn't go amiss at times. Especially when a straightforward pursuit of some bank robbers turned into an elaborate ambush.

A rumble from behind made Kim peer into her side mirror. The door to the warehouse slid shut, plunging the interior into gloom and shadow. The police, when they caught up, would see no sign of the Justice Wagon. There would be no escape, and no rescue.

Well, Crusher would be able to open the door, or knock a hole in the warehouse wall if necessary. She switched her gaze to him.

He was sliding sideways. Kim blinked, confused. Crusher's legs were perfectly motionless, but his feet skidded along the floor, one slow inch at a time. Finally one shoulder bumped up against a tarpaulin-covered shape against the wall.

Carter squirmed, the metal suit mimicking his movements, and suddenly the suit pivoted and thumped against the tarpaulin with a muffled clang. Crusher was now pinned like a beetle with his back against the wall.

As he flailed, the tarpaulin slid down, exposing thick coils of wire in a metal frame. It was some sort of electromagnet, tremendously strong, and it rendered him helpless.

Kim saw the Harpoonist hurrying toward his teammates. Then the floor of the warehouse trembled and the Harpoonist froze.

The wall at the far end of the warehouse exploded inward, and the Harpoonist threw up an arm to protect himself as splinters of wood showered him. Something moved in the darkness, then lumbered forward into the light, and Kim gave an involuntary squeak of dismay.

It was a metal man. That was her first impression, and she glanced at Crusher, comparing the two behemoths.

The new arrival was bigger than Crusher in every way. Nine or ten feet tall, it had legs as big as Crusher's torso and a body the size of the Justice Wagon. There was no head, just a massive steel body with enormous arms sprouting from each shoulder. The pincers it used for hands were big enough to crumple a man's chest.

Its movements were smoother and more graceful than Crusher's as well. Behind a cloud of horror a part of Kim's brain coolly analyzed what she saw, and as she watched the colossus advance the pieces clicked into place.

There was no operator inside the machine. With no need to make allowances for human limbs the machine could do things that Crusher's suit could not. It advanced, the hips flexing in unnatural ways, the elongated arms reaching out as it moved toward the heroes.

A cloud of vapor burst from the harpoon gun as the

Harpoonist fired, not at the advancing behemoth, but at Crusher. The steel harpoon hit the wall above the electromagnet, and a cable separated in a shower of sparks. Crusher staggered forward as the magnet released him.

The metal man advanced, and Crusher came forward, hopelessly outclassed, to meet it. Crusher raised his metal fists like a boxer, and the behemoth swung one massive steel arm. Steel clashed against steel and Crusher's metal feet briefly left the floor. He crashed hard on one shoulder, skidded across the warehouse floor, and landed with a thud on his back.

The Harpoonist moved in, firing rapidly, and half a dozen barbed missiles bounced harmlessly from the behemoth's metal skin. Crusher, meanwhile, sat up and began ponderously shifting around, trying to get to his feet. The behemoth reached him in two quick steps. One pincer closed on Crusher's right arm, and the behemoth's arm spun along its axis like a spool of thread. There was an angry screech of metal as Crusher's steel arm twisted and bent.

The Harpoonist advanced, firing carefully now, aiming for the behemoth's joints at the shoulders and hips. "No," Kim shouted, banging her fists on the dash in frustration. There was a much more vulnerable target. "Find the operator!" she yelled. The Harpoonist didn't hear her, of course. He was totally fixated on the target in front of him.

Kim's hands went to the door handle beside her. Then the behemoth pointed one arm at the Harpoonist and a gout of flame shot from his wrist. Kim froze, shrinking down in her seat. She couldn't face that, not for anything.

The Harpoonist went into a roll, coming up behind some crates, and fired another shot at the metal monstrosity. The behemoth, meanwhile, caught Crusher's metal arm in two hands and heaved Crusher, suit and all, into the air. The behemoth's legs didn't move, but his whole body spun at the waist and he threw Crusher bodily through the air, straight at the Harpoonist.

For a long moment Kim could see nothing but clouds of billowing dust. Her hands went to the Justice Wagon's control levers, and she hesitated, longing to throw the machine into reverse and batter her way through the doors behind her. It would be the best thing, she told herself. She would let the police in. She didn't move, however.

As the dust settled she saw the three bank robbers gathered around the Harpoonist's inert form. Then a shape moved in the darkness at the far end of the warehouse, a tall figure in a long duster and a Stetson, his face hidden in shadow. His voice boomed out.

"Bring him here! Never mind the others for now. They're trapped. Bring me the stick-pin boy. He's the biggest threat. We'll do him first."

Kim watched, frozen in horror, as they dragged the Harpoonist across the floor. Gas lights sprang to life at the far end of the warehouse. The man in the Stetson had his back to her now, and he fiddled with a contraption that stood on a tripod. Kim recognized it as a camera.

"Throw him in the chair," the man boomed. "We only get one chance at this. I want to get it just right."

The henchmen dumped the Harpoonist's unmoving form onto the chair, where he flopped back, arms splayed, face pointing at the ceiling. Two men watched him carefully, hands on the butts of their pistols, while the third man drew a wickedly long knife and ran his thumb along the edge. Meanwhile, the man in the Stetson kept fiddling with his camera.

Kim felt her stomach twist. She could only think of one explanation. They planned to kill the Harpoonist, and capture the moment of his death in a photograph.

She squeezed her eyes shut, trying to block it all away, but her analytical brain betrayed her. She wanted to scream, to weep, to give in to her rising panic, but she found herself cataloging the room, the people, the objects, with a clinical detachment.

And she discovered that she knew what to do.

Her eyes snapped open. She double-checked the position of everything. It was all as she remembered. The only missing ingredient was courage. Could she do what needed to be done?

The sour taste of bile on the back of her tongue made her realize how close she was to vomiting. She wanted a moment to gather herself, but the camera would be ready soon. She rose from her seat, surprised to find herself moving, and wriggled through the hatch leading to the back of the Wagon. The rear door was down, and she slipped out.

Crusher's bulk provided a vestige of cover so long as she kept herself low. She reached him in a crouching run and knelt beside him.

"Dan!" she hissed. "Can you hear me?"

"Kim." She sagged in relief when he spoke. He sounded hurt and weary, but he was alive. "Get out of here, girl. Save yourself."

"Can you get out of the suit?"

"No. I'm lying on the side of the hatch. And the pneumatics are all busted up. I can't move."

"Okay," she said, "I'm opening the hatch from the outside."

"It's no good," he said, "I can't do anything without the suit. You need to go for the police, it's our only hope now."

She ignored him, reaching her hand out to feel across the frame, searching for the hatch that hid his emergency release handle. The metal scorched her fingers, and she snatched her hand back with a low cry.

"The cooling system's a bit smashed up," Dan said.

"My God! You must be cooking in there!"

"It's a bit toasty," he admitted, "but I'll be all right. So long as you go right now," he added firmly.

She pulled out her handkerchief and used it to protect her fingers as she popped open a small panel on his chest. A wave of heat came rolling out. She leaned forward, looking inside.

She could see the release handle, painted bright red. All she had to do was grab hold of it and pull.

There was a length of copper tubing beside it, and she saw

that her hand would have to press against the copper. She eyed it dubiously, then moistened one fingertip and touched the copper tube.

There was a hiss of steam and she flinched back. A tiny blister now decorated her fingertip. She muttered a curse, moistened another fingertip, and touched the handle. It was hot as well, but not as bad as the copper tube.

For a long moment she stared helplessly at the handle. She knew she ought to search around for something to protect her skin, but there wasn't time. The Harpoonist was going to die in a matter of minutes if not seconds, and then the gang would come after Crusher and Typhoon. She had to act now.

She squeezed her eyes shut, remembering the night of the fire, her helplessness, her terror. Her home destroyed, her flesh burned, and nothing she could do about it.

"Not this time," she murmured. "This time I choose it. This time I decide what happens. I choose!"

She wrapped her handkerchief around her hand, grabbed the red handle, took a firm grip, and pulled. The metal was hot against her fingers, but not painful, and the handle slowly moved upward. She could feel the heat of the copper tube scant fractions of an inch away, could smell the fabric of the handkerchief burning. She gritted her teeth, knowing she dared not scream, and pulled the handle all the way out.

Her hand sank against the hot copper tube. The handkerchief burned away in an instant and her skin made a horrible hiss, not quite drowned out by the low wail that started in the back of her throat. For an endless second she pressed her own flesh against the metal, and then something clicked inside Crusher's suit. Kim pulled her hand out, cradling it against her stomach, and the hatch slid open.

She grabbed the steel hatch before it could clatter to the floor. She set it down gently, then helped Carter wriggle out of the contraption. His clothing was hot to the touch and soaked with sweat.

She wanted to curl up and nurse her burned hand, but there was no time. She leaned close to his ear and hissed her instructions. "You've got to release Typhoon. Use a harpoon."

"They'll see me," he protested.

"No they won't. I'll be distracting them."

"No, you can't—"

But she was already moving away from him, stooping to pick up a fallen harpoon, sliding to her left so the behemoth was between her and the gang. Behind her she heard a stealthy rustle as Carter dragged himself along the floor.

Kim held her breath as she approached the huge machine. With all the villains gathered around the Harpoonist and no one manning the controls, it was as harmless as a parked locomotive, but her heart still thumped unheroically as she pressed her back against a steel leg.

She peered around the behemoth and spotted a cable snaking across the floor. That would be how they controlled it, then. She took a deep breath, stepped around the behemoth's legs, raised the harpoon in both hands, and brought it stabbing down into the cable.

The cable was cloth-wrapped and as thick as her arm, and solid enough that the impact jarred her to the shoulders. The cloth covering tore, and she saw a cluster of rubber hoses inside. She swung the harpoon frantically, chopping again and again, and a jet of hydraulic fluid sprayed into the air.

She managed half a dozen more swings before someone shouted behind her. She ignored the shout, continuing to chop. In the corner of her eye she saw Carter, in plain sight, using a harpoon to heave himself onto his feet beneath the net that held Typhoon.

A second hose burst, hydraulic fluid arcing across the floor. A gun fired, the bullet ricocheted from the behemoth with a loud clang, and Kim dropped flat. Another shot rang out, she heard the whip of the bullet passing above her, and she sprang up, darting around the behemoth, using its legs for cover. More shots made her flinch down. She could hear running footsteps. The air stank with cordite, and she felt her whole body tremble. Gunfire was terrifying!

She watched as Carter, his legs trembling, raised the harpoon over his head and jabbed at the cargo net. After three jabs a hand shot out of the net and plucked the harpoon from his hands. Carter fell to a sitting position.

"Don't move, Missy."

Kim twisted her head around. One of the men had circled around the behemoth. He stood a dozen feet away from her, a pistol rock-steady in his fist. Kim crouched, frozen, as another man darted around the other side. A hand closed around her upper arm and yanked her to her feet.

The three gunmen gathered around her, eyes menacing behind their masks, smelling of sweat and dust and coal smoke. One man turned and called to the leader, "It's just some broad!"

"Kill her," the voice boomed out.

Three pairs of cold, impersonal eyes focussed on Kim. Then the man in front of her seemed to spring forward, crashing into her. She fell, the man sprawling on top of her.

Typhoon descended on the gunmen in a blur of motion. A pistol swung toward him and he knocked the wrist upward. The pistol fired into the ceiling, Typhoon's hand smacked into the man's lowest rib, and Typhoon was past him before he finished doubling over.

The man with the shotgun flinched backward, and a foot shot out, catching the shotgun and sending it spinning into the air. Typhoon stepped in close, delivered a kick to the man's chest that sent him stumbling back, and then stuck out his hands and caught the shotgun as it fell. He stepped forward, used the butt of the gun to thump the man across the forehead, then dropped the weapon and turned to face Kim.

The man sprawled on top of her started to rise. Typhoon sprang onto his back, kicking off, flying into the air and driving the man back down onto Kim. Typhoon flew at the third man, who was again trying to line up his pistol, and slammed kicks into his face and chest. The man toppled backward and Typhoon landed nimbly on his feet. One foot lashed out and the man on top of Kim went limp.

She wriggled out from under him and stood. Behind Typhoon she saw the man in the Stetson lifting an enormous pistol from beneath his coat. She opened her mouth to scream, knowing she would be too late, and the Harpoonist clubbed the man soundly over the head with his chair.

For a long moment no one moved. Kim wanted to sink to her knees, cover her burned hand, and have a good cry, but her racing mind wouldn't let her. She strode deeper into the warehouse.

The Harpoonist, weaving on his feet, made his way gingerly toward the Justice Wagon. Typhoon took Carter's arm over his shoulders and heaved the man to his feet, then helped him walk to the Wagon.

Kim knelt over the leader of the ambush party and patted him down, tossing aside a small pistol she found in his boot, a couple of knives, and a straight razor. There was a wallet in his coat, and she pocketed it. Then she grabbed the shoulder of his coat and started dragging him across the floor.

"Kim, what are you doing?" Carter's voice sounded puzzled and infinitely patient.

"We're taking this one with us." She continued dragging him toward the Wagon.

"We don't take prisoners," Carter said. "We leave them for the police."

She gritted her teeth. They should be helping her, not making inane arguments. "We need to ask him a few questions."

"He won't talk."

"We'll make him talk," she said.

"We don't torture prisoners," the Harpoonist said sharply.

"It's not our way," Typhoon agreed.

Kim turned to face them. Three sets of eyes bored into her, stern, disapproving. She had been deferring to these men for two years, and she nearly gave in again. But the smell of burned flesh still rose from her hand, and it stiffened her resolve. She'd earned the right to be heard.

"You know we won't torture him. I know that." She glanced down at the man in the duster. "He doesn't know that. My conscience is fine with scaring him a bit."

Carter's eyebrows rose. "But why, Kim? He's just a bank robber."

She stared at him. "A bank robber? With an elaborate trap set, just for us? Who wanted proof that he'd killed us? There's something bigger going on, Dan. Someone is hunting us, and I want to know who."

He frowned, looking unconvinced, but Typhoon walked over, grabbed the cowboy's other shoulder, and helped her drag him into the back of the Wagon. McClane followed, and she closed the back and returned to the cab.

She turned the Justice Wagon around, backed up as far as she could, and took a run at the warehouse doors. The doors crashed open, revealing a crowd of curious onlookers and half a dozen special constables, nearly half of the city's fledgling police force.

The closest constable walked up to stand beside the cab, frowning in at her. She smiled as sweetly as she knew how and said, "We caught your bank robbers. They're just inside."

"I don't think we need—" he began stiffly, but the excited crowd pressed in and jostled him aside.

A fresh-faced young man with a notepad in his hand hooked an elbow over the top of her door. "I'm Harry MacRae with the Daily Colonist," he said. "Can you tell me what happened?"

It was the team's policy to never speak with reporters or the public. Team Justice was to be aloof, mysterious. It was yet another policy Kim didn't endorse. The public's good will was a resource they would be foolish to squander.

"We came as soon as we realized citizens were in danger," she said. "We pursued three men into this warehouse and apprehended them. While we have every confidence in the abilities of the police, we feel it's the duty of every Vancouverite to lend assistance when they can."

There was a pause as MacRae scribbled furiously. A

woman behind him shouted, "Hey! Who are you?"

Kim glanced at her injured hand, tucked in her lap out of sight. She hesitated, then looked up and said, "I'm Firebrand."

"And what do you do for the team?" MacRae asked. "Are you the driver? We haven't seen you before."

She smiled. "I'm the mastermind. Now if you'll excuse me, our work here is done." She kept the brake on, but gave some power to the back tires, making them grind and spin. The crowd edged back.

"But I have so many questions!" MacRae cried.

"Another time," Kim promised.

"When? How will I find you?"

The Justice Wagon rolled forward, and she leaned out, shouting above the chug of the pistons. "Wherever the forces of crime gather, that's where you'll find us. Whenever the good people of Vancouver are in danger, Team Justice will be there!"

Then she gave a blast on the steam whistle, waved to the cheering crowd, and the Justice Wagon rolled away.

BRENT NICHOLS is a steampunk, fantasy, and science fiction writer, book cover designer, bon vivant, and man about town. He likes good beer, bad puns, high adventure and low comedy. His military science fiction novel *Stars Like Cold Fire* was released in 2016 by Bundoran Press. Look for Brent's other works wherever fine ebooks are sold or at steampunch.com. See his book cover designs at coolseriescovers.com.

THE FIRE MAGE

By Lee F. Patrick

Arlyn walked briskly from the cottage in the early fall morning but didn't react as his magic stirred protectively. That feeling was back. The one that said someone was watching him. It had started a week ago. Maybe longer, but that's when he'd first recognized what he felt.

Eight people were near enough for him to detect the heat of their bodies. Two were near windows, a few others on the paths that wound through the village. He noticed his aunt Wendolyn standing on her porch.

She was staring at him with a disdainful look. As usual.

It must be her, he decided. She didn't approve of magic in general and him in specific. It was *CHEATING,* she said, every chance she had. She'd voted to send for a mage collar when his gift manifested at thirteen. It was voted down, but barely. He openly did the techniques on the elders' list of approved uses of his gift. Other things he did in secret. For the past few months he'd been hiding that his ability was getting stronger. Far stronger than most of the villagers might be comfortable with.

He shrugged and entered Taryn's smithy to get the fire ready for the day's work. His current task was making nails for next spring's repairs. He'd try using his gift to help draw out the stock. Keeping metal hot was easy now and Taryn approved of his early efforts to hold the glowing iron.

"Morning, lad," the smith said. "All set?"

"Just about, Taryn," Arlyn said. He held his left hand over the pile of charcoal to encourage the fire to spread from his initial spark. The smith also liked that with his gift, they didn't waste the hard-to-make charcoal.

"Good. The elders suggested we cut peat for a few days. We can also build up our supply of bog iron. The elders think another barn is necessary and that means more nails. We'll also have lots of peat to keep us warm this winter."

Arlyn sighed. He'd hoped to do some minor repairs to the cottage in this lull between harvest and winter. "The peats won't dry fully, will they? Not unless the weather stays warm."

"Perhaps not, but the iron will be useful in the spring. Everyone can stack their share of the new peats to provide extra shelter from the wind. We're leaving first thing tomorrow so we can cut longer."

His family's cottage was on the side of the village next to the grazing meadows. The large garden was fully harvested and the results hung in the rafters, the kitchen area and the cool cellar under the floor. It had been a good year and the flock of sheep were all healthy, even the twins who'd been sickly for their first two months. This was the best harvest they'd had in the past few years.

"You're going with the others cutting peat tomorrow?" Mama asked as she stirred the stew.

"Yes. My nail making went well. Nearly a hundred smaller nails done and I'm not exhausted this time."

"Good. Come and eat. I'll get my spinning and keep you company. Karlyn is at Aunt Wendolyn's for the evening, helping wind bobbins for the big loom."

He sat down and ate the stew slowly. Despite his pay from the smithy and the good harvest, there wasn't much extra in this household. Karlyn was nine and helped as much as she could with the chores in the cottage and garden and the shared duties, like minding the sheep. Mama had refused to give up the cottage and take them to live with her sister and her large family when papa died of a flux. Arlyn had been very happy with that decision, even though he'd just turned fourteen and suddenly had to do all of papa's chores, in addition to his own and working in the smithy to learn about using his gift of fire.

"I'm going hunting after these peats are stacked," Arlyn said. "Karlyn can help me with the peats. I think I can use my gift to see where the deer are hiding. Even one young buck would give us plenty of meat for the winter and a pelt for my new forge apron."

"That could be dangerous, going out on your own," mama said. "Why not go with the other young men?"

"Because they make too much noise, Mama." He shrugged. "Always talking and making jokes that frighten away the deer. I'd rather go out alone. Maybe I could go with just one other person. We'd bring home at least one, maybe two, instead of empty bellies and a lot of work to finish before the snow comes."

"I suppose you're right."

Arlyn sopped up the last traces of the broth with a heel of barley bread. "I know I am. I'd best pack my gear now. Taryn wants to leave early."

The sun was barely over the horizon as they left the village: the young men, two adults and a two-wheeled cart carrying all they'd need. With any luck, the cart would be lighter on the way back, but Arlyn knew Taryn would keep them cutting until they found enough bog iron nodules to satisfy him. A few days after they returned, the more onerous task of bringing the peat back to the village would begin.

As Arlyn walked along he tried to sense if there were any deer coming down from the higher hills. There was something out there but it didn't feel like a deer. Was it a person? The feeling of being watched was the same as he'd felt in the village. That was really strange. No one went up into the hills unless they were hunting. There weren't any villages out that way so there were seldom any travelers.

The feeling vanished. Arlyn started to worry. Someone had been watched him in the village. Aunt Wendolyn wouldn't come out all this way just to glare at him, would she? Who else could it be? His stomach cramped at that thought.

"You feeling all right, lad?" asked Taryn, on his left.

"Yes. Just thinking about what's left to do to get the cottage ready for winter," he lied. The elders didn't know he could sense living creatures. Yet.

By noon, a brisk walk brought them to the section of the bog currently being harvested. "Get the tents up and then everyone take a cutting tool so we can get started," Taryn said loud enough so no one could claim they hadn't heard him. Everyone sighed and pulled the oiled canvas out of the cart.

The next morning Arlyn heard groans as his tent-mates woke and started to move. Or tried to. As the lads roused and used the pit trench, Dartha, Taryn's wife, called them to the fire. "I've got willow tea nice and hot. And the porridge is nearly ready."

He'd drink the willow tea because it was hot, not because his muscles ached. Another advantage of his gift. He could redirect warmth anywhere in his body now. But that was also one of his secrets. Like sensing people's body heat. The elders might still send to Merthara for a mage collar to control him if they thought he could lose control of his magic. Of if he did things they didn't like and frightened them.

There were tales of magic out of control and others about the dangers of mages who sought domination over normal people. In most stories, the mage died. So did a lot of innocent people, caught up in the conflict.

As he tidied his bedroll after eating, Taryn appeared outside the tent. "I've a question for you, lad. Meet me by the cut when you're done here."

When Arlyn joined the smith he was playing with a small iron nodule, tossing it from hand to hand. "Can you sense the iron down there in the bog?"

"I don't know," Arlyn admitted. "I've never tried. Is metal sensing part of the fire gift?" He'd never tried that on his own.

"Your great-gran had the Fire gift, same as you. But her uncle had Water," Taryn said with a shrug. "From what I've heard, there's only the four types. Earth and Air are the others. Met a fellow years back who had a bit of the fire gift. He said it's in some families but which type of mage a person is doesn't always breed true. Could not have a gift at all, or a different one from their parents."

"Why didn't you tell me this ages ago?" Arlyn asked.

"Didn't seem to be the right time."

"That sort of makes sense. Why didn't anyone write down what she could do? It would have made my training easier."

"I don't think anyone here knew their letters back then. People's memories fade, or they've listened to the tales and believe all the other bits that were put in over the years. Take the nodule and walk out onto the bog. Not too far, mind. Someone heard wolves calling the other night."

"All right." Arlyn didn't smile. Sanctioned exploration of his gift! He took the small nodule and faced the bog.

Find, he thought. He shut his eyes and held out his left hand. It was easier to regulate fire from that hand. The nodule stayed warm in his right. As he looked down, there were pinpricks of light, scattered and small. His head went back and forth, and he took small steps so he wouldn't trip in the tussocks.

"Didn't see any really dense areas," he admitted to Taryn when he returned to the camp. He wasn't sure just how long he'd been out there, but the sun was well up now. "One area that's about double what we usually see. But it's only a couple of paces across and maybe my height deep. It's hard to tell how far down it goes. We'll get to it next summer, I think."

"But you could sense the nodules?" Taryn asked. "Good. Will you need a sample again?"

"I don't think so. Not for iron anyway. I can try to sense the depth of the cut to figure out how deep the other nodules are."

"Reasonable. Hard to put samples down that far without leaving evidence of digging."

"True. Should I try finding other types of metal when I have time?"

"Might not be a bad idea. Lost coins, any nails or such."

"Or arrows lost during a hunt. Metal heads, not flint, though," Aryln said.

"I'll talk to the elders about that. Put the nodule back with the others." He turned to the lads stacking yesterday's peats so they would start to dry in the wan sunlight. The lads all groaned as he smiled. More cutting.

On the way back to the village three days later the sensation of being watched was back. He was slightly behind the others and he sensed the villagers' bodies easily. He reached out with his right hand. How far could he sense other people or animals? The village ... some people but not clearly. Mostly outside, he thought. The goats and sheep were huddled close to the village today. A few geese were out with one of the children. He let the magic fade.

He looked out to either side, hurrying a little to catch up. There was a faint flicker among the aspen trees to the south, then it was gone. Maybe a deer? No. A deer couldn't run out of his range that quickly. Or could it? He needed to do more work with the heat sensing. Could someone hide behind a big enough rock or lie in a dip in the land to prevent him from sensing them? All the cottages in the village were wooden and he could sense people through the walls if he thought about it. He'd try sensing if someone was on the other side of a stone fireplace as soon as he could.

It was soon his turn to help pull the cart but he kept thinking about that flicker. Could it be another mage? Why would one come out here to stare at him and not come to the village to talk to him? Or was it a bandit scout, come to steal their iron and whatever they thought the village had of value? Frankly he didn't think bandits would bother. There wasn't anything worth their effort.

Over the next week he sensed the watching flicker twice more when he was out of the village. It was getting frustrating but he couldn't admit what was happening to the elders. If it was a mage, they could hide behind dense objects. His stomach cramped at the thought.

Mama commented that he wasn't eating as much as usual at dinner that night. He smiled and told her she should be glad he wasn't growing any more.

He joined a group of young hunters instead of going out by himself. Safety in numbers. Maybe. He used his father's bow but all the arrows were of his making. Taryn had taught him how to make steel this past summer. An exacting process, but his arrowheads would last a long time if he took care of them. Taryn said there was a way to make steel that didn't rust, but he'd only seen one sample years ago and had never learned how to do it. Could magic be involved?

He didn't sense any watchers the first three deerless days. He sensed a few animals but the noise from the camp made them flee for the safer hills. Then that flicker was back.

It had to be another mage. He'd been trying to remember the winter tales about mages when he couldn't sleep, which was often in the past weeks. Most mages were the defenders of the places they lived. Other mages sometimes tried to take over those places. Mage duels could kill everyone nearby who couldn't shield. If the flicker was a mage, the entire village was at risk of death. Because of him. What did this mage want of him?

He was on guard duty late that night. The crescent moon set during the first watch and the fire was banked so there was no glare to ruin his night sight.

The glow of the watcher appeared not far from their camp. Not just a flicker this time. Solid.

Here.

Arlyn managed to shout but no one roused. His hands were sweaty with fear. He was not ready for any kind of confrontation with another mage.

"They won't wake until I let them," a tenor voice came from the glow. "If you do as I say, mageling, they will wake normally once we're well away. Unharmed. I promise."

"Who are you?" Arlyn asked. "A mage, that's obvious, but ..."

"Yes. Like you. I learned of you some months ago. You need a teacher if you wish to learn to truly control your gift. I can provide that lessoning."

"Why didn't you just come to the village and ask me to join you in front of witnesses? Like anyone seeking an apprentice?" Arlyn tried to stay calm but a glance toward the hunters, still sleeping, didn't help. He had to face this danger alone.

"You represent a very valuable asset to your village. One they will be loath to see leave without recompense. I refuse to line their pockets for nothing. What is your name, by the way?"

"I prefer not to share it, given your actions so far."

A snort. "Some sense. And I suppose you won't tell me anything about your family? The details I have are rather sparse. That you have the fire gift is about the only real fact. Parents are obvious, but siblings? I hope so but…" The mage smiled, awaiting his response.

"I wasn't raised a fool," Aryln said.

"Tedious," the other mage said. "Well, I hope your village can prosper without these men. Nine of them. Relatively young. Ah well, perhaps it's for the best. They're excitable and easily replaceable."

One of the rumbling snores cut off abruptly.

"What are you doing?" Arlyn asked, glancing back at the camp. The lights of their internal fires were dimmer than before.

"I'm drawing their energy out as they breathe so I'll have more than enough to put my collar on you. And it ensures that they'll stay asleep while we have our little discussion. Once the collar is in place you won't be able to act against me. And you'll tell me about your family, especially any siblings you have."

"No. I won't let you hurt these men. Or any of the villagers."

A silvery laugh this time. "You have spirit, mageling. Come, submit to me and save your comrades' lives."

The banked campfire flared up as he reached for it. Arlyn drew the heat of the fire to him, not the night air. His fists grew warm, then hot.

"Not bad. Fire can be powerful. But I control Air."

Arlyn tried to draw a breath and couldn't. The mage came forward, visible now that the fire partly banished the darkness. Moving golden wisps covered the mage's body.

Seeing them reminded Arlyn of how he handled the hot metals or the charcoal without being burned. Red flames surrounded him now and he took in a deep breath of energy and air. The mage's power couldn't work through his shields, if that's what the wisps were. How much energy would it take to keep him breathing?

"Oh, you're going to do such good work for me," the mage said, but his voice contained a note of concern.

Arlyn wondered how strong he was compared to the Air Mage. Enough to survive, he hoped.

He took several steps toward the mage and his anger flared. The rumbling snores started up again. The other mage's yellow wisps got thicker, sort of. His shielding increasing?

Aryln's hand went into his quiver, still on his back. There were two loose arrowheads in a side pocket. Steel that he could reshape into a better weapon.

"Did someone put a collar on you when you were my age?" he asked to gain time. Reshaping the steel into a spike was hard with one hand, but the mage could see him by the fire's light.

"No, actually. Although I did leave in the middle of the night once I knew what they planned. Didn't you think of running when your power first manifested, magelet? Knowing that you would only be able to do whatever the elders allowed you to? Never to be a free man ever again?"

"The elders voted not to collar me. But you want me to tamely submit to it? To do whatever you order. How is that different from what the elders might choose?"

"Do those elders know everything you are capable of? I think not. Join me and you'll have a good life. I have quite a nice manor to the north of here. With your help, it will prosper even more. I also have a share in an iron mine not far into the mountains. That brings gold into my coffers. My ore is so much easier to work than the tedium of refining the pitiful nodules from your bog. I want you to learn and get better at what you can do. Not stifle your gift as your elders have done."

"And you need to collar me to do that? Why not just teach me?"

"Because I don't trust another mage not to try to act against me. Especially as you grow stronger and more experienced. So you will wear my collar. Forever mine. And your siblings, of course. One mage in a family is not the norm. And I'll breed your mother and sister if you have one so I'll have my own gifted children. Collared from infancy to make sure they never do anything unfortunate."

It was getting harder to hold his shielding fire and form the spike. The wisps of flame shielding him moved slower than before. It was harder to breathe. He needed to end this quickly.

"You are tiring," the mage said, voice full of satisfaction. "Still young, with little control over your abilities. That will change soon under my tutelage."

"But you never had anyone formally teach you," Arlyn said. "And I have a different element. How could you teach me about fire?" A little whine in his voice. The mage seemed to relax as Arlyn's shielding continued to fade. By his own will this time, not because he was getting weaker.

"One element has a certain method of using power. Having two elements under my control more than doubles that power. Imagine stopping a forest fire. I can keep the wind down so the fire won't spread, and you could bank the flames to save a village. With a Water Mage as part of our group we could summon a storm to douse the flames once they were contained."

"Or you could increase the winds and have me spread the flames to destroy anyone who tried to stop you from taking over a town."

"True. I'd actually hoped you were an Earth Mage. They can encourage crops to grow far beyond what is normal. My villagers would always be free of the fear of famine, unlike the normal run of events. That yearly surplus would bring a lot of gold to my coffers."

"Or such a mage could blight an enemies' fields so his own crops were the only source of food," Arlyn said. "And starving people would pay or do whatever you wanted to feed their children."

"You seem to think I do what is evil, mageling. My people are happy and prosperous. They appreciate me and my gifts."

"So you say. How do you control them? Spying on me and hiding from the villagers doesn't fill me with trust. You've also threatened to kill my friends unless I submit to you. Saying I'd wear your collar until I die and that you'd rape my mother and any sister I might have to breed more captive mages don't sound like the actions of a good man."

Within easy speaking distance now. It seemed like the mage's wisps muted as he decided that Arlyn wasn't to be feared. Was going to submit. Arlyn absorbed the heat from the spike back into himself with a breath.

He took another two steps forward, then seemed to trip. But he hadn't. A roll and he stood next to the mage, his hand within those golden wisps. The spike slid into the mage's chest from under his ribs, piercing the heart. As the blood pulsed down Arlyn's hand and forearm, he pulled all the heat he could out of the mage through the steel.

The mage's mouth opened in shock and surprise. The expressions faded as the body slumped to the ground.

Arlyn pulled the spike out and stared down in the flickering light of the fire at his hand and the spike, dripping with hot blood.

He'd just killed a man. Not a sheep or deer. A person. A mage who wanted to enslave him and would have taken him, his sister and mama back to that manor as his slaves.

His throat was tight with emotion but his eyes were dry. He had no regrets. Not now. The blood smell almost made him heave.

He looked back toward the fire, burning normally now that he wasn't pulling energy from it. Should he tell the elders what happened? No, he decided. He could make the body disappear. The bog was the best place for that. First, he had to ensure the men stayed asleep. Having them wake now would ruin not only his life, but mama's and Karlyn's. He'd have to make a choice. The elders would send for a mage collar and he'd have to submit in order to stay with mama and Karlyn. Or he could run, like the Air Mage had. Hope to find someone to teach him.

Arlyn's attention shifted so he could see the men's energy. He reached out and pulled a little from each man. More snores started. Good enough. He cauterized the wound on the mage's chest to stop any further blood leakage and pulled the mage up and over both his shoulders to distribute his weight more evenly. The mage didn't weigh as much as he'd thought. Because he'd removed most of the Air Mage's energy?

Two hours later, he stood by the edge of the bog, breathing heavily. This area was harvested five years ago. The villagers wouldn't be back here for at least another generation. A good burial site. He stripped the mage's clothing off first, letting the bloody garments soak in the water. Then he removed his jerkin and shirt and set them to soaking as well.

He looked up at the stars. He should have enough time before daybreak to finish what he needed to do. He put both hands on the corpse and started pulling every last bit of energy out that he could. The husk that was left sank quickly with the addition of some rocks tied to the midsection.

Arlyn took a deep breath and turned to the mage's clothing. There was a pouch the size of two hand-widths he'd ignored at first but it clinked as he picked it up. Pulling a small coin out he stared at it for a moment. Gold? He'd often felt copper and iron, and mama had a silver pendant she only wore on holy days. This was heavier, solid. Unchanging. Despite the small size.

He reached in again and he held a mage collar made of links the size of his thumbnail. He wasn't sure what metal it was made of. Just touching it made his skin crawl from the controlling spells.

He rinsed the blood out of the mage's clothing, dried them and wrapped everything around the pouch. A gnarled bush nearby with an animal burrow beneath it gave him a hiding place he could easily find again, now that he knew what gold felt like. He sensed no inhabitants and placed the heaviest rock he could move over it.

Back at the bog's edge, he finished washing himself and his own clothing. Checking the stars again, he knew he had to hurry. Dawn would be coming soon.

Spare energy dried his damp clothes as he trotted back to the camp. When he returned to the spot where the mage died, he noticed dark stains on the ground. A tiny, controlled flash of fire turned that blood into ash that blew away in the morning breeze. No one would see anything amiss once the sun was up.

As he stood next to the firepit, he returned the energy he'd borrowed to the men so they'd wake normally. He sat down on his bedroll, then let himself slump to the side with his bow in hand, pretending he'd gone to sleep while on guard. Better be made fun of than chance anyone asking why he hadn't woken the next sentry.

He'd have to be very careful in the future. If the elders knew what he could do, they'd want to collar him. Because he'd killed. Maybe this spring, once planting was done, he'd dig up the clothing and bag of coin, leave the village and try to find a mage who would just teach him about using his gift, so he could make a good home and bring mama and Karlyn to live with him. Because he was sure now: his sister was a mage. Their fields had been more abundant than their neighbors. Only an Earth Mage could have been responsible. She was only nine.

He swore to all the gods that he would keep his family safe from predators like the Air Mage.

Even if he had to burn them all.

LEE F. PATRICK is a resident of Calgary, AB and lives with her wonderful husband Gary and two cats (Romulus and Remus) who help her write. She enjoys going to other worlds, since this one has too many rules. She writes science fiction, fantasy and hybrids that cross several genres, except for romance. The only one of those she tried turned out to be a 'horse and his boy' story with the girl an also ran.

EMBER

By Christopher M. Chupik

Rel stood naked on the surface of a dying planet. All around her was desolation, a lifeless brown wasteland stretching from horizon to horizon. This planet's geomagnetic field was nearly gone and most of the atmosphere stripped away by the pitiless solar wind. The storm of radiation and heat tingled against her skin.

Her chosen form was that of an Early Galactic female, humanoid, her skin a dark golden brown, hair silver-white and eyes emerald green. She and her bond-mate, Kaem, who was still aboard the ship, had embodied themselves in these synthetic forms to honor their ancestors as they searched for Origin.

Rel knelt, placing her right hand on the ground, the rocky soil rough and hot against her palm. She looked up into the sky. A bright amber sun burned there, dominating the heavens. Once a yellow dwarf, it was now in an unstable phase that would end with it swelling into a red giant, destroying this system's inner planets, including the one she stood on.

The scientist glanced over her shoulder at *Seeker*. The starship resting on the blasted plain was spherical, thirty meters across, its mirrored hull shining a dull bronze in the reflected sunlight. The hull rippled as Kaem stepped out of the ship. His body was similar to hers, masculine as hers was feminine. He was completely hairless and he had eyes of bright violet.

Rel rose and turned.

"It's beautiful," she said, words and emotions transmitted instantaneously across the quantum medium of Mindspace.

"You have a strange idea of beauty," Kaem replied.

She smiled, feeling her bond-mate's love. Such "body language" had been strange, back when they first embodied. Now it came naturally.

"Just because it's beautiful doesn't mean it can't be sad, too."

Another dying world. They had seen so many. This one had been found by one of their probes and fit the theoretical parameters of Origin. But there was little time. Already the planet's equator was beginning to liquefy into an ocean of magma, a giant burning scar dividing the hemispheres.

"If only the moon were still intact," Kaem said. "It might have had ruins and other traces of Early Galactic or even Primordial civilizations."

"We were fortunate enough to arrive before the surface was completely destroyed," she replied. This planet was encircled by a wide series of debris rings, the remains of a natural satellite destroyed in some ancient cataclysm. Between the impact of falling debris and the melting equatorial regions, much of the planet's fossil deposits might already be lost.

Kaem nodded. "We should get started."

Rel sent a command to the ship's Mind. Clouds of effectors rose from the hull like thick metallic smoke. Another command, and the clouds divided into thirty smaller masses which started to gather matter from their surroundings to replicate and grow.

Searching a planet was an enormous task, even with modern technology. Searching an entire galaxy with one ship was a fool's task. Yet Rel and Kaem had done just that for the past century.

Their native Sodality was ancient, advanced, and stagnant. Even their Consensus of Knowledge, which had once probed the mysteries of Time and Space, had abandoned the pursuit of exploration, relying instead on Mindspace simulations rather than direct observation.

She looked to Kaem. Of all the members of the Consensus, he was the only one willing to follow her on her quest to find the home world of humanity. Together they had created *Seeker* and set out. In regions of the Near Galaxies where the ancient wormhole network had collapsed, they traveled at relativistic speeds. Decades were moments to such as they, but while they traveled, the universe grew older.

Were they too late?

Rel averted her eyes from Kaem's. She could not let Kaem sense her misgivings, not now.

"Rel, was there something—"

"No. Nothing."

She sealed her doubt away and Kaem did not press her, though she felt his concern.

When the effector clouds were large enough, Rel tasked them with detecting and uncovering fossils. Then she ported the clouds away in a quantum blink, dispatched across the globe to locations believed to contain fossil deposits.

"Now we wait." Kaem said.

So they waited, while the world died.

Rel was a patient being. She had already lived for more than a millennium and had spent a century searching for Origin. But every second spent waiting for the effector clouds was time lost forever.

Finally, after two hours, the ship's Mind spoke.

Report: Fossils located

"Finally," Rel said.

After the Mind relayed the location they ported.

They materialized with a soft crack, a wave of dust displaced from where they stood. It was nighttime there, pleasantly cool after the searing heat of the day. Rel and Kaem were in a deep rift valley located in the northern hemisphere of the planet at the base of towering cliffs. Layers upon layers of rocks, the geological record of billions of years exposed to the open air. Above, the debris rings arced across a sky packed densely with stars. This planet was located in the Newborn Galaxy, actually a pair of galaxies which had collided and coalesced. Before the Consensus abandoned the search for Origin, the oldest traces of humanity had been found in Newborn, so it became the focus of their search.

A few meters away, the effector cloud was still clearing an opening into the base of the cliffs, spinning slowly like a liquid vortex. It burrowed through the sedimentary rock, converting its matter into new effectors. When it finished, the cloud dispersed, effectors remaining on standby.

Kaem and Rel entered the tunnel. It was not necessary for them to be physically present, any more than it was necessary for them to set foot outside the ship. Mindspace data flow was sufficient. But being embodied had imparted certain desires, including the need to experience things with their own senses.

The tunnel opened into a small chamber, the fossils still partially embedded in the rock. Rel switched her vision to multispectral. It was the remains of a quadruped, a horned ungulate, herbivorous by its teeth. The basic physiology was similar to life-forms found on other human-colonized worlds.

Analysis: Fossils are Original life the Mind confirmed.

"And the age?" asked Rel.

Estimate: Five point two billion years

"Early Galactic Era," Kaem said. "That's encouraging."

Perhaps, but it was no older than anything else they had found in Newborn. She sensed his eagerness through Mindspace and it shamed her. When she looked at Kaem now, she saw the optimist she had once been. Once, she had believed they might find Origin. Now, she feared they were too late.

"Scan and store," she commanded, hiding her doubts.

Effectors scanned the fossils and reduced them to quantum memories in Mindspace. When they returned to the Sodality, the fossils could be recreated for further study.

Soon the Mind announced the discovery of two more fossil sites. Kaem and Rel each chose one and ported away. Rel found herself in daylight, in a mountain range in the southern hemisphere. She examined a shale formation containing hundreds of shelled brachiopods. Again, similar to Original life, and again, not significantly older than previous finds.

Data flowed from Kaem. His fossils were of simple single-celled prokaryotes which had apparently survived the rising temperatures and thinning of the planet's atmosphere for almost a billion years. But even they had perished in the end.

Rel spent the next few days porting from site to site, enthusiasm waning with each discovery. No traces of humanity, only a litany of extinction. She started to avoid her bond-mate and withdrew, afraid he would sense her growing despair. Every day the sun expanded a little more and the devastation of the equatorial regions spread.

Now she stood alone on the edge of a vast escarpment, watching debris from the ring make fiery streaks across the night sky as it fell.

Had she been wrong?

Life in the Sodality was easy. Effectors to create whatever they required. Mindspace to communicate with ease. Wormholes to travel between galaxies. They lived for millennia, in any fashion or form they desired. There was no more reason to explore. Even the Consensus of Knowledge now believed humanity had reached the limits of its understanding.

She had once believed that if she could find Origin or Primordial humans or both, she might be able to answer the ancient questions. Who were they? Where had they come from? And where were they headed? And in doing so, she hoped to rekindle the Sodality's lost yearning for discovery.

But what had she learned so far? Stars died. Planets died. Eventually the universe itself would die. And what would it all have meant?

It had to mean something.

"What's wrong?" Kaem demanded, his concern bleeding across Mindspace.

Rel tried to shield her feelings but she felt Kaem gently push through her defences.

"Please, Rel. Let me help."

Opening herself, she let him see her doubts. She should have known better than to hide her feelings after having been bonded so long.

"This may not even be Origin at all."

His words were meant to comfort her, but they gave her no peace.

"What if it is, and what we're looking for is gone?"

"I have to believe that we'll succeed."

"It's just that I've brought you so far…"

"Rel, I'm exactly where I want to be."

In a quantum blink, her bond-mate was there. They held each other close for a long time, saying nothing.

The rim of the mammoth sun rose in the east, painting the escarpment with sullen crimson light. Rel had left the Mind in charge of the fossil search. The search was nearly complete. There was no more reason to remain.

And then:

Report: Possible human fossils detected

Rel immediately accessed the site. It was near the equator, a small rocky island in the sea of magma.

Caution: Region is unstable. Recommendation: Effector clouds can handle the task

"No. Human fossils are why we came."

Caution: Physical harm is—

"Mind, this is not a debate," Rel said, and ported before it could object.

She found herself in a rocky highland region. A hot wind blew, ashes and volcanic gasses swirling around her. The ground burned beneath her feet. Looking to the south, she saw the magma sea, a vast, glowing mass of orange flecked with black. Smoke rose where solid rock mixed with molten and began to turn red and flow.

Rel looked down at her hands and saw the outer layers of her skin flaking away under the onslaught of heat. The effectors of her body struggled to replicate and repair.

Kaem ported in seconds later.

The Mind spoke.

Observation: You are intent on ignoring my warnings. Response: I am en route to your location to render assistance

Rel smiled.

"Thanks, Mind. How deep are the fossils?"

Information: One hundred twenty-two meters

"We have to shield this site as long as we can," she said. Minutes later, *Seeker* hovered overhead, casting the excavation site into shadow. At her command it deployed an enormous roiling cloud of effectors, a shroud that darkened the air around the site. Under the shroud, the air began to cool slightly.

Information: This region will be destroyed within forty-six minutes. Caution: This Mind cannot guarantee your safety if you remain

Noted Rel replied.

She and Kaem waited. A faint tremor shook the ground. The effector cloud kept tunneling downwards. Twenty two agonizing minutes passed.

The instant the effectors dissipated, Rel and Kaem ported directly to the bottom of the pit. She knelt before the fossilized bones, her eyes scanning them. They were brown with age among the gray sedimentary rock which had once encased them. A jawbone, half of a skull, ten ribs, two segments of vertebra, a thighbone, part of a hand.

Unmistakably human.

How old? she asked, hoping, fearing.

Estimate: Five point eight billion years

The oldest human remains ever found. Excitement flared Mindspace, but she had to be certain.

A Mindspace simulation was generated as the Mind extrapolated the probable appearance of the Primordial, completing the fragmentary bones and clothing them in flesh. It was like no human variant she had ever seen. Like their own forms, this creature was bipedal but it was shorter, about one point six meters tall standing nearly erect. Its brow was low and sloped, its nose flattened and its brows heavy.

"It's old. Are you certain it's Primordial?" Kaem asked.

She interpreted the data before answering.

"That vestigial tailbone is completely lacking in all Galactic specimens to date. Brain capacity is too small. Simple tool use and basic reasoning, yes, probably primitive vocalization, but there's no possibility that they could have developed spaceflight."

He looked to her, shocked. "Then it's …"

She smiled. "Origin."

No time to celebrate. Rel turned her attention back to the fossil.

"Who were you?" She asked as data flow washed over her. "Male. Omnivore. Approximately thirty Standard years at time of death."

"Young," Kaem said.

"Old, actually, for someone living in extreme primitiveness," she corrected. "Hard to imagine an entire life in so short a time." Rel examined the left femur. "Femur was broken, you see? Healed badly. I'd say ten years before death. He would have had a limp for the rest of his life."

"And yet he kept going," said Kaem.

In spite of everything, this Primordial persisted. Against sickness and starvation, against predators, even against the pain of his own body. And the species survived and evolved. Stone tools became metal. Civilizations rose and fell and rose again. Wars, plagues and famines threatened to destroy them, but they survived. Not only survived, but thrived. Trapped at the bottom of a gravity well, they dragged themselves out of it and spread across the universe.

And now she understood why.

Because they burned to know.

That same fire burned in her. It burned in Kaem, as it burned in all those who were driven to explore. Those embers might cool, but never faded. Nothing short of the destruction of the universe could extinguish it.

And when that time was upon them, she knew that whatever humans had evolved into would keep fighting. Life was tenacious. Like the prokaryotes that struggled on when all other life on Origin had perished. Against the ending of all things, those last remnants would strive. Perhaps in vain, but they would not yield.

Rel had her answer. She did not know if it would reawaken the Sodality's lost sense of wonder. But it had reawakened hers.

There was a second, more powerful tremor.

Critical: Geologic instability growing. Recommendation: Abandon region immediately

Kaem placed a hand on her shoulder.

We have to go he said.

The fossils were scanned and stored. Kaem ported back to *Seeker*, but Rel lingered a moment. If only they had more time. But she was grateful to have stood on Origin with her own feet, looked upon it with her own eyes.

She closed her eyes. When she opened them she was back aboard *Seeker*.

The ship rose on a wave of gravity, reaching orbit in minutes. Kaem touched the hull, turning it transparent, giving them an unimpeded view of Origin's ancient, ravaged face. Far below, the island began to fissure as rivers of lava flowed across it.

"Sad," Rel said.

"But beautiful," replied Kaem.

And it was.

A million years would pass before the planet would be

completely consumed by its sun. But they decided to linger a while. Someone had to witness and remember.

Reaching into Mindspace, Rel recreated the Primordial skull. Taking it in her hands, she contemplated it, like a child gazing into the face of their parent.

CHRISTOPHER M. CHUPIK has worked at bookstores and libraries. In his increasingly rare spare time, he reads (too much) and writes (too little). His short story "Grasshoppers" appeared in the 2015 *Enigma Front.* He is also an occasional guest-blogger. Christopher lives in Calgary, Alberta and wishes to assure you all that he does not make a habit of referring to himself in the third-person.

THE DEMON OF P-CITY

By Elizabeth Grotkowski

My day started with a hangover, sunlight leaking through the crooked motel blinds, and a second-string Hurry Girl, whose name I forgot. Anna? Agnus? Christ, she was already talking matching curtains and china patterns. Just because she gave me a discount rate for her services didn't mean I needed to produce a ring.

"Chris, honey. You gonna give me a call?" she asked as she pulled up her stockings.

I reached for the bottle of hooch on the bedside table, tipped it upside down then sighed. Empty. "Sure thing, sweetheart."

She still smiled even as I gently pushed her out the door.

My tee-shirt stuck to my back like flypaper in the furnace-hot room. I ran out of dough and couldn't afford air conditioning. Pain ricocheted in my head when a shaft of light hit me square in the eyes as I parted the blinds to check on the Charger. The car didn't look like much with her mismatched-colored doors and dust-filmed windows, but she had plenty of attitude under the hood. The fastest ride in P-City.

Shoshee called at noon. Between my narrow escape from

little Miss "I Don't Remember" and my five alarm hangover, something told me not to answer, but listening to reason isn't my strong suit so I picked up the mobile, my hand still dripping from the shower.

"Kellerman." I grunted.

"Hey Kells, my man—up for a job?" Shoshee's deep rumble of voice rolled out of the receiver, hearty, insincere, and a little off.

"Half in cold and hard, upfront?"

"Of course, baby. What kind of operation do you think I run?"

A slight shake vibrated the soothing bass that oozed over the phone. Made my right eye twitch. But I recalled my wallet and how Miss "I Don't Remember" emptied it and how I'd sleep in my car tonight if I didn't find some shekels to jingle in my pocket.

"What's the deal?"

"It's a pickup and delivery, Kells baby. Simple and sweet." The unmistakable strain in Shoshee's voice made my ears prick up. A high risk job meant I could ask for more cash up front.

"Really? Who's the customer?"

"Ah, there's the rub, Kellerman. The client wants to keep that to himself."

"Then this deal doesn't sound simple or sweet, Shoshee. I want triple my rate." Unheard of—Shoshee is cheaper than a fourth-string Hurry Girl— but I opened high so I could negotiate to double.

"You got it, Kells. Done deal." What? Shoshee paying triple with no back and forth? My chin dropped so fast my jaw clicked.

"Pickup is at Swaller's. Gunderson will give you the delivery address when you arrive. You gotta deliver by 3:00 am or—"

"Or what, Shoshee?"

"Just be there, Kells. Funds in your account…" I heard a key tap, "Now. Deal specs coming down the pipe." Then a click and dead air.

I brought up the specs on my tablet and they looked mundane, so what made Shoshee pay triple? I checked my account and sure enough, my balance breathed air again.

No backing out now.

A convoy of asses clogged up the streets and their riders cursed me in Farsi as I leaned on my horn. By the time I rolled up to Swaller's front entrance, night reduced the swelter of P-City to a tolerable, sticky hot. Water hung in the air, but the dampness only teased. It never rained in P-City, or at least it hadn't since the day I landed here on my butt in a cloud of dust and camel dung.

Don't know how long I've been in Purgatory.

Yeah, Purgatory. The place you go if you're not sweet enough for heaven or rotten enough for hell. "The state of purification and the refuge of last chances." At least, that's what the ragged flyers stapled to the dead trees on the city boulevards said. Everyone calls it P-City because who wants to remember they live in a place where evil is purged from the soul with heat, dust, flies, and the ever present smell of camel—that fetid perfume of sour milk, urine, and musk.

I used to be a high end transporter, working for anyone who'd pay me enough to keep me in fast cars, pretty girls, and Jack Daniels. Then, for some inexplicable reason, I stepped in front of a gun aimed at a junkie with big blue eyes. My resumé should've landed me in hell, but apparently taking a bullet for someone gives you squatter's rights in the place between the bottomless pit and the pearly gates. For some it's an in-and-out gig, for others it's more a holding pattern. But once the big guy makes up his mind it's a done deal and you find yourself either polishing a halo or sitting on the business end of a pitch fork.

When I arrived in P-City I didn't know what to do. Purgatory is a big, sprawling town and you could drive for hours before you ended up where you started. Tried making an honest living at the city salt mine, but I worked hard and made crap so I fell back on what I knew. I scored a car then started transporting again.

And the stuff I usually move is blue.

Blue Ice. It showed up on the streets of P-City around the same time I did. A drug tailor-made for demons that dopes them up then leaves them squirrely and begging for more.

And he don't like squirrely. Yeah, him. The big cheese, the prince of darkness, the destroyer—the one and only Lucifer aka Satan. No one knows who the supplier is, but Shoshee manages to keep some on hand. I'm busy these days, moving ice, using up my last chances, and trying not to cross paths with the nastiest dude of them all.

Where's Pauli? I wondered as I walked up to Swallers's awning covered doors. The bar's three-hundred-pound doorman never left his post. Two first string Hurry girls burst out of the club, clutching ripped garments to their chests and sobbing.

"What's going…" But they disappeared down the street before I could finish.

Cautiously, I pushed one door open. As I walked across the bar's scuffed marble tiles, my steps echoed in the silent room. Though customers crowded the tables, no one said a word. Gunderson, the cantankerous bar owner, sat on a bar stool beside a good-looking kid. I carefully circumvented a red puddle on the floor which grew by steady drips from something suspended from the ceiling. I didn't need to look up to know I'd found Pauli. As I walked up to Gunderson, I slid my right hand into my coat pocket and caressed the hilt of the shiv nestled there.

"Hey, Gunderson. What's up?" Gunderson didn't say a thing, which unnerved me because he always had something to say.

"Howdy," said the kid with a big grin. Girls would dig the way his dark hair hung over his forehead.

Then his eyes glinted red.

I'd never seen such a high level demon before. Usually they had animal features, misshapen bodies, and stank of rotten eggs. But I did recognize the dilated pupils and blue lips—the kid liked to skate on blue ice.

"This my pick up?" I murmured. Gunderson nodded vigorously, shaking sweat off his face like a dog after a bath.

"And where do I deliver?"

His eyes bulged and his pudgy face turned bright red, but his mouth remained clamped shut.

"Cat got your tongue, Gunderson?" I asked.

"Actually, I do," said the kid as he lifted up his hand. Pinched between two fingers wobbled a fleshy piece of meat. I tightened my grip on the shiv's handle.

"He wouldn't shut up. I asked him for 'ice' but he kept saying he didn't have any. A man who owns a bar should have some ice, shouldn't he?" The kid cocked his head.

"You would think so," I replied, every inch of my skin crawling. "Ah, any chance he could get his tongue back? I need to talk to him."

The demon shrugged. He rubbed his fingers together and the meat vanished in a wisp of smoke. "Wasn't real—ripping his tongue out would've got blood on my shoes."

"Those are sweet kicks." I nodded as I took in his pristine sneakers.

The kid beamed. "I like you." He turned to Gunderson and waved his hand dismissively. "You can talk now."

Gunderson blinked. "Deliver him to Fierro Tower by 3:00 A.M." The words he rushed out sounded like they were covered with rust.

My mouth went dry. There are two portals in P-City. One takes you to the pearly gates and the other takes you to hell. No one knows where the former is, but everyone knows the latter's address. Fierro Tower.

"That's the problem!" The kid threw his hands in the air. "I don't want to go there. I WANT SOME ICE!" The glasses shook on the bar shelves and the customers covered their ears. Someone whimpered.

I plastered a smile on my face. "Well, you're in luck, because I've got some blue candy in my car."

The demon perked up. "Is it a cool ride?"

"It's the fastest car in P-City. And the ice is top grade, my friend—you won't find any bluer."

"Sweet." The demon jumped off his stool. "Let's go." Gunderson slumped in his seat, the relief on the old bastard's face profound.

Then all hell broke loose.

Three Nephilim burst through the front doors breast plates blazing, wings unfurled. Blinding light sent terrified customers diving under tables and chairs. The heads of the angels skimmed the ceiling as they scanned the room until their glittering, silver eyes focused on the kid.

One opened his mouth and breathed out fire as his voice shook the ground and walls.

"Spawn of Satan, foul offspring of Belial—return to the abyss, accursed one." The Nephilim leveled his flaming sword at my pickup.

Without thinking, I grabbed the doped up demon by the scruff of his neck and hauled him to the ground as a volley of holy fire sizzled through the air where his head had been.

The angels unveiled and bellowed as white light scorched our eyes. Flaming swords held high, they charged our position where we cowered with our hands clamped over our ears. But below the tenor of the voices of heaven, the floor rumbled with the bass of ironclad feet.

A troop of snout-faced demons the size of linebackers charged out of the kitchen swinging battle axes, their razor sharp tusks gleaming. Grunting and squealing, they plowed through tables and chairs, sending hapless patrons flying as they attacked the Nephilim.

"We need to go!" I yelled over the squealing, the angelic roars, and the screaming customers. "Back door!"

The kid didn't listen. Instead, he rolled on the ground, laughing at the chaos that surrounded us. I grabbed his arm and shouted in his ear. "Let's get you some ice."

That got his attention.

We crawled toward the kitchen, gagging from the stench of burnt feathers, fried pork, and sulfur. To my dismay, another white robed angel walked into the bar from the back, ducking through the kitchen doorway, before straightening to his full nine feet.

The Nephilim pointed his sword at the kid. "Son of Shaitan, foul—" Several oinking demons bowled him over. They stomped on his wings with their horned boots, breaking them until they stood out at obscene angles. The cracking sounds made my stomach wrench.

Something grabbed the back of my jacket with thick, blunt fingers and yanked me off the floor. A moment later, two porcine demons stuffed the kid and me under their arms like footballs. Eyes watering from the rank smell emanating from my demon's armpit, I watched helplessly as they formed a wedge with another demon before they charged through the melee of battling angels, demons, and exploding holy fire.

My burnt hair still smoked when I hit pavement face first, outside Swaller's front entrance. The kid landed beside me with a thud. The demons grunted before returning to the bar to block the doorway. A burst of light etched my retinas and one of the demons fell backwards, squealing in agony as flames consumed him.

"Move!" I yelled, grabbing the kid's arm. We ran to the Charger and dived into the car. I jammed the key into the ignition then floored the gas pedal as we tore out of the parking space and down the street in a cloud of atomized rubber and dust.

"You okay, kid?" I asked, once we cleared the Nephilim.

The kid turned to me, his face cold, his eyes glowing red. "Where's the ice?"

My gut twisted. "Ah, it's in the glove box."

The demon rummaged through the compartment until he found the blue ice suckers I kept on hand for bribes. He looked up at me and grinned.

"Want a lollypop?" he asked.

"I'm good, bro—I'll party later," I said, my knuckles white against the black leather steering wheel.

"Okay." He smiled inanely as he stuffed one into his mouth. He crunched hard and pulled out the white stick with only a jagged piece of blue remaining. He closed his eyes and leaned back against the seat, the smile still on his face. His bare, unguarded neck made me think of my shiv, but I kept my hands on the wheel as I drove down the wide road to hell.

Two burly security guards pulled the entrance doors open for me as I carried the unconscious kid in a fireman's lift into the foyer of Fierro Tower.

Onyx pillars towered above us and a marble-tiled floor so black that I seemed to fall into a void with every step I took. The cavernous room loomed dark and empty except for a circular wood desk that sat in a pool of light. Behind the desk, an elevator door stood out in sharp relief against the black wall like a single tooth in a giant maw. Richly embossed with gold, the door was alive with undulating snakes and contorted bodies.

A babe of a girl in a beige suit sat at the desk. She looked up. Her pink frosted lips parted into a smile revealing white, jagged teeth and oversized incisors. A whiff of sulfur mingled with the Chanel No. 5 perfume she wore.

"Mr. Kellerman, you're expected. May I see the package?"

I turned around so she could see the kid's face.

"Excellent. You can take him to Mr. Zagan." She pointed to the elevator.

"Sorry, but the deal specs didn't include restricted delivery. I'll just leave him here and go on my way." I dropped the kid to the floor and the sound of his skull hitting marble echoed throughout the foyer.

"Mr. Zagan's instructions are clear. You're to deliver the package in person." She continued smiling. Three porcine demons moved in from the shadows and the guards from the front door walked toward us, one of them rapping a baton in his hand.

"Ah, I guess if that's what Mr. Zagan wants ..." I pushed the words past the lump in my throat. One of the guards flung the kid over his shoulder and followed me to the elevator. The gold door slid open without a sound. My knees shook like maracas as I walked through the gates of hell.

Don't know what I expected when I walked into the room, but a spacious, modern office wasn't it. Plush, gold broadloom carpeted the expansive floor and black cherry wood paneling flanked the walls. Behind a huge antique desk sat a lean, dark-haired man in his early thirties wearing a gray suit. A gold pen glinted in his hand as he wrote on a sheet of paper, the only item other than a laptop on the wood-grained expanse of his desk.

"Mr. Kellerman, I presume," said Zagan as he looked up. I stifled a gasp. His eyes gleamed silver like those of the Nephilim and his face—well, if I swung for the other team, he'd be my everything. His eyes locked on the kid now propped up by the guard.

"Got some ice?" the kid slurred, a dopey smile on his face.

Zagan sprang from his seat, stalked over to the boy, and hit him with the back of his hand. The crack of knuckles against bone made me wince as the kid's head snapped sideways before it lolled on his chest.

"Take him to the basement and get that blue shit out of his system." The guard grabbed the kid's collar and dragged him out the door.

Zagan returned to his desk, straightened his tie and sat down. I contemplated what would happen if he found out about the candy store in my glove box. I needed to leave. Now.

"Great to meet you, Mr. Zagan," I said, backing away from his desk, "You have your package now, so guess I'll be on my way." I turned to follow the guard out of the office.

The door slammed shut in my face.

I turned back to Zagan, who now studied his laptop. He closed it and beamed at me. Something inside me shriveled.

"Well, Junior has certainly taken a shine to you."

"Ah, what makes you think that?" I asked, my voice hoarse.

"For starters, your entrails aren't wrapped around your neck, and you still have all your limbs. I take these as signs he likes you." Zagan folded his hands on his desk. His fingers were long and graceful, perfectly designed to play a stringed instrument.

I moistened my cracked lips. "When you say Junior, do you mean—?"

"The beast, the anti-Christ, the profane and wicked prince—yes, Junior is my boy. Mine and hers." He pointed to something hanging on the wall behind me. I glanced over my shoulder.

The Mona Lisa?

"I put that smile on her face. That's the original, by the way. Leonardo owed me— most brilliant artists do. The portrait worshiped in the Louvre is but a pale imitation." Zagan said.

"So he's half human?"

Zagan nodded, "Yes. That's why, unlike me, he can stroll the streets of purgatory, looking for a fix." Rage flickered across his face, so virulent I almost fell to my knees. "That's the deal. Bubba doesn't go there so I can't go either. It's a reciprocity thing."

"Bubba?"

Zagan pointed up.

"Oh."

"You may have noticed that Junior has a few issues," said Zagan. An angry crimson glow still managed to leak through the closed blinds behind him. No sky in P-City ever looked that red.

"He is a…spirited boy."

Zagan threw his head back and laughed. The sound ripped

into my eardrums like shards of glass. "Spirited. Yes, I'll grant you that." The laughter faded and his expression grew contemplative.

"I have a job for you, Mr. Kellerman."

"A job?"

"Yes. I need someone to look after Junior in P-City. Show him the ropes, up his social game, and…," Zagan reached in a drawer and dropped my remaining stash of suckers on his desk top, "Keep him clean."

An arctic chill ripped down my spine and coiled up in my bowels.

"I already have work, thanks." The carpet started moving as if legions of bugs, worms, and rotting things crawled underneath it. I wiped away the drops of sweat beading on my upper lip.

He smiled. A smile that made me work hard to swallow. "Yes, I know all about your current situation, Mr. Kellerman."

Oh shit.

I stood frozen in place as my shoes sank in the carpet and the crawling things underneath wiggled against my ankles. The silence in the room grew louder than the screaming in my head.

"Do you know much about the end times?" asked Zagan.

The carpet stilled.

Blinking hard, I shook my head, both confused and relieved by the sudden change of topic. My feet stood on solid ground again.

"Let me give you a condensed version." Zagan leaned back. "It all started with a pissing match. Bubba thought his creations would follow him no matter what. I said they wouldn't if they had a choice. We set a date—the end times—and whoever owned the most souls on that day would win."

Zagan leaned forward across his desk, smiling. "Well, mankind couldn't get enough of me. War, human sacrifice, incest—his children built alters to me drenched in blood.

And I'm winning." His smile faded into a scowl.

"So Bubba sends in a game changer and is it a cracker. He delivers his son to humanity just to show he cares. Bubba Lite spouts some mumbo jumbo about forgiveness, gets himself nailed to a piece of wood, and the sheep change direction."

"Well, that sets me back until this." Zagan pointed to his laptop. "The Internet.

"Greatest perdition delivery system since the apple tree. Now all my vassals are IT associates and executives in Silicon Valley. Best of all, I'm winning again.

"The timing couldn't be better. Judgement day is fast approaching and, because of the reciprocity clause, my son gets his shot at mankind. And he's perfect for the job. Charismatic, smart, and gifted with my silver tongue, nothing can stop him. With the help of the global network, he'll preach my message to the world and the sheep will flock to him."

"Until this shows up." He picked up the baggie holding the blue ice and stared at it morosely. "Another game changer. Bubba uses my own weapon against me—even I have to admit it's genius.

"Of course, Junior has to give it a whirl and boy does he like it. He has the voice of command—demons must obey—so when he gets a hankering for something blue, he skips off to purgatory unprotected, where he's fair game for the Nephilim scum." Zagan's lip curled. "Worse, Junior loses his soft touch and now relies on his baser instincts to achieve his ends. While I'm all for having fun, some restraint is necessary to gain a human following. Junior must become the ultimate politician not a butcher.

"And you, Mr. Kellerman, have people skills."

A long silence formed.

I cleared my throat. "As much as I appreciate the offer—"

"What made you believe acceptance of employment is negotiable?" asked Zagan.

"Don't think you'd explain things so nicely if I didn't have a say," I said.

Zagan chuckled as he tapped his head with his finger.

"You're smart. And likable with above average looks. Such a winning combination." He shook his head. "I had great hopes for you.

"Could you explain why you did it? Why sacrifice yourself for an addict that you didn't even know? The act confounds me." Zagan's brow furrowed.

Suddenly, I was back in the bar, the girl pressing her knee against mine, her eyes luminous with need, her face still pretty. She couldn't have been more than eighteen. Me, swirling the whiskey in my glass, knowing that the stuff I transported would devour her looks and her dreams and her soul…

"Guess I got tired of seeing people suffer."

Zagan sighed. "Yes, he would like that." He folded his hands. "Look at your feet."

I looked down. A laser-like red line bisecting the floor of the room almost touched the toes of my boots.

"That's how close you are to damnation. The line moves, Mr. Kellerman. One more botched job, one more Hurry Girl crying in the night, and you're on the other side." Zagan smiled. "You'll crochet barbwire dollies, and watch "Barney and Friends" reruns with your eyelids pinned back for eternity. It's just a matter of time."

He tilted his head. "Or, we could come to an arrangement.

"You keep Junior off the ice and tutor him so he'll have a fighting chance when he ascends to the earthly plane, and I'll rescind any claim I have on you. You'll remain in P-City until Bubba decides your fate."

"Can't imagine he'll want much to do with the Antichrist's nanny," I muttered.

Zagan shrugged. "Perhaps." Then he leaned forward. "However, don't you think it's a curious coincidence that you, arguably the best transporter of your generation, arrived in Purgatory the same time the blue drug did?" My mouth opened and closed as I tried to comprehend what he said.

Zagan's mouth brushed my ear. "Bubba moves in mysterious ways, Christopher," he whispered. My lips parted and I longed for him to touch them. With his elegant fingers, with his cruel mouth ... I blinked. Zagan watched me over caged fingers from behind his desk. I cleared my throat several times.

"And if I can't keep Junior on a leash?" My voice a harsh whisper.

"Then you'll get to know me better." Zagan smiled. Though the sculptured splendor of his face didn't change, something hideous shone through. Something feral and hungry—like a Rottweiler eyeing a juicy T-bone steak.

Zagan cracked his knuckles. "Decision time, Mr. Kellerman. Do you become Junior's new best friend or do I start looking for my Barney DVDs?"

"Guess I don't have a choice after all," I said.

His eyes glowed red. "There's always a choice."

I managed a weak smile. "So where I do I sign?"

"Your word will do. Arrive here tomorrow morning at eight sharp. Junior will be waiting." He resumed writing on the paper before him. Guess he dismissed me. Don't run to the door, Kellerman. Just one foot before the other. One foot, and another and—

"Stop."

My hand rested on the doorknob. A bead of sweat slipped down my forehead, onto my nose, and dropped to the carpet. I turned around.

"You'll need these."

A pair of keys sailed through the air toward me.

Ten minutes later I ran my finger along the burning flames painted on the sides of my spanking new black Charger. Air conditioning cooled the car's windows while her headlights glowed demon red. And though he scared the hell out of me, I had to admit it.

The dude had style.

LIZ GROTKOWSKI loves reading and writing YA, science fiction, and fantasy. A loyal member of IFWA and several writing critique groups, she is happiest pounding on her laptop after midnight, while listening to indie rock and ignoring pleas from her family to go to bed.

Made in the USA
Charleston, SC
15 July 2016